Where Are They?

The Missing Men from Marlowe Mansion

DAVID COCHRAN

An East Blawenburg Publication
http://www.dcochran.net

ABOUT THE AUTHOR

David Cochran's writing/publishing credits include 12 books, many professional education articles, 40 technology education newsletters, 30 science magazines for middle school students, and over 80 issues of his blog, *Tales of Blawenburg* (blawenburgtales.com). Visit his website at http://www.dcochran.net.

ACKNOWLEDGMENTS

Thanks to Olinda Young for offering suggestions early in the writing of this book.

This book would not have come to fruition without the diligent editing of Barbara Reid. Thank you, Barb

Contents

THE ANNIVERSARY

The unsolved case that baffled retired Stillwell PD detective Harvey Hawkshaw for two decades was the farthest thing from his mind as he waited impatiently for his microwave to tell him that dinner was ready. He stared at the old kitchen TV as if it wasn't there and half listened to Channel 8 News reporter Heather Compton recap the news of the day. When she broke into a story about the missing Marlowes cold case, he perked up, ignored his microwave buzzer, and turned up the TV volume. "My case," he said to his cat, Fluffy, as if she cared. The Salisbury steak, mashed potatoes, and overcooked peas could wait. Twenty years had gone by since those three men went missing from the Marlowe mansion, and Heather Compton commanded his full attention.

"Good evening. I'm Heather Compton reporting to you live from Quarry Road in Stillwell. Behind me, you can see the infamous Marlowe mansion, where 20 years ago today, March 15th, three men associated with the Marlowe family inexplicably disappeared within a short time of each other. Two were members of the Marlowe family, and one was a family associate.

The scene of the crime, if indeed there was a crime, was the Asa Marlowe homestead, where Asa built a fortune as a health guru—selling books, conducting seminars, and peddling what some called 'snake oil' remedies to his over 100,000 followers. He died many years ago… presumably of ill health. (She chuckled.) Sorry, I couldn't resist that one. His son, Asa Marlowe II, is also known as Junior, and he was the first man to disappear. Junior invested his father's fortune in local real estate and lived comfortably in the mansion. His son, Asa Marlowe III, is called Three, and he disappeared shortly after his father. The third man, Roscoe Savini, is believed to be Junior's son from a previous relationship, and he disappeared around the same time as three.

Here is what retired Stillwell Police Department detective Harvey Hawkshaw had to say about the case 18 years ago when he was the lead detective on the missing Marlowes case at the time. He was being interviewed by the late Channel 8 reporter Sylvia Ronstadt."

Harvey moved closer to the TV and sat in the counter chair. He put his hand over his mouth as a younger, leaner version of himself appeared on the screen.

"Detective Hawkshaw, the Marlowes have been missing for two years. What progress are you making on finding them?"

"Well, Sylvia, I wish I had good news to report, but we still have no solid leads, and we haven't heard from any of the men."

"Do you think they are alive?"

"I don't know, but we've talked to a lot of people, including the two women who lived in the mansion. I think they're the last to see them alive. We keep hitting brick walls. But mark my words, Sylvia. Somebody knows where these men are, and I won't give up until we solve this case."

The camera came back to the live coverage with Heather Compton. "Well, Detective Hawkshaw retired last year without reaching his goal, but I understand that he is now a private investigator still working on this case. We reached out to Detective Chapman Chan of the Stillwell Police Department, who filled Detective Hawkshaw's shoes, and he is with me today."

The camera panned to the short, thin, Asian detective with black hair dressed in a neatly tailored suit. He looked like a man on a mission, eager to be somewhere else as he talked.

"Detective Chan, can you tell us about the progress being made in the Marlowe case?"

"As you know, Heather, I can only give you a general update. This is an ongoing investigation, so I can't tell you anything that would compromise this case. We still receive information from time to time, but we have no strong leads on any of the missing men."

"So where do you start, Detective? It's been a cold case for a long time."

"Well, Heather, my mentor, Detective Hawkshaw, spent years trying to solve it without any luck. I agree with what he said in that clip you played. We know that someone around here knows something about what happened to these men. We urge any person with information to contact our hotline at 1-800-555-1212. As far as we can tell, the men disappeared around the same time, but we don't think they disappeared together."

"So, these are three unique events?"

"Possibly, Heather."

"Any new clues?"

"No obvious clues from the Marlowe mansion or its current residents, the three women associated with the missing men."

Heather raised her eyebrows. "Three women? I heard Detective Hawkshaw mention two women."

"Things change over time, Heather. This case is confusing because we have so little information and so many people that have connections to the Marlowes. We've put thousands of hours into this case over the years, and it's still a cold case."

"That must be frustrating."

"It sure is. Everything we've tried to figure out all these years ends up with no leads, no suspects, and no victims. We think we know the motive, and we believe whoever was involved had the means and opportunity to carry out these events. We have our suspicions but no solid proof. It's a mess."

"I guess that explains why this case has been cold for so long. Detective Chan, thank you for your time."

"Well, folks, there you have it, such as it is. Where are they? Maybe you can find them. There's still a $150,000 reward for anyone who provides information that results in the resolution of this case. So, put on your double-brimmed, Sherlock Holmes caps, grab a magnifying glass, and help find the missing men or their perpetrators. You just might solve this cold case and pocket that $150K reward."

The TV cut to a commercial break, and Harvey said aloud to his cat, who was always close by at mealtime, "Same as it was 20 years ago, Fluffy. I thought those biddies did it, but I couldn't crack that case. Cold then and cold now. Where are they, Fluffy?" He reached into the microwave, pulled out his dinner, and smiled. "Wouldn't it be great to get all that money?" Fluffy meowed, wanting some of his food.

TOOTIE'S CAFÉ

Harvey ambled into Tootie's Café at eight o'clock the next morning to have some breakfast and catch up on the local gossip. The reminder of the Marlowe case was still fresh on his mind.

"Mornin' Harv," Tootie said with her usual big smile.

"Saw you on TV last night. Quite a looker in your younger version."

Harvey yawned. "Yeah. Younger and skinnier. I was just a kid then."

"Who you kidding, Harv," Rexie said. "You weren't a kid then, and you're definitely not one now." Rexie Jackson was a short man with unkempt hair, dressed in a Hawaiian shirt, and looking like he was ready for a vacation. He always started his day at Tootie's when he was in town. No one knew where Rexie got his money, but he never held a job. He lived what he called "a freelance lifestyle."

"Be nice to Harvey," Alice Gemmel chimed in. "That must have been stressful for you to see yourself looking so young and not having that potbelly, Harv." She winked at Harvey. Alice owned the U Nique Boutique just up a few stores from Tootie's on the square that defined the center of Stillwell. Middle-aged and single, she always started her day with the gang at Tootie's before opening up the boutique at 10:00 a.m. She could hold her own in this group that was characterized by quick wit and jibes.

"Ooh. Zing. You be nice, Alice," Oscar Rhinehart said. Oscar, like Harvey, was a retired detective from the Stillwell PD. Tall and gray-haired, he had worked on the Marlowe case from time to time and shared Harvey's frustration that it was still a cold case.

"Here you go," Tootie said as she put a cup of Joe on the counter for Harvey.

"Thanks, girlfriend," he said, displaying his first

smile of the day. Harvey liked Tootie's Café. Everything about Tootie's was comfortable, like an old, worn shoe. Unpretentious. He and all the "regulars" treated the café like a second home, and Tootie treated everyone like they were her best friends. She always asked them if they wanted some "Joe" when they walked in and always had menu suggestions that matched their eating style. She treated all her customers like guests.

Tootie's Café had been a landmark for more years than Harvey had been alive. It was established by Ernie Gringwald, who named the Café after his wife, Gertrude. He and Gertrude had one child, also named Gertrude, who everyone called Tootie. She grew up in the café, and when she became an adult, she took over the business, running it much as her father did.

The bell attached to the front door, which opened onto the town square, jingled to let Tootie know a customer had arrived, and Jeb Wheeler, an English professor at Jefferson County Community College, walked in. He was tall and always wore a tie and jacket, even when he wasn't teaching. Jeb arranged his classes so that he could have what he called "quality time" every morning at Tootie's.

"You can start now," he said. "Sorry, I'm a little late. Got busy reading Shakespeare's *The Tempest* and forgot about the time."

"*The Tempest* sounds like our group," Rexie said. "Like a tempest in a coffee pot."

The group gave a weak laugh. They didn't want to humor Rexie too much, or he'd get carried away.

"More Joe, Harv?" Tootie asked with a coffee pot in hand.

Harvey nodded, still not alert.

"Josephus Daniels," Jeb mused. He liked to throw out names and phrases that people didn't know.

"Who the hell is Josephus Daniels?" Rexie said.

"You and your obscure facts, Jeb,"

"Former Secretary of the US Navy."

"And you're saying this because?"

"That's who they named coffee after. Joe. Joe Daniels."

"That's important information, Jeb. Thanks for sharing that with us. I knew his brother, Jack." Rexie tried for another laugh but got head shakes instead.

"Hey. You never know when trivial things can help you. Something we say here might help Harvey solve his case."

"Yeah," Rexie responded. "Like a killer named Joe."

Alice joined in. "So, you still think it's those 'biddies,' as you call them, had something to do with the disappearances? And by the way, Harv, those biddies aren't much older than us."

"I probably shouldn't have said that," Harvey responded. "I'm finding myself with a looser tongue now that I'm not in the department."

"I know an ear, nose, and throat doctor who could tighten things up, Harv," Alice said.

"You mean an otolaryngologist, don't you, Alice?"

"Shut up, Jeb. You know how to ruin a joke."

"You still think those ladies up at the mansion did it, don't you Harv?" Oscar asked.

"Actually. I'm not sure. Not as sure as I used to be," he replied. "It seemed obvious that they were involved, but the more I talked to them, the more I had doubts."

"We need something to turn this case, Harv," Oscar said. "You know, like new information."

"Where am I going to get that?" Harv said. "I have been looking for that for years."

"What about that third woman in the mansion that Chan mentioned in that TV interview?"

"Old news, Oscar. I knew about her. Carmela, Three's wife or partner or whatever she is. She came and went from the mansion over the years but seems to be there more often in the past two years. I think she was running out of money. But she's been no help."

"How 'bout Junior's wife? I think she's been there the whole time," Rexie said.

"Ever talk to her, Rexie?" Alice said. "A real charmer. She talks like she drinks vinegar for breakfast."

Harvey smiled. "Acid tongue. I think she's fermented."

"I hear she's pickled most of the time," Rexie said.

"I know there's another one that they keep locked up in that turret," Oscar said. "I forget her name."

"Rapunzel," Jeb replied. "Rapunzel. Rapunzel. Let down your hair," he said in his most dramatic voice.

The group laughed. "I don't think she's locked in that tower," Harvey said. "She's very quiet, reclusive. A loner who needed a place to live after Roscoe disappeared."

"That's right," Tootie said. "I always forget about that one. Never seen her. She's certainly never been in here. What's her name?" She looked at Jeb. "I know it isn't Rapunzel."

"Felicia. Felicia Savini," Harvey replied. "We called her an associate of the family because we aren't sure of Roscoe's real relation to Junior. It could be his son. Junior might also think he's Roscoe's father, but he really isn't. I don't think anyone did a paternity test, and DNA wasn't around when Roscoe was born. He'd be about 40 now. Same age as Three."

"So, Harv, if you had to pin this on someone or a couple of someones, who would it be?" Tootie asked.

"I honestly don't know, but it would be a big payoff in more ways than one."

"What do you mean, Harv?"

"Well, Tootie, money is one thing, but finally solving this case would be a big deal."

"From what Heather Compton said last night, it would be a $150K payoff," Alice said. "Not bad."

"A $150K puzzle. You know how I like puzzles," Jeb said.

"You are a puzzle, Jeb," Rexie said.

The group laughed.

"Seriously, when you're doing a jigsaw puzzle, you can easily get the outside pieces because they're obvious. Straight edges, often the background color, like a blue sky."

"So, what's your point, Jeb?" Rexie asked.

"I always reach a point where I get stuck. There are a bunch of pieces that look like they might fit in, but I can't see the connection. I turn the pieces every which way, but I'm stumped. Then, I move on to a different piece, often one I haven't picked up before. I find where that piece fits, and bingo, it suddenly becomes obvious where the other piece fits."

"So, again, what's your point?"

"If I were trying to solve this mystery, which I'm not because I'm busy writing my bestselling novel, I'd stop looking at the piece that is getting me nowhere and start looking at the new pieces."

"I hear you, Jeb," Harvey said, "But we've done that over and over. We've gotten nowhere with new leads."

"You're a PI now, not a detective, Harvey. You've got some new freedom to talk to people and explore some new pieces of the puzzle. You may not even know they fit into the puzzle until you start looking at things from a different perspective."

"Thank you, Professor," Rexie said. "I couldn't have said it better myself."

"You couldn't have said it at all, Rexie," Alice said.

The group laughed again.

"It's trite to say, Harv," Oscar said, "but he's saying think outside the box. You're not in the SPD box anymore, so you aren't constrained by department rules."

Harvey nodded in agreement. "You're both right. Thanks, Professor, my old colleague. I need some new leads from a new source."

"You know what that whispering voice said in Field of Dreams, Harv?" Jeb said.

"If you build it, they will come," Harvey replied.

"And Shoeless Joe Jackson showed up."

Harvey smiled. He understood Jeb's point. "I've wanted this badly for a long time. Maybe it's time for me to start whispering for help."

"If you need help reaching Shoeless Joe Jackson, let me know, Harv. According to my genealogist, he's a distant cousin of mine." Jeb grinned.

Alice threw her balled-up napkin at him, and the whole group laughed.

THE NIGHT VISITOR

After he left Tootie's, Harvey ran errands around town, and everywhere he went, he ran into people who recognized him. "Saw you on TV, Harvey," they said. Or, as the more insulting commenters would say, "You sure were skinny 20 years ago." It was an exhausting day.

"What did Thelma think about the interview, Harv," Burt Arnold, owner of the Happy Hammer Hardware store, asked when Harvey went in to pick up some screws to fix his deck.

"Didn't see it. The wife's out of town again."

"Helping Grandma?"

"Yeah, Grandma thinks she's in her 20s instead of her 80s."

"Still ice skating?"

Harvey nodded his head and smiled. "Collar bone this time."

Harvey picked up his screws and thanked Burt.

"Happy bachelorhood, Harv."

Harvey waved to Burt as he headed out the door, looking forward to a relaxing evening.

After yet another TV dinner, Harvey sat in his favorite recliner and turned on a March Madness game. It could have been the Metropolitan opera or a Bugs Bunny cartoon for all the attention he paid to it. All he could think about was that cold case that would never end. It wasn't long until he was fast asleep with visions of reward money dancing in his head.

Later that night, Harvey was still in his recliner, snoring at full throttle. The TV on low volume showed an Asian man twirling sharp Ginsu knives and telling anyone listening that these utensils could slice and dice like no other knives. Harvey was oblivious to it all. Dead to the world.

The doorbell rang, playing "Take Me Out to the Ball Game!" Harvey awakened with a start, sputtering saliva. "Wha?" He shook his head, trying to figure out what was happening. He heard the same seven notes again as the doorbell rang a second time.

"Knives. Where am I? What the…? What time is it anyway?" He pulled his cell phone out of his pocket and groaned. "Two o'clock! Who rings doorbells at two in the morning?"

He pushed Fluffy off his lap, maneuvered his stiffened body out of the recliner, and stretched. "Man, I must have fallen asleep." He yawned and started for the door, promptly tripping on the leg of the coffee table and falling to the carpet atop Fluffy, who let out a shrill yowl as she bolted from beneath him. "Leap'n Leana. What's going on here?"

Harvey slowly ambled to the door, rubbing his elbow to soothe the carpet brush burn. He was awake enough to remember he was a private investigator, so he turned on the porch light, making sure he didn't open the door as if he was welcoming a long-lost friend. Carefully, he looked through the glass panel next to the door but saw no one. When he turned on the front floodlights, he saw the tail lights of a dark vehicle go out of his driveway, turn in the cul-de-sac, and leave the neighborhood.

Then he remembered. "The video doorbell. Just installed. Great." He reached into the pocket of his flannel lounge pants covered with Steelers football images and pulled out his phone. He opened the video doorbell app and the most recent file.

"Well, I'll be," he said. "Looks like one of my friends left me a present." On the stoop, he saw a bright red, medium-sized suitcase with several tags and scuff marks on it. He was really curious now, but he couldn't just open the suitcase. *What if it has a bomb in it*, he thought. *Here today and gone a minute later. Maybe one of those biddies saw me on TV and wanted me to disappear like the Marlowe men.*

Harvey wasn't a pessimist, but in his line of work, anything could happen. After all, he was a well-known detective in the Stillwell Police Department until that "catastrophe," as he called it, a few months back accelerated his retirement. He rescued a cat from an icy tree, ending up needing to be rescued himself. As he was just getting back in shape after physical therapy for his broken leg, he was offered an irresistible early retirement package. But his new lifestyle didn't work for him, so after two boring months, he went back to what he did best, reinventing himself as Harvey Hawkshaw, Private Investigator.

As his sleep fog cleared, he mentally reviewed the latest cases he was working on and got no help in figuring out why someone would anonymously leave a suitcase at his doorstep. *Can't rule out a bomb*, he thought again.

He looked at the video from his doorbell again, more carefully this time, and saw a man take a suitcase out of the back of his SUV and bring it to the front door stoop. The man wore regular street clothes with a dark jacket and a knitted ski cap. He slipped on the black ice that had accumulated on the lawn and sidewalk and then placed the suitcase on the stoop (very gently, Harvey thought), rang the doorbell twice, quickly walked back to the SUV, and drove away. "Suspicious," Harvey said aloud. "Better be careful."

Cautiously, he opened the door and stepped outside to give the suitcase a closer look. "I see why that guy slipped," he said to no one. Black ice was a typical March event in Stillwell. He had a quick flashback, perhaps a premonition, about the incident with Binky, the rescued cat. Harvey no sooner stepped out on the stoop when his feet slipped, and he went headlong toward the red suitcase. Instead of having it break his fall, he pushed it onto the icy lawn. He grabbed the railing to avoid cracking his back on the steps. He spun, tumbled, and ended up atop the mysterious red container just off the sidewalk on the slick, frozen grass with his foot caught in the handle.

"NO," he yelled as he heard a ticking sound

coming from the now horizontal suitcase. "It's going to explode!" He tried frantically to get up, but the black ice on the slope in his front yard prevented him. As he slipped and slithered on the shiny grass, he realized he had wrenched his back and landed on his shoulder. He couldn't move anywhere, and his foot was still trapped in the ticking bomb container that had so rudely interrupted his nap. His butt stuck up in the air as he again tried to get up. He laid still for a minute and then tried to get up, unsuccessfully once more. He lay immobile for several minutes, which seemed like an hour.

Soon, he saw a flash from a camera and wondered why anyone was on his lawn at that hour. "Help," he yelled and saw his neighbor, Bob Gilpain, a reporter for the Stillwell Gazette, holding his cell phone out, taking pictures of him.

"For God's sake, Gilpain, help me."

"I already called 911. Help is on the way. It's too slippery for me to reach you," he said as he continued to snap pictures.

Harvey continued to hear the ticking and had more thoughts of the Marlowes' revenge. His breathing became harder as he panicked. "Call (wheeze) 911," he said aloud as he started to hyperventilate. He tried to reach for his phone in the left pocket of his lounge pants and yelled as the sharp pain increased. He finally reached underneath his prone body with his right hand. It took a couple of tries for him to wriggle the phone out. With his butt in the air and his head down to minimize injury if the bomb exploded, he pushed the emergency button on the phone to dial 911.

The 911 dispatcher, Darla Machem, answered immediately. "911 Dispatch Center. What is your emergency?"

Harvey was cold and still hyperventilating. He wheezed and sputtered and couldn't get a word out.

"Sir, I have your address, and someone just called this in. But state your problem."

He took a deep breath, almost passing out, and replied. "Suitcase bomb (wheeze) on my lawn. Help."

"We have contacted EMS, and I will now contact the bomb squad. I'll stay on the phone with you. Where are you?"

"(Wheeze) Lawn. On the lawn next to the bomb."

"Good Lord," she said. "Move away. Move away immediately."

Harvey attempted to heed her orders, but each time he tried, the pain in his back and shoulder prevented him from going very far. Every time he moved, the suitcase moved with him.

"Are you away from the bomb?"

"(Wheeze) No." He paused to catch his breath. "Bomb's following me!"

"Sir?"

"Oh, man, (wheeze). The foot caught in the handle. I move, and it moves. (Wheeze)"

"Don't move. Pray."

"Pray? Oh no. I'm gonna (wheeze) die!"

Just then, he heard a siren in the distance. And then he heard another and another. It sounded like all of Stillwell was under nuclear attack.

Three police cars arrived first, followed shortly by the EMS. The police didn't park at his house but kept the cars across Azalea Court, closer to the end of the cul-de-sac, in case they were called off to another emergency.

Police Chief Milton Jenkins, a good friend of Harvey's, got out his bullhorn.

"Harvey, are you okay?"

"What (wheeze) do you think, Milt? I'm laying (wheeze) injured on the ground with a (wheeze) bomb about to blow me to (wheeze) smithereens! Get me outta here."

"Chill out, Harv. Bomb squad is on the way. Hold on a while longer. Hey, I saw you on TV tonight. Of course, you were 18 years younger and 30 pounds lighter.

Gotta shed some of that weight, Harv."

"Ho-ho-hold on, Milt. Get my foot outta this thing."

"I hear the bomb squad siren. They'll be here in a minute, and we can take care of you after they take care of the bomb. Don't want too many casualties."

"(Wheeze) Casualties? That's what I am? (Wheeze) I'm a frigging casualty!"

Donnie Nutkiss, aka Donut, backed the ambulance into the driveway and walked up to where Milt was talking to Harvey.

Seeing Donnie, Harvey yelled. "Oh my God, it's Donut. He (wheeze) wears Velcro shoes 'cause he can't tie his (wheeze) shoelaces right."

"Evening, Harvey," Donnie said. "Got yourself in a real pickle, don't ya?"

An emergency medical technician was slowly creeping toward Harvey. He threw Harvey a thin rope and told him to pull it toward himself. Harvey wiggled on the ground until he got to the end of the rope and found a paper bag clipped to it. He unclipped it and looked inside. Nothing. The bag was empty.

"What? (Wheeze) What's this, a bag for me to pack my (wheeze) lunch?"

"Put it over your mouth, Harvey," Donnie yelled. "Breathe into the bag."

"(Wheeze) Where'd you guys do your EMT training, Donnie, (wheeze) at the takeout deli?"

"You're hyperventilating, Harvey. You're breathing out too much carbon dioxide, and your blood flow to your brain needs more carbon dioxide. Nervous system stress. Put the bag over your nose and mouth and take some deep breaths. NOW!"

Harvey called Donnie a name between gulps of air but realized that his wheezing was slowing down, and he could breathe more comfortably. "Better," he said. "Much better."

Chief Jenkins checked in with Harvey. "You okay now, Harvey?"

"Sure, Milt. I'm not having mental stress, except that I'M HOOKED UP TO A TICKING BOMB! Geez."

An SUV hauling a trailer with a large, blue, metal barrel marked EOD pulled right up on the lawn. Two men wearing thick green suits that made them look like a cross between the Jolly Green Giant and the Incredible Hulk came toward Harvey.

"Who are these guys in space suits? They think I'm an alien?"

"It's the County Explosive Ordinance Disposal team, Harvey," Chief Jenkins said over the bullhorn. "They're better known as the bomb squad. They're wearing blast suits. You know, so they can withstand the pressure of a bomb blast and shrapnel...."

"Stop," Harvey interrupted. "I don't want to hear this."

The two people walked up to Harvey and gingerly wiggled his foot from the handle of the suitcase. But as his foot was released, his leg muscle twitched, and he kicked the suitcase, popping it open.

The EOD guys dove to the ground as far away from the suitcase as they could get. Harvey yelled, "Goodbye! Take care of Fluffy." he covered his head and tried to wiggle away from the suitcase.

Nothing happened. No one except Harvey moved for what seemed like an eternity. When they thought it was safe, the EOD team got up and headed toward the suitcase. Harvey continued his painful crawl across the icy lawn, teeth chattering, and other EMTs left the security of their warm ambulance and headed toward Harvey.

As the EOD looked in the suitcase, a dark van pulled up, and a man dressed in dark clothes wearing a knit cap got out. "What's going on?" he asked Chief Jenkins.

"Possible crime scene. Bomb. Better get back. We're still not sure if it's safe."

The man laughed. The more he looked at the mayhem on Harvey Hawkshaw's lawn, the louder he laughed. "Can I just go get the suitcase?"

"You crazy? Want to get blown up?" Officer Boileau said. "Say, what do you know about that suitcase?"

"I put it on his stoop."

Chief Jenkins stepped back, put his hand on his holstered gun, and motioned for two other officers to come over to him. "This guy says he put the suitcase on the stoop. Go verify it with Hawkshaw."

An officer talked with Harvey, nodded his head, and then returned.

"He's the guy. Harvey has him on video dropping off the bomb."

"Bomb? You guys have a good imagination. I would have been blown up already if it was a bomb."

"But it's ticking," an officer said.

Another officer came over to Chief Jenkins, holding something in his hand. "Here's your bomb, Chief. Just got it from the bomb squad." He opened his hand to reveal a small, old-fashioned travel alarm clock ticking away. "They also told me bombs don't tick anymore. They're digital."

Officer Jenkins turned to the suspect. "So, who are you?"

"Alonzo. Alonzo Bilken. The delivery guy. I came back because I realized I had put the suitcase in the wrong house. I moonlight for East-West Airlines, delivering suitcases that don't arrive on the same flights as their owners. Pretty good money, but you have to work in the middle of the night."

The officers looked at each other and then burst out laughing. "Poor Harvey. An evening of overtime for us at his expense."

The EODs told Harvey his bomb was a clock and assured him he was never in danger.

"Geez," he said. "All that for nothing except a

racked-up body."

The ambulance backed closer to Harvey on his lawn. "What are you doing?"

"Protocol, Harv," EMT Tony Fribish said. "Whenever you get hurt, and you have the police, EMS, and bomb squad on the scene, you need to get checked out at the hospital."

"Oh, no," Harvey said. "I'm fine. I'll call my doctor later."

"Sorry, Harvey," Tony said. He motioned for the other EMT to take care of Harvey. Before he knew it, he was strapped to a board, lifted onto a gurney, and put into the back of the ambulance.

"Who's driving this rig?" Harvey asked.

"I'll be with you in the back," Tony said. "Got your favorite driver up front."

"Donut?"

"Yup. He's the only one who likes to come out in the middle of the night to drive. He's usually up half the night playing video games, so he's ready to go... wide awake."

"Oh no. I've seen him in action. Just like a video game. I'm not sure I'll make it."

"You'll be fine. You won't be in the ambulance long, Harv. I guarantee you. Lead foot and empty roads make for a quick trip."

As the ambulance rolled out of the neighborhood to take Harvey to Stillwell Medical Center, the lights were on in all the houses, and many neighbors were standing in pajamas and winter coats, talking about the terrorist attack that occurred in their quiet cul-de-sac. Bob Gilpain called in his story and sent his pictures of Harvey to the Stillwell Gazette so they could make it in the morning edition. Heather Compton arrived on the scene in time to get some video for Breaking News on Channel 8.

Even though there was no one on the road and the hospital was less than a mile away, Donnie had the siren wailing the whole way, waking up half of Stillwell.

"Thank God," Harvey said when they pulled into the Medical Center complex. "Didn't think I'd make it here with Donut at the wheel."

THE ER

As the ambulance pulled into the bay at Stillwell Medical Center, Harvey had a strange thought as he looked around. "Looks familiar. Seems like only a few months ago, I was here. Oh, that's right, I was here, only I had a real reason to be here. Injury, not protocol."

Tony Fribish laughed, "You'll be just fine, Harvey. Sorry, we have to put you through this, man; we have to make sure you're okay. Capiche? After all, you're still recovered from that cat rescue."

"Don't remind me. First, that cat mess, now this. The guy with the suitcase makes a mistake, and I end up floundering like a walrus on ice. But I'm not suing anybody unless my lawyer tells me to."

Tony laughed again. "Some scene. I won't forget this call for a long time." He laughed again.

"You weren't there for the whole mess, were you?"

"No, but Don Gilpain, the reporter, was there. Had video rolling on that cellphone much of the time."

"Always nice to have somebody nearby to capture every scene you hope will be forgotten."

"Yeah, Don doesn't miss much. He's like a roadrunner when he hears a siren or something come over the police radio. He monitors that 24/7. This time, he only had to walk next door. Heather Compton arrived, too. That's how they got Breaking News coverage so fast."

"Geez, so it's on the news already? How lucky can a guy get, having the media right at his doorstep!"

Tony laughed again, then got serious. "Oh, Harv. I forgot to tell you. We brought you in as a trauma patient."

"What?"

"They might treat you a little more aggressively than if you were coming in with a tummy ache."

"What? What do you mean more aggressively?"

"Uh. Well. You know, they have their protocol, too.   They'll cut your clothes off first and then probe all

21

your orifices."

"Get out of town. Nobody's probing me. Not my orifices. I got Constitutional rights. Life, liberty, and the privacy of my orifices. Tell them I'm fine."

"I can't stop them, Harv. Protocol."

"At least save my Steeler's pants."

"It's out of my hands, Harv. Sorry."

The ambulance came to a stop and backed into the bay to unload its cargo. A team of people in scrubs and white coats was standing at the bay like vultures alongside the highway, waiting for the traffic to clear so they could dig into the roadkill. They opened the back door and whisked the gurney out. Its wheels popped down so fast that Harvey couldn't imagine what was going on.

"I hope you know what you're doing," he yelled as four pallbearers in white coats pushed and pulled the gurney down the crowded hallway at high speed. No one else said a word except Harvey, who yelled "slow down" incessantly.

He was wheeled into a brightly lit examining room. "Who are these dudes?" he asked as he gestured toward the eleven people assembled in the room who looked like they were ready to perform surgery.

An older man, who appeared to be in charge, smiled at him and said, "Mr. Hawkshaw, these are residents at Stillwell Medical. They're here to observe how we help our trauma patients, and they will participate in your examination."

Then he turned to the residents. "Doctors, Mr. Hawkshaw has been here before. It seems he tried to rescue a cat, which I understand he did, but he ended up with two broken intermediate leg bones, his tibia, and fibula. His femur was fine. He's still in recovery from that, so that's part of the reason he is being treated as a trauma patient."

"I'm not a trauma patient. I'm a doof who slipped on some ice and couldn't get up. I'm fine. See."

He tried to get up and was immediately pushed down by two of the white-coat guys who looked like bouncers at the Starlight Lounge. "Relax, Mr. Hawkshaw. We'll just relieve you of some of your clothes, examine you, and then maybe run some tests."

"Don't touch me. Don't mess with my Steeler's pants. You understand? I want my clothes on, and I want out of here." His comments fell on deaf ears.

What happened next was like a piranha feeding frenzy. Nurses with scissors cut his shirt and pants, ripped them off, and threw a sheet over him to protect his self-esteem.

Next came one of the residents donning latex gloves, who checked Harvey's body from head to toe, poking and prodding in places where few would want anyone else to put their hands. Meanwhile, the assistant was explaining his every move to the residents in far more detail than Harvey wanted to hear.

When the check was over, the attending physician spoke to him. "Harvey, we don't find any problems, but we'd like to take some CT scans to make sure you don't have any hidden issues."

"Hidden schmidden," Harvey yelled. "I don't want any tests. I'm fine."

"Ah, but that's how people always get into trouble. They feel fine, but they don't realize that there is something more sinister going on inside. If they don't address the problem, big danger, even death, could be lurking around the corner."

The grim reaper knew he had a platform with the residents, so he continued talking to the residents about Harvey as if he wasn't there. "Patients often deny their conditions. Even when they are presented with evidence, they want to fall back on their old beliefs. Take Mr. Hawkshaw, for example...."

"Don't take Mr. Hawkshaw anywhere for anything," Harvey interrupted. "Look, Doc, I know you don't want to get sued because you missed something, so I'll sign off on the testing. No tests, no problem. Deal?" Harvey lifted his arm up to give the doc a high five, but Doc didn't reciprocate. The bouncer pushed his arm down.

The doctor looked at the residents. "This is where we enact Protocol 99, which says that the ER doctor has the right to determine whether or not it is in the patient's best interest to have a test." He nodded at the bouncers, who smiled like NASCAR drivers just before a race. Lickety-split, they whisked him down the hallway for a CT scan.

By the time the testing was over and Harvey was returned to the ER, all the individual rooms were full, and there were patients wherever they could put a gurney. Harvey's gurney was parallel parked between two other gurneys. One held a groaning old man and the other a teenager who kept saying it wasn't his fault. Maybe it wasn't, but no one knew what he was talking about.

A nurse in blue scrubs came up to Harvey. "Ok. Mr. Harvey. We have to get you into a gown." An older woman right across the aisle from Harvey was glaring at him. She didn't look happy, but Harvey thought he recognized her. Her face was ashen, and she looked exhausted. He couldn't tag a name to that face.

"Where am I going to change?" Harvey asked the nurse.

"This is like Macy's at Christmastime in here this morning. You change where you are. If you want me to hold a sheet up, it might give you more privacy. Remember, the gown's open in the back." She had an impish smile. "If you want, I can put the gown on you."

"No, no. I've had enough southern exposure for one day."

"Open in the back. Undies on," the nurse said as she turned away to tend to the old woman.

"Yeah, yeah." Harvey immodestly followed orders.

The nurse saw that the woman across from Harvey

was awake. "How are you doing, Mrs. Marlowe?"

Harvey's eyes widened, and he looked toward the old lady. *Mrs. Marlowe? THE Mrs. Marlowe? Wife of the missing Asa Marlow Jr.? She's really aged since I saw her last.*

The sullen Mrs. Marlowe, with glazed eyes, stared at nothing in the distance.

When the nurse walked away, Harvey cleared his throat to break her trance. "Hello. Mrs. Marlowe. I heard the nurse use your name."

Without looking at him, she said, "Eavesdropping. I could tell."

"Well, I wouldn't call it that. You can hear a lot more than you want in these tight quarters."

Mrs. Marlowe had no response.

Harvey used his most casual voice. "Say, you wouldn't happen to be related to the Marlowe family up on the mountain, would you?"

"Why would you care?"

"Are you related to Asa Marlowe Jr.?"

"None of your business. What are you, a cop?"

Was I a cop? Harvey thought. *I was the lead detective on the Marlowe case 20 years ago, but she doesn't remember me.*

"Well, not anymore. I'm just curious. You know, you can take the cop out of his job, but you can't take the metal out of an old copper like me."

"Cut the comedy, Seinfeld."

Harvey gave a fake chuckle to humor the old lady.

He tried again. "Say, you wouldn't be Asa Jr.'s wife, would you?"

"Still none of your business. Don't you get it? I don't want to talk with you."

Just then, a woman wearing a clerical collar came up to Mrs. Marlowe. "Hello, Eunice," she said. "I'm Chaplain Nancy. I know this is a difficult time for you. It's been 20 years since your husband disappeared. And now this."

Harvey was all ears. *This is? What's going on? Come on.*

Tell me more.

"No surprise, Chaplain," Eunice said. "Long gone... years ago. Just didn't know where he was or if we'd ever find him."

"How long were you married?"

"Counting the years, he was missing? 25."

"Oh, so you weren't married that long before he disappeared."

"Not to him. If he'd lived, it might not have been much longer, either."

Harvey was all ears as the chaplain continued.

"So... uh... is Three your son?"

"No, thank goodness. Another bum. He was the only child of Asa and his first wife. What was her name? Valerie, no Vanessa. He must be 40-some now. A bum, just like his father."

"Are you feeling okay, Eunice?" the chaplain continued.

"I'm fine. They thought I was going to have a heart attack when I heard that they found Asa, so they brought me here."

Harvey's eyes widened. *Found Asa?*

"No heart attacks. That's good news, Eunice," the chaplain said.

"No heart attack and no Asa either," Eunice replied. "Mark my words. Don't know who the unlucky person was that they found up on that mountain, but it wasn't Asa."

"Oh, that's interesting. The reports say it's him."

"They're wrong. Dead wrong. I wish it was him, but I know it isn't. They'll find that out soon enough."

The chaplain didn't know how to respond and stood silently next to the gurney. Eunice's cynical smile spoke volumes to Harvey.

A nurse came up to the chaplain and Eunice. "Doctor discharged you, Eunice. Said you were in great shape and expressed his condolences. Your ride is waiting

26

at the ER entrance."

"Forget the condolences; send money," she said.

Two bouncers wheeled her gurney out of the ER, and that was the last Harvey saw of her that night.

Harvey rang the buzzer three times for the nurse to come to him. It seemed like forever, but when she arrived, Harvey got right to the point. "I need to get out of here," he said. "I want out like Mrs. Marlowe."

"You have to be discharged by a doctor, Mr. Hawkshaw," she said.

"Then, can you get me a doctor? I've got an appointment soon."

"It's 4:00 a.m., Mr. Hawkshaw. Who are you meeting before sunrise?"

"I got friends that are vampires. I got to see them before the sun comes up."

The nurse rolled her eyes and started to walk away. "I'll see what I can do," she said as she continued walking.

Harvey picked up his phone and called the only person he thought would pick him up. The phone rang and rang until a very groggy voice answered.

"Who's this?"

"Me, Donut. It's me, you know, Harvey. I'm going to need a ride soon."

"Where are you?"

"Where you left me, wingnut. At the ER."

"You discharged?"

"Not yet."

"Call me when you're discharged." He hung up.

Every 15 minutes or so, Harvey would buzz the nurse, and she would eventually arrive at his gurney. He would ask where the doctor was, and she would always say, "Busy with other patients." This went on for a while, and then the nurse stopped coming to him.

Finally, at 6:30 a.m., the doctor showed up and told him that his CT scan did not show any major problems but that he needed rest and some medication for anxiety.

"So, does this mean I'm discharged, Doc?"

"Well, yes. But it will take a while for me to complete the paperwork before you can leave."

"You need help? I was a cop. I can do the paperwork. I'm fine, so I can help you."

"Not that easy. We need records in case there are questions later."

"Here we go again. CYA. Don't let anyone sue us."

The doctor didn't want to hear about Harvey's theories of medical practice or malpractice, so like the nurse earlier, he said, "I'll see what I can do" as he walked away.

By 8:00 a.m., there had been a shift change, and a new nurse approached Harvey.

"Who are you?" he asked.

"Chenille. But you can call me Chenille!" She chuckled.

"Oh boy. A comedian. Where were you when I needed you? Can you check to see if I'm being discharged anytime in this century?"

Chenille looked down at her iPad and found Harvey's name. "Hmm. Says here that you could be discharged at 7:00 a.m."

"It's 8 o'clock now."

"So, you're overdue. I'll get your clothes, and we'll wheel you right out of here. Got a ride?"

"Yeah, but I got no clothes! They mutilated them when I came in."

"Ooh. That's right. You came in as a trauma patient. You call your ride, and I'll find you something. We have what we call loaner clothes."

"Do I want to know who loans clothes to a trauma unit?"

"No. Just wear them home and then burn them," Chenille said. Then she giggled. "Just kidding. They're fine. Old, but clean. The previous owners don't need them anymore."

Harvey shook his head in disgust and got right on his phone. Donut picked up on the first ring this time. "Where you been, Harvey?"

"Don't ask. They forgot about me. Hurry up. Come to the ER entrance. As soon as they find me some clothes, they'll wheel me out."

"Ambulance?"

"No. Definitely no ambulance. A car is fine."

The nurse returned with well-worn sweatpants, a stained sweatshirt with the logo of Gerber baby food, and Harvey's slippers, the only thing the piranhas hadn't destroyed. "Looks like these should fit you," Chenille said. "Don't worry. We washed these cadaver clothes."

Harvey looked pale. "What? Cadaver clothes?"

Chenille shrugged her shoulders. "You can recycle the clothes, too. We don't want them back. Just go home, get cleaned up, and catch up on lost sleep. This is no place to get rested."

"You got that right, Chenille. But I'm not going home."

"What, are you crazy? After all, you've been through?"

"Got to see my homies. I think they're counting on me showing up for breakfast and stories."

"You've sure got a story to tell."

"More than one!"

BACK TO TOOTIE'S CAFÉ

Donut pulled into the parking lot behind the café.

"Let me buy you a coffee and donut… uh, Donut." Harvey laughed. "Do you eat donuts, or is that like cannibalism to you?"

Donut shook his head. "Guess you're feeling better, Harv. Sorry, I can't stay. Work, you know. The boss won't understand if I show up late with donut dust on my face."

Harvey thanked him for the ride and walked into the rear entrance to Tootie's Café. He was greeted with cheers, hoots, and high fives as he walked through the dining room up to the U-shaped counter near the front entrance to the café. His breakfast friends were all smiling when Harvey arrived.

"Little late, Harv." Tootie greeted him with a big smile. "Actually, I didn't expect to see you at all today. You doin', okay?" Tootie and everyone else in the café knew all about the bomb incident from the Breaking News on Channel 8 and the Stillwell Gazette, the morning newspaper.

"Yeah," he muttered in a low tone. "Been better, though. A lot better."

"Nice clothes, Harv," Oscar said. "Did you stop by the clothes bin over by the Quick Stop on the way here?"

Everyone laughed.

"Nah. It's a long story, but I got my cadaver outfit on." He swept his arm the length of his torso and legs like a model on a runway. "Cadaver sweatshirt, cadaver sweatpants. At least they let me keep my slippers."

"Ooh, gross." Alice shivered at the thought of wearing a dead person's clothes. "Where are the clothes you wore to the hospital?" she asked.

"Probably in the incinerator. They cut them off me before I knew what had happened. Even my Steeler's pants. They brought in Edward Scissorhands on the graveyard shift to do the dirty deed."

"Oh, no, Harv," Alice said. "Your favorite loungewear."

"So, you haven't been home?" Tootie asked.

"Nope. I need some Joe and seeing normal people if you could call yourselves that."

Tootie poured a cup of Joe black and put it on the counter. Harvey reached for his wallet.

"Oh, no, my friend. You've been through the mill. On the house. And the refills, too."

Harvey smiled at her. "How do you know what happened, Tootie?" he asked.

Rexie overheard Harvey's conversation from two seats down the counter. "You asked how does she know, Harv? How could she not know? You're all over the media in Stillwell."

"And that picture in the Gazette," Alice said, and then she giggled. "You really had that butt sticking up in the air. You'd make a good plumber, Harv!"

"You didn't see the Channel 8 News morning edition?" Rexie asked.

Harvey shook his head. "You kidding? I've been busy having my orifices probed and having photo shoots of my innards."

"You really have to see the coverage," Rexie said, and then he started to laugh. "In your case, we'd call it poor coverage. I really like the part where that EMT throws you a rope, and you have a hissy fit 'cause he won't come over to help you."

"Hysterical, Rexie. Really funny," Harvey scowled at him.

"But the best part," Alice said as she continued to giggle. "The best part was when those bomb guys go up to the suitcase, and you kick it over." She giggled again. "They dove to the ground, and you all thought it was going to explode. Great scene. Better than a made-for-TV movie."

"And check this out," Oscar said as he held up a copy of the Stillwell Gazette. "Just came out this morning,

Harv. Bobby Gilpain's shot seen all around Stillwell!"

There on the front page was a big picture of Harvey, butt in the air, foot entangled in the suitcase, and his hands covering his ears.

"Oh no," Harvey said.

The café erupted in laughter.

"Let me see that," he said as he reached for the paper. He shook his head as he read Bob Gilpain's account of what happened. The article was filled with quotes as well as an event-by-event reckoning of the bomb event. "How'd he gets all that information? Must have stayed up all night writing that article."

As he went to hand the paper back to Oscar, his eye caught another story on the front page. He pulled his arm back quickly as he grabbed the paper, knocking over his half cup of Joe. It was a painful reminder that his shoulder was sore from his fall on the lawn.

Tootie quickly came to the rescue with a towel in hand, mopping up Harvey's mess.

"Time for another Joe, Harv?" Tootie's question didn't require a response as she set a fresh cup of coffee to his right and threw him a dishtowel to dry his counter stool.

"Sorry, Tootie," he said as he soaked up the Joe. "I just saw this other article, and it got my juices going."

"Yeah, Harv. That's your juices all over the counter," Rexie said. "Some things never change. A regular Inspector Clutz-o."

Harvey gave Rexie an evil look and turned his attention back to the Gazette. The headline read: Skeleton Found as Marlowe Cold Case Marks 20th Anniversary. "You see this other headline, Rexie?"

"How could I? Your body takes up half the front page." Rexie laughed.

"Seriously, the article is all about my Marlowe case."

Harvey scanned and paraphrased the article. "It

says that Marlowe was a rich guy who lived up the mountain in an old Victorian-style mansion. True. It was built as a vacation home in the 1890s by a rich dude who wanted to get away from it all. The first Marlowe bought it in the 40s, that's the 1940s. He was the father of the guy they think they just found, Marlowe II, the guy they call Junior. He was your age, Rexie, ready for retirement, but he didn't work either, so he didn't need to retire. Kind of like you. Says here that he was an heir to the Marlowe fortune. Old news. We all knew that 20 years ago."

"Well, what I've heard is that the old man, Marlowe Senior, was a real shyster. Made his money as a self-appointed health guru," Rexie said. "Would sell you a cure for whatever ails you. But the old man was a shrewd one. Could sell sand to nomads in the Sahara Desert."

Good stuff, Harvey thought. Information from a new source. "How do you know all this, Rexie?" Harvey wanted to know. "I thought you were just a dumb schmuck that hung out here at Tootie's."

"Well, I am, and I do hang out here with other dumb schmucks. But I've been listening to a lot of gossip over the years, and after a while, you begin to know what's true and what's not."

"So, what have you heard about how the old man made his money?"

Rexie tapped his spoon on the counter as he recalled the Marlowe story. "He called his 'practice' the Marlowe Health System. Of course, he liked his name on it, and calling it a practice sounded like it was real medicine. People bought it big time. If you bought his health books, you became part of his cult. Of course, he never called it a cult. Then he'd sell you more books or have you taken courses at his private university."

"Sign me up, Rexie. I wanna get healthy," an eavesdropper yelled from the back of the café.

"Sure. Just give me $25 per book in 80-year-old dollars. A real bargain when it comes to your health. By the way, that's over $400 each for his books in today's dollars."

Alice brought the conversation back. "That's interesting, Rexie. So how many of these cult followers bought his books?"

"I've heard over 100,000, maybe more. Not bad, huh?"

Harvey started to fill in the gaps in the story. "I'll just give you the abbreviated version. So, the old man, Asa Sr., is going like gangbusters on his health business, and then he dies. He was a widower, so Asa Junior, his only child, got all his money. Junior marries Vanessa and has a kid they name Asa Marlowe III. They nickname him Three. Meanwhile, Junior finds another girlfriend. Vanessa wants no part of that, so they get divorced. You following me so far?"

"Just keep going, Harvey. If you want, I can give you a marker to draw a family tree," Alice said. The group laughed.

"Ok. Then Junior marries his second wife, Eunice. You've heard of sweet and charming Eunice, I'm sure."

"Sweet like a lemon," Jeb said.

"It continues. We think Junior has a kid with his girlfriend and names him Roscoe. But Roscoe has a different last name. Roscoe Savinni. I guess Junior's girlfriend had another boyfriend. Very confusing. Then five years later, all of a sudden, Junior disappears. Woosh! Vanishes like a lady behind a sheet in a magic show. Then Three leaves town, and so does Roscoe."

"And none of these guys were ever found?" Tootie asked.

"Nope. Spent a lot of time on that case. Way too long. I guess that accident I had was a wake-up call."

All of a sudden, Rexie started laughing, and his laughter got louder and louder. Tears flowed from his eyes.

"What's with you, Rexie? What'd I say?"

"Your recent accident, Harv. Your 'catastrophe.' Rescuing that cat in the tree."

"Since when are broken bones and bruises humorous?"

"I remember you hobbling in here on crutches with a cast on your leg." He started laughing uncontrollably again.

"Ignore him, Harv. Remind us how you were injured," Tootie said. "I know you retired because of your injury."

"Injured in the line of duty," Harvey replied.

"Line of duty! Ha." Tears streamed from Rexie's eyes.

"Wasn't it an animal rescue, Harvey?" Alice asked.

"Well, yeah. I guess you could say that."

"Tell us the straight scoop, big guy," Oscar said.

"Well, a call came in on 911 from just up the street from my house. I was just getting off duty and on my way home, so I stopped at the Cavendish house. I knew them. Thought they were okay people. They sent me to the backyard where there was a cat meowing up about 20 feet in the tree."

"I heard it was 10 feet, Harv," Rexie chimed in and then laughed again. "Story gets better each time you tell it."

"Whatever. They had a ladder up to the tree, and I figured I could climb up, stand on a branch, and grab the cat by the scruff of the neck to bring it down."

Harvey paused as if he didn't want to tell the rest of the story.

"So why did you fall down?" Tootie asked.

"Well, I went up the ladder to almost the top rung. No big deal. I used to be a volunteer firefighter back in the day. I reached for the cat and tried to grab his neck. But Binky, that's the cat's name, jumped to avoid me and landed on my neck. He dug in with his claws, causing me to lose my balance. Before I knew it, Binky and I were victims of gravity. I hit the ground first and buffered Binky. He just jumped off me and scampered away. The Cavendishes were squealing with joy as I lay motionless on the ground."

"But you were hurt."

"Hurt ain't the word for it, Tootie. I was a train wreck. Bruises, broken bones, you name it."

"That was a few months ago, right?"

"December 23, at 4:30 p.m. to be exact, Alice. A date that will live in infamy."

"Not original, Harv, but dramatic. I think President Roosevelt beat you to that line when Pearl Harbor was attacked," Jeb said.

Harvey glared at Jeb and continued. "I thought I would be back on the job in a couple of weeks, but I decided that I had 25 years in with SPD, so I could retire with bennies. I talked with my family, and they thought I should stop the crazy work schedule and retire."

"But there's a murder to solve, Harvey," Oscar said. "Paper says they found Junior."

"We know they found a skeleton, but we don't know yet who it is or if it was a murder," Harvey replied.

"Ok, so you've been a train wreck for a while, and now you're thinking about getting on the train again," Oscar said.

"Choo choo," Rexie said. "All aboard. Chug-a, chug-a, chug-a, chug-a."

"Back to the crime," Oscar said, staring at Rexie. "Enough busting, Harv."

Alice tried to turn the conversation back. "This guy you call Junior all of a sudden disappears. Did anyone see him that night?"

"Nobody did, or at least nobody's saying they did. It was early spring. Kind of like now. Cool nights, warmer days. Eunice says she was out, but she can't remember where. Three, the spoiled playboy, said he was out 'somewhere.'" When Eunice comes home, Junior's nowhere to be found."

"Oh yeah," Tootie said. "There were lots of questions about that case. You used to come in here frustrated. Said everything was too neat. Said there was no evidence like somebody scrubbed the place, so there'd be no clues."

"Yeah, so I talked to Mrs. Marlowe very early this morning." Everyone perked up.

"Get out of town. How could you?" Alice was surprised.

"She was in the ER when I was. A real charmer. She didn't remember that I was the detective on the disappearance, and I didn't tell her. She figured out I was a cop by the questions I asked. I just told her I was retired now."

"What did she say about all this?" Alice continued.

"Nothing to me, but I couldn't help but hear her talking to the chaplain who stopped in to see her. I was surprised by her comments."

"What did she say, Harvey?" Alice persisted.

"You know me," Harvey said. "Even though I'm not a detective, I am a PI. I consider this an active case for me, so I can't say anything that might ruin a lead."

The group issued groans of disappointment.

"You and your leads," Harv," Rexie said. "I remember when you said you thought Junior was murdered by Professor Plum with a wrench in the library. But you didn't have a clue."

The group groaned again.

"What do you guys think?" Harvey turned the conversation away from himself. "Junior goes missing, and 20 years later, a skeleton turns up in a hole on his own property. Way up on the hill near where the old limb maker lived."

"Limb maker, Harvey? You making this stuff up?" Jeb said. "I'm the one that's supposed to know this trivia."

"You probably haven't been up on the mountain on the Marlowe estate. There's a stone foundation of an old house where they said a limb maker used to work. He made prosthetics for people after the Civil War. He was there before the mansion was built, and when he died, the house went to ruins, and nobody cared."

"The paper says some kids were digging behind this place and found the skeleton," Alice reported.

"Inside job," Rexie said right away. "Has to be."

"Yeah, but who was on the inside? Eunice, Three, Roscoe, Three's wife Carmela, Felicia. Who else?"

"You been to the mansion, Rexie?" Tootie wanted to know.

"You think I'm a suspect?"

Everyone laughed.

"Any of you been up there to the mansion? Can't even see it from the road except in winter. It's off Quarry Road." Harvey said.

"I only know about it from people talking around town, but you know who lives near there?" Alice said.

Harvey shrugged his shoulders.

"Noah."

"That's right," Harvey said. "Otto. Otto Zark. With a name like Zark, everybody calls him Noah."

"Cute. Harvey. Noah Zark!" Rexie said.

Another collective groan came from the regulars.

"He used to work for the Marlowes. Maybe he still does, but I haven't seen him in a few years. I talked with him about the case years ago, but a fresh conversation might help. Thanks, Alice."

"So, let's think about another lead," Alice said. "What did Junior do when the old man died?"

"Got rich the old fashioned way," Oscar said. "He inherited it. Gobs of it. The old man owned hundreds of acres up on the mountain. I heard he was going to build a thousand houses there for people who believed in his health system. But that never happened."

"Why not?" Tootie asked.

"Probably died of poor health," Rexie said.

"Don't be stealing Heather Compton's jokes, Rexie," Jeb said. "I heard her say that last night on the news."

Harvey continued. "Marlowe Sr. croaks, and Marlowe Jr. is now rich."

"I heard he got into real estate. Junior used his inheritance to buy up everything imaginable around the area," Rexie chimed in.

"Asa Sr. was smart and put the money in Wall Street. When the market fell and everyone was selling, he was buying. I heard he bought stocks that survived the Great Depression in the early 1930s," Harvey said.

Oscar smiled. "I heard the old man bought into the good stuff like movie production companies, Coca Cola, Standard Oil, US Steel, and many more. By the time Junior got the money, the whole market was way up. Then it was time to sell. Junior used the money to buy cheap properties around Stillwell and sat on them. As they doubled and tripled in price, he sold them."

"So, did Three get all this property when his father went missing?" Alice asked.

"He had enough to live on, but it wasn't long until he disappeared. Junior's wife, Eunice, can draw on the trust. That's probably how she's survived in the mansion all these years. I think Three had money, plenty of money that he got from Junior."

"Did Three and Eunice get along?" Oscar wanted to know.

"What do you think?" Harvey replied.

"I heard Three is a playboy," Alice chimed in. "He married somebody named Carmela. She's not from around here. A lot of shenanigans were going on in that mansion."

"So now we've got this married playboy with a lot of money partying in a big mansion, and he suddenly disappears," Harvey said.

"That's two," Alice said.

"No, he's Three. Two is also missing," Rexie said and laughed.

"You know what I mean, Rexie."

Harvey clarified the rumors. "Three didn't

disappear like we're gonna find him in the next fort kids build. No, he's sending postcards from the Caribbean and who knows where else."

"Postcards, Harvey, really?" Alice asked.

"Not literally. I think he's alive and can be found with a little work."

"We already did a lot of work," Oscar said. "We need a break, in this case, to pull some of the clues together."

"I thought you were retired, O," Harvey said.

Oscar smiled. "Just like you are."

Tootie flashed back to Junior's disappearance. "I remember Junior. He used to come in here and just hang out. It was like he wanted to get away from the mansion."

"Did you meet Eunice?" Harvey asked.

Tootie rolled her eyes. "Memorable. Nasty. Customers used to call her the Wicked Witch of the North."

"Played by Margret Hamilton in the Wonderful Wizard of Oz. 1939."

"Thank you, Jeb," Tootie said. "I remember one time Junior and the Wicked Witch came in here together. Big mistake. They couldn't agree on anything and ended up yelling at each other. I encouraged them to calm down and get takeout."

"I remember when Junior disappeared. I was in here for lunch," Oscar said. "The Café was buzzing with gossip. The place was full of armchair detectives trying to figure out where Junior was."

"Detectives like you, Harvey, only you would have probably fallen on the floor and spilled your coffee if you tried to get out of your armchair!" Rexie said. The eavesdroppers erupted with spontaneous laughter.

"So, nobody knows anything or says anything for twenty years? I think it's safe to say someone knows something." Harvey said.

"You may find this harder than you think," Jeb

chimed in.

Harvey smiled. "We failed the first time. You remember Oscar?"

Oscar nodded.

"But mark my words; I'm not going to fail again. I may not have the answers, but I have more questions this time. And I may not know who to ask now, but I will out. I need to dig deeper into this."

"Go get'em, Clouseau!" an anonymous voice yelled from a table in the back.

The Café filled with laughter again, and Harvey smiled. He surprised himself with his own words.

FLYWHEEL

"Sounds like party time here," a voice said as a 45-year-old black man sauntered up to the counter at Tootie's. "Flywheel," Oscar said, extending his arm for a high five. "Where you been, man? Haven't seen you since Hector was a pup."

Jeb couldn't resist. "In Greek mythology, Hector was the son of King Priam of Troy and his second wife, Hecuba. He participated in the siege of Troy."

"You never give up, Jeb," Oscar said.

"My uncle had a dog named Hector, and he wasn't Greek," Rexie said. "Liked olives, though."

Flywheel shook his head. "So, I see things haven't changed much here."

"Nope," Rexie said to his old high school buddy. "How you been, Fly? You're looking skinny as ever."

"You know me, always snoopin' for metal. Puttin' the pedal to the metal." He smiled his big toothy smile.

"You know Harvey?" Rexie continued.

"Sort of, but not really. You're a cop, right, Mr. Harvey?"

"Harvey Hawkshaw, former cop, now a private investigator. Call me Harvey."

"You can call me Flywheel, just Flywheel. No first name or Mr. or any of that stuff. Former delinquent, full-time upcycler."

"Upcycler?" Harvey asked.

"Yup. Collect old metal and sell it. Kind of like recycling, but classier... upscale... but just metal, no dirty cardboard."

"We were just talking about the missing Marlowes. Remember that case?" Oscar asked.

"Sure. Couldn't forget that bunch. Messed up. Used to pick up metal at the Marlowes all the time. Let's see. First, there was Vanessa. The nice lady who deserved better than Junior. Then there was Eunice. Ugly. Not her looks,

42

her personality. She'd spit at you as soon as look at you. Never saw her smile. Not once."

"How about the other women at the house?"

"Woman, not women. Felicia. Quiet. Kept away from people up in the turret. Like Rapunzel locked up in her tower."

"Hey. Now you're stealing my lines, Fly," Jeb said.

"Wasn't there a third woman?"

"Well, let's see." Flywheel stroked his chin. "Three's wife, Carmela, would come and go, and then she left and didn't come back. Three didn't either. I guess if you count her, there'd be three."

Harvey nodded. "That's helpful to know, Mr. Flywheel."

"Flywheel. No, mister, remember?"

"Oh yeah. Sorry."

"What's all the interest in the Marlowe gig all of a sudden?"

Harvey explained that a skeleton had been found, and the police thought it might be Junior. "I don't remember talking with you 20 years ago," Harvey said.

"That's 'cause I wasn't talking to cops. Last people on earth I wanted to talk to, especially then."

"I'm not a cop now, just a PI trying to solve this case."

"Think there's a difference? Cop. PI. Still got the law on your side."

"You seem to know about the Marlowes and this case."

"Doesn't mean I'm gonna tell you what I know."

"I think you might be interested in talking with me, though."

"Fat chance."

"Ok, what if I contact you, and we talk about the old days?"

"Not my old days."

"No, no. The old days at the Marlowes. Your old

days with them."

"If it's their old days, I'm cool with that. My old days are in the vault. Sealed tight." He made a motion like he was zipping his lip.

Harvey extended his right hand to seal the deal. Flywheel pulled his hand back.

"Just one question, Harvey," Fly said. "Why are you so interested in this case?"

"Why do people rob banks?"

Fly shrugged his shoulders.

"For the money, Flywheel. Money, moola. You know?"

"Now that sounds good. How much?"

"Big reward on this one."

"How big is big, Harvey?"

"We can talk about it soon, but not here."

Flywheel smiled a big, toothy smile as he handed Harvey his business card. "Come by soon. Money sounds good to me."

"We'll be in touch." Harvey smiled.

Flywheel talked with Tootie and got an order to go. Harvey slowly got off his stool and groaned as he awakened his sore shoulder and healing leg. He started to leave when he turned back to the counter. He'd forgotten something.

BREAKFAST FOR PHILIP

"Whatcha need, Harv?" Tootie asked.

"Almost forgot. I'll take a coffee and Danish to go."

"Hungry today, Harv?"

"Nah. Not for me. Throw in a few extra napkins, too."

"Oh. I know where you're going with this."

Harvey smiled and winked at Tootie. Instead of going out to the parking lot the way he came in, he went out the front door onto the square. Stores were opening, and shoppers were pulling their cars into the diagonal parking places that outlined the perimeter of the square.

Harvey wasn't on a shopping trip to one of the boutiques that dotted the square. Instead, he headed like a man on a mission to the gazebo on the island in the middle of the square. He saw Philip sitting alone as he did on most days at his usual spot on a bench in the raised gazebo. Philip was bundled in several layers of clothing, including a stained winter coat, frayed knit ski hat, worn jeans in need of a wash, and well-traveled work boots. He looked and smelled like he could benefit from a shower.

Philip lived in Stillwell all his life, but few people knew his past. They just knew he was a kid no one wanted. He was immediately placed in foster care after birth and remained in foster care until he became an adult, moving from family to family frequently. It was hard to live with Philip and his gruff ways. He seldom talked, and when he did, it was usually a short, strident response, the kind of reply that cut off further conversation. Most people thought Philip was likely the offspring of an unexpected teenage pregnancy.

Several people thought about adopting him, but Philip's obstinate ways quickly changed prospective parents' minds. It was unclear who his biological parents were. People speculated, but no one knew for sure. The social agency in Stillwell was not about to reveal his origins to anyone. What was very clear was that no one wanted a steady dose of Philip.

Despite his crude ways, Philip was befriended by many people. Some pitied him, others liked to learn the town gossip from him, and still, others felt good about bringing food to a down-and-out homeless man. The townsfolk were good to Philip, providing him with enough food and money to survive.

"My man," Harvey said as he mounted the steps to the gazebo. "How ya doin', Phil?"

Philip stared at the bag Harvey was carrying.

"Philip. My name is Philip. You know that."

"Sure. Got something for you, Phil ... ip." Harvey proffered the bag.

Philip looked in the bag and smiled. Without looking up, he raised his right hand, offering Harvey a high five in mute gratitude. He made short work of the Danish and drank the coffee as if he hadn't had food or drink in a long time.

Harvey knew that timing was tricky with Philip. He'd learned not to say anything until Philip finished eating. Sometimes the silence grew uncomfortable. Philip was a man of few words and a limited attention span. But when it came to local happenings, Philip was the go-to source. A Stillwell encyclopedia. He picked up a lot of gossip at the gazebo, and people gave him copies of the Stillwell Gazette to read. Others liked to sit across from Philip and tell him what the news on Channel 8 had to say about local events. Some people treated Philip like a therapist or a priest at a confessional, spewing out their troubles to a silent Buddha. But everyone knew that you had to choose your words carefully, or Philip would shut down.

"What you want, bringing me food and looking like a bum?"

"So, you think I look like a bum?"

"A poor homeless guy like me. Look at you in old beat-up clothes."

"Oh yeah. I had a rough night. I'll be outta these soon. So, I wanted to talk with you about the Marlowe case. Remember that a while back?" Harvey began.

"Ancient. Long time ago. Already told you plenty."

"I know, Philip, but things change," Harvey said.

"We need to talk like in the old days."

Philip nodded. "Cop then."

"Yup. Not anymore. Remember, we could never figure out where Marlowe II, Junior, was."

"Not we. I told you. You didn't listen."

Harvey knew to ignore the insults. "Yeah. I'm getting older now, Philip. Remember what you thought happened to him?"

"Sure."

"What happened?"

"I said he wasn't far away."

"Alive or dead?"

"I didn't say. Just not far away."

"Well, you were right, Philip. He wasn't far away for all these years, and he also wasn't alive."

"Hm. Hadn't heard that. Where'd they find 'im?"

"Up on the mountain. Behind the limb maker's house. Know where that is?"

Philip nodded.

"Some kids were playing, you know, digging a hole to make a fort. They found a skeleton."

Philip furrowed his brow and shook his head. "Not him. He's not there."

"How do you know, Philip?"

"I just do. That's all I'm saying."

"You know the cops could arrest you for withholding evidence."

"They wouldn't."

"Why not?"

"I know too much."

"Hmm. You worked for Junior years ago, right?"

"Back when I could. Worked for Marlowe on the farm."

"So, what was he like?"

"Pretty good guy. Not too bossy. Didn't care much about what happened on the farm."

"How about others? Were they okay?"

"No way."

"What do you mean?"

"That wife of his. What was her name?"

"Eunice?"

"Yeah. Witch."

"Yeah?"

"Marlowe. He'd say the sky's blue, and she'd say it was pink. Couldn't agree on anything."

"How 'bout the son?"

"You mean the third Marlowe? Everybody called him Three. Spoiled rich kid. Thought the world owed him a living. Never did a lick of work in his life."

"Sounds like things weren't so good up on the hill."

"Nasty. Always fighting. Marlowe II with Eunice. Eunice with Three. Three with anybody that asked him to do anything."

"Like who?"

"Noah, for one. He managed things for Marlowe, but Three thought Noah was his servant."

"Like?"

"Wanted him to run errands for him. Polish his shoes. You name it."

"What did Noah do?"

"Told Marlowe or Eunice. More fights. Like a battleground up there some days. And Roscoe was a mess, too."

"I didn't think he was at the mansion. What did he do?"

"Came when he needed money for drugs. Stirred up trouble and left."

"So, was Roscoe Three's brother or half-brother?"

"Don't know whose kid he is. Mother's name is Savini. Felicia, I think."

"This is confusing, Philip. So, is Roscoe Junior's son or the Savini guy's son?"

"Beats me. Hard to know who's related to who."

"Like, who's on first and what's on second?" Harvey said. "Remember that old Abbot and Costello joke?"

"Nah. You would. I'm too young."

Harvey smiled. Philip's insults were endless.

Philip looked down at his empty bag, put his cup in it, took out the napkins, wiped off his face, and blew his nose. He looked more relaxed. That was Harvey's clue. More talk required more food.

"I gotta go, Philip," Harvey said. He was exhausted from his sleepless night in the hospital and wanted a nap in the worst way. "I know how to find you."

"Sandwich," Philip replied.

"Sure. Next time I'll come with a sandwich. Be thinking about those days workin' up on the hill."

Philip nodded and handed Harvey the bag with the empty cup and dirty napkins in it.

"See you soon," Harvey said as he headed down the stairs and tossed the bag in the trash can.

"Maybe, but you be careful, man. You're playing with fire with that family."

CHAPPY CHAN

As Harvey left the gazebo and crossed the square, he remembered that he had no ride home. Donut had brought him to Tootie's, so he'd have to call someone or walk home. He stopped on the sidewalk and took out his cell phone when a neatly dressed Asian man walked up to him.

"Harvey, how are you?"

Harvey looked up from his phone and smiled. "Hey. Chappy, how 'ya doin'? Saw us both on TV the other night."

Chappy rolled his eyes. Always well dressed and well groomed, Chappy looked more like he just stepped out of GQ than someone trying to solve a cold case. His suit was perfectly tailored for his trim 5'7" frame, his shoes were shined like he was in Army boot camp, and as always, he looked bright and focused.

"How are things at the department, Chappy?"

"We're doing okay, Harv, but we miss you."

Harvey gave his modest smile.

"But I see you're getting a lot of media attention these days."

"Don't start, Chappy. People were having a field day with my lawn incident last night. Must be boring around here if that's all they have to do."

"Not boring on my front."

"Yeah?"

"Your old case, the Marlowe mess. You know we found a body up there on the mountain?"

"I heard about it. You think it's Junior?"

"The media thinks it is, but we need forensics to tell us who it is or at least who it could be."

"You have your doubts, huh?"

Chappy nodded his head. "I haven't been a detective as long as you were, but I don't think it's him. Don't know who it is; just my gut is telling me it isn't

Junior."

"That gut is important to listen to." Harvey patted his paunch. "I got two other people who would agree with your gut."

"Really? Who?"

Harvey explained what he overheard Eunice say in the emergency room and what Philip had told him.

"Wow. Two people that could know something."

"Say, my friend, I know you're here on company time, but I'm wondering if you could give me a ride home. Donut gave me a ride here, but he's at work, thank goodness. I want to get home safely and get out of these clothes."

"You're not making a good fashion statement, Harv. Sure, I'd be happy to take you home. I can fumigate the car later."

When he got home, Harvey turned off his phone and immediately fell into a deep sleep. At 2:30 in the afternoon, he was awakened by Fluffy, who was kneading his leg and purring loudly. She wanted what all cats want, food and attention on their own terms.

"Oh, alright, alright, Fluffernoodles," he said to her as he lumbered to the kitchen to replenish her food.

Out of habit, he looked at his cell phone and realized it was shut off. He turned it on and noticed a big red 11 on the text message icon. "Geez, Louise," he said to no one. "I can't get away from people. Maybe I should go on vacation. Aruba sounds good."

He made a cup of coffee to wake up and then began to tackle the messages. Reporters, friends, acquaintances, and people he didn't know were all wanting to talk with him. The only message he wanted to read was from Chappy.

"Good seeing you today," Chappy had texted. "Let's talk some more about the body. Need some background. I think you can help."

Harvey thought it was a good idea to return the text

with a call. "Hey, Chapster. I can help you with what happened 20 years ago, but I'd like your help with what's happening now."

"Why do you care about what's happening now? You're retired."

"Well, I spent a lot of time on this case and got nowhere, and, well, you know, the other part of this case."

"No, I don't."

"The reward money. I couldn't think about that while I was in the department, but now I'm a private investigator and eligible for all that reward money."

"I hear you, Harv, but I can't give you much to go on. Not much to snoop or scoop yet. We have the forensics team all over the site where they found him if it's Junior."

"You agree with Philip and Eunice?"

"Don't really know yet. Ollie Kingston, the medical examiner, picked up the skeleton from the gravesite, but the skull wasn't on it."

"What? You gotta be kidding. Grave robbers?"

"Nah, just the kids, those Hopper kids that were making the fort and found the bones."

"Souvenir hunters?"

"Yeah, kind of. The kids brought the skull home. You know, kids, Harv."

"Not those kinds of kids. That's sick, isn't it, Chappy? Taking the skull off a skeleton isn't normal. Most kids would be freaked out."

"Not normal, but what's normal when you're 12 years old? The next step is to comb the area for any 20-year-old evidence. We'll have to call in for help using GPR. We don't own the equipment. Very expensive.'"

"I'm not up on this technology, Chappy."

"You know, ground penetrating radar that lets you see what's underground. It's like an x-ray of the ground. They'll scan the whole field. Never know what else you'll find."

"Think they have enough to identify the person now?"

"Good question, Harv. Hey, it's great talking to you, but I've got to run. I have to go meet with Milt to figure out what we're saying at the press conference this afternoon. If you snoop and find something, let me know. But remember, you're off the books. You can't be doing too much snooping, or they'll invalidate what you find in court."

"Look at you, Chappy. Giving me advice like I used to give you. I'm proud of you, son."

"Son. Ha. Are you fishing for a Father's Day gift? Don't answer, Dad. Bye."

After his call with Chappy, Harvey's mind began racing, so he went to his garage. Some might call it a man cave or just a place to escape to, but he did some of his best thinking there. He called the third bay in the garage The Situation Room, his fortress. It didn't look like a garage, with no oil stains from his car, no junk except his "man junk." Harvey had painted the walls and floor. He made it homey with his well-worn sofa, a 65-inch TV for football, basketball and baseball seasons, a cupboard filled with snacks, and a refrigerator filled with beer. "What else could a man want?" he often asked.

The key elements of The Situation Room were his "boards." He had a whiteboard where he could use markers to make notes and diagrams. He always felt like a football coach when he drew his diagrams. He also had a pin board where he could post pictures of possible perpetrators, newspaper articles, and other ephemera. He had a computer with internet service there, too, but Harvey had enough trouble mastering the cell phone. He always planned on learning more about computing tomorrow.

He grabbed a marker and let his thoughts go into overdrive. He wrote anything he could think of that related to the cold case on his whiteboard:

Marlowe family: Eunice, Junior, Three, Carmela,

Felicia, and Roscoe.

      Suspects: Eunice???

Who is the third woman that Heather Compton mentioned? Carmela? Someone else?

      People who know something: Eunice, Philip

      Evidence: grave, skull, see Hopper kids

      People to talk to Flywheel, Noah

He clipped the Marlowe story, including that now famous picture of him from the Stillwell Gazette, and stuck it to the pin board next to the faded picture of the Marlowe mansion that had been put there 20 years ago. Satisfied that his brain dump was complete for the time being, he grabbed a beer from the 'fridge, turned on the TV, and promptly fell back to sleep.

NOAH ZARK

Otto Zark lived in the last remaining worker's house on the Marlowe estate. It was a small bungalow just off Quarry Road, south of the long driveway that led to the mansion. He and his wife, Earlene, had no kids, so the house was just the right size for them and their dog, Diesel. They lived there rent-free since he was an employee of the Marlowe family for many years. There used to be other houses for the employees, but those were torn down when parcels of land were sold off by Junior. Now, the Zark's house sits among trees near an upscale housing development that was developed by Junior. Almost no one called Otto by his first name. He was known around town as Noah, a nickname his parents had called him since birth.

Harvey drove a mile to the west side of town, crossed the railroad tracks, headed a mile north to Quarry Road, and then to Noah's, halfway up the mountain a quarter mile from the mansion. As he parked the car and started to get out, he saw Noah's dog sitting attentively on the front porch. Diesel was a three-year-old black lab with a shiny coat and a playful spirit. He was carefully trained by Noah, who walked out on the porch to see who was arriving.

Noah was in his early 60s, thin but rugged looking from his years of work on the farm. He has been very cautious ever since his house was burglarized two years ago. Noah recognized Harvey and gave Diesel a nod. "Go say hi, Diez."

As Harvey closed the car door, he saw Diesel coming at him at full speed. He tried to avert his welcome by turning his back just as Diesel leaped to greet him. Too late. Diesel's front paws pushed the middle of Harvey's back, and he slipped on the muddy ground, falling face forward into a mud puddle that still had remnants of last night's late winter freeze in it. Diesel immediately started making whimpering sounds and licked Harvey's face as he struggled to get up from the slippery slurry. Every joint in his body seemed to remember yesterday's event in his front yard.

Noah ran over to him and helped him stand up. "Sit, Diesel," he said, and the dog obeyed after finding a dry spot to rest his haunches.

"Sorry, Harv," he said. "He got a little carried away trying to make a new friend."

Harvey didn't say a word as he wiped off his wet face and made a vain attempt to clean off his jacket and wet pants.

"What do you need?"

"How 'bout a towel, for starters?"

Noah got a towel, and Harvey wiped himself off.

"Kinda like taking a shower with my clothes on," Harvey said.

"So, what brings you here, my friend? It's been a couple of years, at least."

"When did you get that rascal, Noah?" Harvey asked. "Still acts like a pup, but he's got some weight to 'im."

"Diesel's great…well, when he's not knocking my friends into mud puddles. Got him a couple to three years ago. I forget; you know how time flies."

"Like a rocket. But do you know that fruit flies like a bunch of rotten bananas?"

Noah laughed. "An old one, Harv. My father used to say that's an old Groucho Marx line."

Harvey was calming down, and Noah invited him to sit down on the porch. He offered him a beer, but Harvey declined. "I'm on the clock, Noah. I don't mix booze and work. After work, well, that's another story."

"What work? I heard you retired."

"Yeah, I don't work for the town anymore, but I'm still a cop at heart. I call myself a PI now. I have a license, too. Legit."

"So, what brings you here? You're not trying to

hide from all that publicity you got, are you?"

"Wish I could, but this is real business."

"You've been the butt of a lot of publicity, Harv."

"Cute, Noah. But I've had my fill of butt jokes, so I need to be serious for a minute."

"Hard for me to be serious when I'm looking at you all covered with mud and thinking about you on the Channel 8 News with your butt in the air yelling about bombs going off." Noah got laughing. "You have to admit it was funny, Harv."

"No, I don't, and I won't."

Still laughing, Noah said, "Ok. So, you want me to be serious." He tried to contain himself but started hilariously laughing before Harvey could say anything. Tears rolled from his eyes, and about the time he was calm enough to talk, he would burst out laughing again.

"You done?" Harvey asked in a deadpan tone.

The best Noah could do was nod his head.

Finally, Harvey just spits out why he was there. "You know they think they found Junior."

"Yeah. That was the second big event on the news. You know I used to work for them? Well, I kind of still do. But just on call when they need help."

Harvey nodded.

"I had worked for the old guy. Two. Some call him Junior, but I call him Two. I worked first as a manager of the crew when he still did a lot of farming. He had quite an operation up there, but after he went missing, Mrs. Marlowe just kept me on as a handyman and rent-a-cop. You know, security."

"You remember Three then."

"Sure. He was like a wild stallion then. In his 20s, he had lots of money and thought he was God's gift to women. I never could figure out what was going on with him. Dressed to kill. Expensive clothes, perfectly tailored. He'd travel alone. Never said where he was going. Seldom took his wife with him."

"What was her name?"

"Carmela."

"First I heard of her. She wasn't there when I was interviewing the two women that lived there."

"Well, she wasn't there much, and when Three disappeared, she did, too. For years, almost two decades."

"Any kids?"

"Nope. Only family was that dimwit of a half-brother, Roscoe."

"Dimwit?"

"Well, maybe I should have called him a druggie. He was pretty smart before he got burned out."

"Really into drugs, huh?"

"You name it. Cocaine, heroin. Today he'd be into opioids for sure."

"So, what happened to him?"

"After Two disappeared, Roscoe left town."

"Sounds suspicious."

"Especially since Three didn't want anything to do with him. They think Roscoe is Junior's son like Three is, but they never did any paternity tests. Junior left his first wife, Vanessa, and married Eunice. He soon found out that his girlfriend, Felicia, was pregnant. Nobody's sure if Roscoe was fathered by Junior or that derelict boyfriend that Felica took up with. It gets really complicated, Harv."

"Let me see if I get this. There's Three, who is the son of Junior and Eunice. Not his first wife."

"No, three is Junior's son, but his mother is Junior's first wife, Vanessa."

"Ok. And then there's Roscoe, who's either Three's half-brother or no relation if the derelict is his father."

Noah nodded.

"Then Junior goes missing 20 years ago. Three has money because his father has a lot of money and gives him a generous allowance. Actually, more than that. Rumors say that he gave Three several million dollars for his playboy spree."

Noah nodded again.

"And then there's Roscoe. Junior could be his father, but nobody's sure."

"Except Junior said no. He didn't accept any responsibility for Roscoe. He disowned him."

"Where did Roscoe live?"

"Not sure. Last I heard, he lived on the streets in Philmont. Bigger town, more drugs."

"Did he ever come back to visit?"

"You mean to beg, borrow, and steal? Sure. I had to drive him back to Philmont many a time."

"So, who would give him money here?"

"Felicia. She lived at the mansion with Eunice at the time. Still does. Two sort-of widows. Widows without corpses."

"You really know a lot about this family and the disappearances."

"Things slowed down at the mansion after the disappearances. Eventually, I got another job over at Higgin's Electronics. They make all kinds of component parts for electronics. A lot of government contracts. I've been there parttime ever since Junior disappeared. The job's pretty easy. Just screen people who come into the plant. Eunice calls on me if she has security issues or needs something done. Pays me sometimes, but I'm not sure she has a lot of cash. It's all tied up in investments and trusts. Bank handles most of the business stuff for the family now."

"Unless someone cleaned it out, that estate must be worth a fortune now."

"Ya think? It was a fortune before Two and Three left town."

"Maybe they left more than a town, Noah." Harvey lifted his head up, nodding toward the sky.

"Oh, yeah. Or not. But Three could be on a Caribbean Island sipping Mai Tai's on the beach."

Harvey smiled. "If that's the case, he took a whale

of a lot of money with him to live like that for this long. Twenty years of Mai Tai costs a lot of money. What about the wife? Did she stick around? Must be getting some of that money."

"Good question, Harv. People knew that Two had disappeared, but they didn't realize that Three had also disappeared. You know, he was away so much. Hard to know where he went or when he was here."

"So, the wife stayed home. What was her name again?"

"Carmela, but she wasn't here long after Three left. She was gone for years like Three was. Then all of a sudden, she returned a couple of years ago. She'd be here for a while and leave. I gave up figuring out what was going on."

"Is Carmela there now?"

"I think so. She was a couple of weeks ago when Eunice had me come up to help her."

"So, what do you think happened up there? Foul play?"

"Nobody knows. Whatever happened, it was a neat and tidy departure."

"Well, this has been helpful, Noah. Confusing but helpful."

"I can't tell you much more, but you know who might have some information, Harv?"

Harvey shrugged his shoulders.

"Flywheel."

"Flywheel. Yeah, I met him at Tootie's yesterday. The metal guy. Thought I knew everybody in Stillwell. I recognized him but never really talked to him before. He stayed clear of cops."

"He doesn't live here, but you know him. He works all over town. You know, that guy with the beat-up pickup? Picks up metal and junk. Says he recycles it, but he's got quite a pile of stuff out there. Calls his place an upcycle center."

"Oh yeah. Can you make a living off that stuff?"

"Better than a living, Harv. Flywheel is rich. Still lives across the railroad tracks in Philmont, a couple of miles out of town and up the mountain. Can't miss the old junkyard. Gets his junk for free, and sometimes he charges people to take it away. He sells it off to flea market types and metal recyclers."

Harvey nodded. "You think he's going to know about the Marlowes?"

"I don't know, but he knows a heck of a lot about whatever's going on. Even stuff that we don't know is going on. He knew Three and Roscoe from Philmont. He's about their age."

"Really?"

"I'd be surprised if he doesn't know something. I'd also be surprised if he tells you anything."

"Great. I love challenges. And, oh, one more thing, Noah. You know Philip, the homeless guy who lives in the gazebo in town?"

Noah didn't say anything at first. "Uh, well, sure. I guess I know about him. Can't say as I really know him. I don't go into town much. Earlene does, but I don't."

"He seems to know a lot about what's going on around here, too. He said he used to work for Junior."

"Gosh. That's right. Many, many years ago. Then he got messed up, and the next thing you know, he was on the street."

"He says it isn't Junior that they found up in that grave."

Noah shrugged his shoulders. "Who else would it be? Three or Roscoe?"

"The medical examiner will do his thing, and they'll figure out who it is."

"Let me know if you find out. I'm curious."

That was Harvey's exit cue. "Well, Noah, it's been nice seeing you again. I'm going to move on. Maybe I'll go home and change my clothes! I seem to be doing a lot of that lately."

Noah laughed as Harvey headed to his old Ford Mustang. "I'll let you know if I find Two or Three," he yelled.

"You won't, and I won't, but we might, Noah. You know, many a mickle makes a muckle."

Noah looked perplexed by Harvey's comment and just waved as he drove away.

Harvey headed back home. His greeting from Diesel and his wetness from that slushy mud puddle aggravated his already damaged shoulder and reminded him of the aches and pains that he thought were subsiding after his bomb event. After he showered again and donned another set of clean clothes, he sat down on the couch and promptly fell asleep. A visit to Flywheel would have to wait for another day.

THE UPCYCLE CENTER

The next morning Harvey felt like he could tackle the world... until he tried to move. Then he remembered being tackled by that pair of white-jacketed lugs in the hospital. He called a few of his favorite contacts to see if they knew anything about Flywheel and found out that Noah was right about him. Everybody said Flywheel was tightlipped and full of knowledge about what was going on in Stillwell as well as Franklin Township, Philmont, and Carney. Rexie knew him from his school days and told Harvey, "You're gonna need a crowbar to pry any information out of that guy. He knows all the good guys as well as all the bad actors. Be careful."

Harvey took the scenic route to Flywheel's junkyard in Philmont, 20 minutes away. As he rode across the railroad tracks, the tranquil farmland was interrupted by an enormous pile of metal parts that rose from the ground like a monolithic sculpture. Noah and his homies at Tootie were right. You couldn't miss Flywheel's metal collection.

Flywheel's place was on Wheaton Road as you headed up the mountain. Harvey parked his Mustang outside the fenced yard beneath a sign that said, "Flywheel's Upcycle Center. No metal refuse refused." He read the sign a couple of times, shook his head, and decided to find Flywheel. He could hear some smashing going on inside the six-foot-tall stockade fence that surrounded the yard. High above the fence line, he could see piles of rusted and faded metal. Old wrecked cars, dented sliding boards, and old metal boilers were strewn about like discarded trophies from an ancient battle. Harvey couldn't see through the fence, so he went over to the solid gate that looked like the only entrance to the junkyard. The doorbell had a sign above it.

• Bill collector? Ring once. Wait 10 seconds and leave.

• Looking for a handout? Ring twice. Wait 10

seconds and leave.

- Got metal? Ring three times and wait.

Harvey scratched his head. "Hmm," he thought. None of these apply." So, he rang the doorbell four times.

Immediately, a large dog started barking ferociously, causing Harvey to jump back from the gate, remembering his greeting from Diesel yesterday. "Not again," he said aloud to no one. This dog had a deep sound like a Rottweiler on a rampage. Harvey jumped back farther. The smashing sound stopped, and in a few seconds, a small speakeasy-style door that Harvey hadn't noticed in the larger fence door slid open, and a skinny brown face peered out.

The barking continued. "Cool it, Bosco," the man looking through the small window said. The dog stopped barking.

"You don't want money, and you aren't giving me money, so what's your business, mister."

"My name is…."

Before he could finish, Flywheel laughed. "I know who you are, Mr. Harvey. Just joshing you. After I saw you at Tootie's, I saw a lot more of you on TV. Must be desperate for news over there at Channel 8."

Flywheel started to open the gate, and Bosco started to bark again.

"Better leash that monster or I'm not comin' in," Harvey said.

Flywheel started to laugh again and opened the gate. A small brown chihuahua scurried out and made a soft, high-pitched barking sound as he nipped at Harvey's heels.

"This is Little Bosco," Flywheel said.

"Where's the big monster?" Harvey walked to the gate, poked his head inside, and looked left and right. No Rottweiler was anywhere in sight.

Flywheel reached up on the gatepost and pushed a button. Immediately, the Rottweiler began barking again.

Harvey jumped back, tripping on Little Bosco but catching himself before he fell in the driveway.

Flywheel laughed again. "You're goosey, man."

"You tryin' to scare the b'jesus out of me?"

"You and the bill collectors." Fly looked intently at Harvey. "You know, I think I know you. Not from being a cop or ex-cop or whatever you are. Somethin' else."

"Everybody's seen me. And don't start with my newspaper picture either. I've heard enough of those jokes this week."

"But you look familiar to me. Someplace else."

Fly put his hands on the side of his head like he was trying to communicate with a deceased relative. After a long pause, he popped his head up, and his eyes widened. "Got it," he said, and then he laughed. "I know how I know you." He laughed some more. "Years ago. Never forget it. I was workin' at that mattress store over there off Route 10. 'Remember that one? Philmont Mattress Company. It's long gone, but I remember you."

"Yeah. Can't say as I remember you, Mr. Flywheel."

"Just Flywheel. Remember. No Mister. Bill collectors and people wantin' money call me Mister."

Harvey nodded. "Ok. Flywheel. Still can't remember you."

"You came in the store askin' me all kinds of questions about mattresses like you were some fancy dancy mattress guru. And then you wanted to try some out." Flywheel shook his head and chuckled. "You tried a couple, bouncing up and down like you were on a trampoline. I asked you to cool it on the jumping, but it was like you were on a bouncy high. And then you wanted to try one of those waterbeds. You know, all squishy and slushy." Flywheel got a big grin on his face.

"Oh, yeah," Harvey said. Then his eyes widened. "Oh no. No...no. We don't need to go there. Let's talk about why I'm here."

Flywheel ignored his comment. "So, you laid on

this waterbed, and you got rockin' and rollin'. Remember? You asked me if it came with seasick pills. Then you wanted to see if you could stand up."

Harvey just shook his head.

"Your wife's there telling you to sit down, but you think you're surfing like one of those California dudes."

Harvey shook his head again. "You don't need to remind me."

"And then you jump up. You see it... the big wave. A bomb." Flywheel jumped up, flung his arms out like a surfer, and laughed. "And you caught it all right. You came down hard, and 'kapow,' the mattress let go. You fall." Flywheel got laughing harder. "Water's flyin' all over the place, and you land on your back on the bed frame. Hurtin' dude, man. You were a sore puppy. I had to help you up."

"Uh, Flywheel, maybe we don't have to remember this anymore, Okay?"

Flywheel was still laughing and sputteringly as he continued the story. "I can still see you slippin' and slidin' out of control. You're yellin', and before you know it, your feet go out from under you. Splat. You flopped like a big old whale."

"Well, maybe we could talk about the reason I came here."

"Sure." Flywheel laughed, shook his head, and slapped its knee. "Splat!" He laughed even harder.

Harvey walked away from Flywheel and toward the huge metal pile.

Flywheel finally calmed down and pointed to the enormous metal pile. "This is where all the action happens."

"What's that smashing sound I'm hearing?"

"Oh, that. I'm so used to it. I forget it's on. Let me turn it off." Flywheel pulled a tiny remote control from his pocket, pointed it toward the office, and clicked it once. The piercing sound of metal smashing stopped.

"I don't get it, Flywheel. You've got a small dog

with a Rottweiler recording. Smashing sounds but no actual work. What's going on here? You printing money in the basement?"

"Can't do that, Harvey. I ain't got a basement." He slapped his knee and laughed again.

"So, you know a lot about what's going on around the area, right?"

"Might say that."

"I'm trying to find out more about the Asa Marlowe case. Remember that?"

"Might say that."

"You were around when he disappeared, right?"

"Might say that."

"Did you know the family—Junior, his wife, Three, and Roscoe."

"Knew Roscoe best but knew them all."

"Roscoe had a drug problem, right?"

"Might say that."

"Can you tell me more about the family or the disappearance?"

"Maybe."

"Will you?"

"Depends."

Harvey was getting frustrated. "Ok, Flywheel. You're like a clam shell. How do I get you to open up?"

Flywheel rubbed his thumb against his fingers. "You know what talks."

"What do I look like, a bank?"

"Might say that."

"I'm looking into this old case because they think they found Junior."

"Think they found him? Where was he? In Bora Bora?"

"Doing underground work."

"Huh? He's a cop?"

"No. Underground, as in buried."

Flywheel jumped back and got serious. "Now

you're creeping me out, man. Dead?"

"Well, the media thinks it's him."

"How do you know all this? You're still being a cop, aren't you.? I knew it."

Harvey just smiled. "Used to be."

"I can't be messin' with no cops. I'd lose half my customers."

"I told you there's a reward for finding Junior. It's been on the books for years, but nobody's claimed it."

"But you said they found him."

"I said the media thinks they found him. It could be somebody else. A couple of people in the know think it's somebody else."

Flywheel took on a more serious tone. 'Hmm. So, I got the knowledge that you want, but you don't have the money I want."

Harvey smiled. "Might say that."

"Hey, that's my line. You can't go stealing my line." Flywheel said with a smile.

They both laughed.

"Ok. I'm not sure I can get a reward 'cause I'm a retired cop, but I'm willing to give it a try."

"I'm not seeing me in this picture."

"If we work together, I might have some info, and you already have info. We pool these ideas and see what we can come up with. Maybe find these guys…and that's when the reward kicks in."

"Reward. I like the sound of that word. Now you're talkin'."

"See. I know we can work this out."

"How much?"

"Depends on how much help you give me. If you can help me untangle this crazy family, you'd probably get the big bucks."

"How much?" Flywheel repeated.

"Was $100K, but I heard it's up to $150K."

Fly stroked his chin as he thought about the

reward. "Here's the problem, Harvey. I know nothin' 'bout you. Who you really are, where you live, what you do for a livin,' except when you're trying to wheel and deal with a poor old upcycler."

"Poor, huh? Like Marlowe. I heard you're loaded."

"Ha! Nowhere near that rich. Doin' okay, but nothin' like that."

"So, you in? It's a win-win for you."

"Well, I guess so, but I might bail if this gets messy."

"You can bail at any time. I'll just get your $75K."

Harvey extended his hand. "Deal?"

Flywheel pretended that he was thinking about it, then shook Harvey's hand. "Ok, deal."

"Great, partner," Harvey said.

"I'm ready, Boss. Where do we start?"

"First off, I'm not your boss. We're partners."

Fly rolled his eyes.

"Well, there's a couple of things we need to do," Harvey said. "We need to know more about the three ladies living in the mansion. I call them the sisters, even though they aren't. But I think there are other people who know things, too."

"Like who?"

"The kids who found the body, for starters."

"Kids? How'd they find the body?"

"It's more than I want to go into now. I'll see if we can talk to them. I know the parents, so I'll give them a call."

"Tell them we aren't using rubber hoses and bright lights."

"I won't even suggest it, Flywheel."

"You can call me Fly. We're partners, remember. If we go bust, it will be Flywheel or Mr. Flywheel. Understand?"

Harvey laughed. "Ok, partner. Give me your cell number so I can let you know what time we'll meet them tomorrow. I'll aim for 1:00 p.m. in the parking lot of Mershon Park. I think it's better if we use my car. I saw your truck."

"Now you're hurting my feelings, Harvey. You know I'm sensitive." Flywheel pretended to wipe a tear from his eye. "I've kept Minerva running for years, Harvey. It's as old as I am. 40 something. She's been good to me."

"Let's hope she still is." As Harvey got back in his Mustang, he heard the smashing of metal and a Rottweiler barking in the background and wondered if this partnership would work.

THE HOPPER KIDS

Harvey called Flywheel the next morning and confirmed that they'd go to meet the kids at 1:30 p.m. He told Flywheel to arrive a half hour early. Harvey arrived at Mershon Park precisely at 1:00 p.m., but Fly wasn't there. He sat there for ten minutes and was growing impatient when he finally heard the old truck clanking up the lane to the park.

"I wasn't sure you'd show," Harvey said.

"Man, of my word, at least some of the time. I'm like the rich dudes today, fashionably late."

Fly got into Harvey's Mustang, and Harvey briefed him on what to do.

"These are kids. Their parents had some reservations about us talking to them, so we have to tread lightly."

"They found a body, but what else could they know?" Fly wondered.

"They were there and made observations about the area. They may not know what they know."

"So, if they don't know what they know, how are they going to give us evidence?"

"I'm not sure, Fly, but we will know when we know."

Fly just shook his head. "You're messing with me, Harv. Don't do that."

"I'm speaking the truth like I almost always do, Fly. They don't know what they know until we ask them about what they saw and found. And we don't know what they know until they tell us. Got it?"

"No. And I don't know what I don't know, and you don't know what I don't know. So, we don't know."

"Right. And we're going to find out what we don't know."

"How?"

"By asking the kids."

"You said you know them, right?"

"Yeah. They're Ed and Janice Hopper's kids."

"Oh, Flush's kids? I know Flush. An old friend of mine from growing up. Good guy. Great kids."

"Flush? Never heard him called that."

"With a name like Hopper, what'd you expect?"

Harvey shook his head and laughed.

"Good guy. Helped me get in and out of trouble."

Fly and Harvey drove over to Greenwood Avenue. It was Saturday, and it was very quiet at the usually bustling Hopper house.

They went up on the porch, and Harvey rang the doorbell. Janice came to the door, recognized Harvey and Fly, and then stepped out on the porch to talk with them. Harvey explained that they just wanted to ask a few questions that might help them solve the case.

Janice hesitated. "Well, you should know that they're on weekend lockdown since they found the body and brought the skull home."

"Really? Ooh," Fly wrinkled his nose. "Didn't know they brought the skull home. Kinda creepy for little kids," he remarked. "Kinda sweet, though. They were probably bringing mom a present. Creepy sweet."

"It's not sweet if you don't know your kids are digging up bodies on somebody else's private property. Suppose they got hurt up there. Who would know?"

Fly knew he'd better not say anything more.

"Let me find Flush. He was in the bathroom."

Flywheel slapped his knee and laughed. "Flush is in the bathroom. Cracks me up!"

"Sorry, Janice. See what I have to put up with?" Harvey said.

"No need to explain. We know Fly."

Janice went off to get the kids, and Ed came onto the porch.

"Hey, Ed," Harvey said.

"Hey, Flush," Fly said. "Got any metal you want to

get rid of?"

Ed pointed to Fly. "What are you doing with this guy, Harvey?"

"Trainee. Teaching him how to catch bad guys."

Ed laughed. "Fly knows where to look!"

"Be nice, Flush."

The 12-year-old twins, who were called Eddie and Jani, came flying out the front door onto the porch like pit bulls escaping from a kennel.

Eddie gave Fly a high five.

Jani jumped into Fly's arms. "Uncle Fly. Where have you been? They locked us up in our rooms for the weekend. Help us escape."

"Sorry, guys. I heard about that."

"Can't you pay them off to get us out of jail?" Eddie asked.

"I don't think that's a possibility," Harvey interjected. "Anyway, you're out of jail because we want to talk with you if it's alright with your parents and you."

"We're your Get Out of Jail Free card like in Monopoly," Fly added.

"Can we, Dad?" Jani pleaded. "And stay out of jail?"

"Yes, and maybe. Depends on how cooperative you are with Mr. Hawkshaw and Fly."

"Yay!" they yelled.

"Maybe, I said."

They went into the house and sat in the living room.

Harvey started. "I read in the Stillwell Gazette that you went up on the mountain to build a fort. Tell us about why you went to that particular place to build it."

Jani spoke first. "Well, we like to build forts in our neighborhood, but Billy Jankowski and his gang always wreck them. He's a big rotten bully. We figured if we got far enough away, they wouldn't wreck it."

Harvey smiled, and Fly responded. "I can see that.

Makes sense."

"Some of the kids in our class told us about this old crumbling building up on the mountain," Eddie said.

You could tell they were twins. By the way, Jani continued the conversation as if it was one person talking. She said, "We took a couple of small camping shovels and put a bunch of small digging tools in a canvas bag that was in the garage."

"Then we rode our bikes up Quarry Road as far as we could. It got too hard to pedal, so we walked the bikes up to the old building," Eddie added.

"Do you know what was there a long time ago?" Harvey asked.

"Billy Chan told me it was a limb maker's house. He said that they made arms and legs for people that needed them after theirs got blown apart in the Civil War. Sounds gross," Jani said.

"Billy Chan. Must be Detective Chan's boy. Little Snappy Chan," Fly said. "Is he a snappy dresser like his dad?"

The kids shrugged their shoulders, and Eddie continued. "We found some nails and stuff behind the house and decided to keep digging near the stone wall to make a fort. The ground was already a little sunken in."

"And then you found the body, right?" Fly asked.

"We hit something hard with the shovel and thought it was a treasure chest. Jani got all excited and thought it was millions of dollars in jewelry."

"You were pretty excited, too, Eddie. Remember you said you were buying a Corvette? You can't even drive yet."

"Doesn't mean I can't buy it and have it sit in the driveway 'til I get my license."

"Ok, kids," Harvey said. "So, you clunked something hard with a shovel and probably kept digging for the treasure. What next?"

"I screamed," Jani said. "I saw these eye sockets

looking up at me."

"I just jumped back from the hole," Eddie added.

"But I came back and started digging around the skull."

"What happened next?" Harvey asked.

"Well," Eddie said. "We were kind of freaked out by it. But Jani said she wanted to take the skull home. She said it would look good in her bedroom."

"I did not, you liar. You know it was you who wanted it. You said you wanted to put a light in it and have her be weird at night."

"Did not."

"Did, too."

"Ok, guys," Harvey said. "So, the skull wasn't attached to the body?"

Eddie responded. "It was until she accidentally smashed it hard with the shovel."

"You did that. Not me," Jani responded.

"But you wanted to take it home. You put it in the tool bag in your bicycle basket and brought her home."

Fly interrupted. "Wait. What do you mean brought her home?"

"Well, we thought it was a girl, but we weren't sure. The rags that were left looked like something a girl would wear."

"Interesting. So, what did you do next?" Harvey asked.

"We got on our bikes and pedaled home as fast as we could," Jani said. "It was downhill, so it was easier than going there."

Eddie continued the story. "After we washed the skull, I dried it with mom's kitchen towel. We put it on the table. Mom came in the kitchen, and when she stopped screaming, she called the police."

"Yeah, I've never seen her like that. She made us take it outside," Jani reported.

"Do you think it was a girl just because of the

clothes?" Harvey asked.

Jani paused. "Uh, well, because."

"Better tell them, Jani," Eddie said.

Jani spoke fast. "Okay, okay. We found a locket wrapped around the neck of the skeleton. Heart-shaped. With a gold chain. But we couldn't open it without breaking it."

"What?" her father yelled. "You never told us about this."

"We were afraid to, Dad," she said. "We figured you'd make a big deal out of it."

"You're darn right. I'd make a big deal out of it, young lady. Now you can add stealing to your crimes of trespassing and removing a body part from a grave."

"Wait, Flush." Fly intervened. "Remember the time you went to the pet cemetery with me and dug up Rin Tin Tin 'cause you wanted to do your own autopsy?"

"Dad. You did that? That's horrible," Jani said.

"Wasn't Rin Tin Tin," her father said.

"Must have been Lassie," Fly laughed.

"I'm sure it was Scooby Doo," Ed said.

"Dad!" Jani exclaimed.

"Let's see. That would be trespassing, removing a body, and who knows what else," Fly said. "How old were we? Hmmm. Twelve, right? I rest my case."

"Alright. Alright," Flush said. "But you two shouldn't have been doing that."

"Did you do jail time, Dad?" Eddie asked.

"Well, no, I didn't."

"Probation?"

"No. Let's get back to the skull."

"Anything?"

"No."

"Not even a weekend lockdown?"

Flush shook his head.

"Why not?"

"Well, only one person knew about it."

The twins looked at Fly.

"Got a lot of mileage out of what I knew. I kept my mouth shut, and your dad always knew what I knew."

"So, you were blackmailing him," Eddie said.

Before Fly could respond, Janice spoke up. "We can talk about penalties for you and your father later. Where's the locket?"

"You tell her," Eddie said to Jani.

"In my room. In an envelope in a box with the cat skeleton we found in the back yard."

"Old apple doesn't fall far from the tree, does it, Dad?" Fly asked.

Flush gave Fly a nasty look. "Jani, go get the locket and give it to Mr. Hawkshaw."

Jani went to her room, brought back a used white envelope, and handed it to Harvey.

"I'll see that Mr. Chan gets this today," he said. "This might be a big help in finding out who the victim is. Sorry, Eddie, we got sidetracked, but that was a lot of good information."

Eddie continued his story. "Mom called the police department, and then Billy Chan's dad came to the house with another guy in a suit. He's a detective. They were taking pictures of the skull and put it in a plastic bag to take it away to the morgue," Eddie said.

"And then mom drove us up the mountain with three police cars following. We showed them the hole, and they asked us questions like you guys did. That was it," Jani said.

"You never saw the rest of the skeleton?" Harvey asked.

"Nope," the twins replied in unison.

"Well, we're going to go up there and have a look for ourselves. Another set of eyes might find a prize," Harvey said.

"Very poetic, Harvey," Fly said. "We might find a box of Cracker Jacks up there."

The Hopper twins giggled. Harvey and Fly thanked the Hoppers, Eddie, and Jani for their help. The parents shook hands with Harvey and Fly, and the twins gave Fly a big hug.

"Say hi to Little Bosco, Fly," Jani said with a giggle.

"And we'll text you if we find some metal," Eddie added.

"Just be careful where you're digging," Fly responded.

As Harvey and Fly were leaving, they heard Eddie in the background.

"Why does Fly call you Flush, Dad?"

"It's a long story, son. I'll tell you someday."

THE GRAVESITE

Harvey and Fly drove up Quarry Road, they could see Noah Zark's bungalow, and then about 200 yards past it, they saw the long driveway that led to the mansion. Fly knew his way around, so he directed Harvey to go past the mansion driveway and continue on to the old mining road that led to the top of the mountain. The old road was seldom used since the trap rock quarry went out of business years ago. It split as they neared the top of the mountain, with one road leading to the quarry and the other to the upper field owned by the Marlowes. The old field road, a pair of ruts worn by tractors and other farm equipment with clumps of weeds between them, led to the top of the field near the wood line. It continued running parallel to the trees to the remnants of the limb maker's house. They continued to the scene of the gruesome discovery.

"Not great on my Mustang," Harvey said.

"Better than Minerva," Fly replied. "She'd never make it up the hill. Gettin' to be an old gal, but she still gets me where I need to go."

As they approached the ruins, they saw the old fieldstone foundation that had survived years of neglect. Most of the boards from the house had decayed and collapsed into what was probably a basement and root cellar.

"Mangy," Fly commented. "Wouldn't stay in this B & B."

They walked behind the house toward the old wall made of stones taken from the field years ago. It was obvious where the gravesite was.

"Just follow the yellow-taped road, Harv. Think they've got enough Crime Scene and Caution tapes around? Guess they have extras and want to use them up."

"Nah. Just being cautious. Crime scenes get a lot of gawkers looking for photo ops so they can put their pictures on social media."

"Really? That's sick. Not a bad idea, but sick." Fly took out his cell phone and took a picture of himself next to the gravesite.

"Want to take a selfie with me, Harv?"

"Who's the sicko? Start looking for some evidence. No evidence means no reward."

Fly put his phone back in his pocket and hustled over to Harvey. "Yes, Boss."

"I'm not your boss. Now get serious and look around."

After a few minutes of careful looking at the gravesite, the house remnants, the field, and the wall behind the site, Harvey asked Fly, "So, Junior Detective, what do we know now that we didn't know before?"

"Junior Detective. I like that. When I'm old, can I be a Senior Detective like you?"

"You want to be a detective? Then answer the question. What do we know?"

"Let's see. Pretty sure it isn't Junior. And it's probably a girl unless it's a guy with a locket."

"Whoever she is, she didn't plant herself here. Somebody put her here," Harvey noted. "And she lost her head."

"Yuck. Can't imagine doing that. I buy chicken parts, so I don't have to cut up the bird. That's a fowl job."

Harvey groaned.

"But the kids said they accidentally cut off the head."

"Maybe," Harvey responded. "It could have been cut off by the perpetrator, and the kids thought they did it."

"Maybe not on purpose. I can see them digging away. Hittin' those rocks. Bam. Snapping that head off before they knew what happened."

"A good theory, Fly, but we'll need to confirm it with the medical examiner."

"The coroner?"

"Ollie Kingston is a medical examiner."

"Right. A coroner."

"Wrong. Coroners are elected, and they don't have to be doctors. Medical examiners are trained and certified."

"So, I could be a coroner?"

"Let's hope not. Remember, you hate cutting up chickens!"

Harvey took out his cell phone in case he needed to use the flashlight app to see in places where the shadows blocked the light in the grave or the wall behind it. They first looked at the foundation of the limb maker's house. Not seeing anything obvious, they turned their attention to the hole behind it that was barricaded with yellow tape that said "Caution. Do Not Cross."

"One of your detective tricks?" Fly said, nodding to the flashlight.

"I've got a lot of tricks, Fly. A cellphone flashlight is easier to carry, but I've got the real thing in the trunk of my car."

"You ever think of being a magician?"

"Being a PI is often like being a magician. That's why all good PIs have rabbits at home."

"Right. Bosco would spend too much time chasing the rabbits. Guess I better stick to card tricks."

When they looked over the yellow barricades, Fly knew Harvey was right. The sun was lowering in the west just enough to cast a shadow that obscured visibility in the grave.

"Clever devil, Harvey. I'll add 'use the flashlight app' to my training manual."

They looked at every inch of the grave, side to side, top to bottom; aside from the indentation where the skull was and the area where the rest of the skeleton had been removed, there were small footprints at the base. They didn't find any more clues.

"Now what?" Fly asked.

"We look at the perimeter of the grave. Sometimes

there are things nearby that can offer a clue, but after who knows how long and the area being disturbed by removing the skeleton, we'll be lucky to find anything."

They moved back to the fieldstone wall about 10 feet behind the grave on the upside of the mountain. Over the years, the stones had shifted. Some had fallen, and others had loosened to reveal crevices between them.

"Let me borrow your flashlight, Harv," Fly said.

"Use your cell flashlight."

"Oh, yeah."

"Don't touch anything. If you find something, we'll take a picture of it."

Fly looked like a hound dog sniffing out its prey as he looked in every crevice and all around the fallen rocks. Meanwhile, Harvey walked around the nearby fields and gave the limb maker's house another look.

The pair worked silently for about 10 minutes when Fly yelled, "Bingo!"

Harvey limped over to the rock wall. "Whatcha got?"

"Taking a picture of this one. Putting it in my trainee manual. I've got a digital manual in the cloud."

"Come on. Whatcha got?"

Fly pointed to a crevice in the wall about 10 yards north of the grave. The top rock had slid off, and a shiny object was resting deep inside as it had been for likely a decade or more.

"Holy moly, Fly. I think you've found something! Don't touch it, whatever it is."

"Metal. A knife. The big E, evidence. Very cool."

Fly took out his phone and turned on the flashlight app. He carefully propped it up on the stone wall so that just enough light shone into the rock layers where the knife was located.

"Have to let this be for the forensic team," Harvey said.

"But it's really neat. Not like a regular hunting

knife." Fly continued to remove smaller rocks so he could get a better view of the knife.

"Be careful. This is like pickup sticks… know that game? A wrong move and you wiggle the sticks, then you're out. But the stakes are higher on this one."

"Just one more rock," Fly said as he wiggled a smaller stone.

When he got the rock out, the stone above it slid down, partially hiding the evidence.

"That's it. You may have already done damage. Do I have to take away your phone and put you in Time Out?"

"No, Daddy. I'll be a good boy."

Fly smiled like a kid who'd just scored the winning home run in a baseball game. "My first evidence. Maybe I should put this on Facebook."

"NO! Maybe we should take a picture of it and show Chappy. Hmm. Wonder why Forensics didn't find this?"

Fly pointed to his face. "Fly the Eagle Eye."

"How'd you find it?"

Fly pointed to his nose. "My upcycle business. I can sniff out metal anywhere—steel, iron, copper, aluminum; you name it. Better than that, I can tell you that the metal in that wall is stainless steel. Wait. You'll see I'm right."

They took a few more minutes to look in the crevices and around the immediate area.

"You know what's bothering me, Fly?"

"Your teeth? Maybe you need to see a dentist. Or if it's your sacroiliac, then you need to see a …"

"Muzzle it, Fly. What's bothering me is that this person was murdered, and someone chose this place to bury her."

"The kids said they accidentally cut off the head, and now we find a knife."

"Good observation, Fly, but don't leap to conclusions. We don't know that the knife is associated with this crime. We always want to know the identity of the victim and why the killer resorted to murder."

"Think he knew her?"

"You know the perp is a he? She could have done this."

"This stuff is hard on my brain. Not as obvious as it seems."

"There's a lot to figure out about this, and we don't even know if the body is related to Junior, Three, or Roscoe. We just know that this victim isn't one of them."

They took a couple more pictures of the new evidence, and Harvey gave Chappy a call. "I think we have something for you, Chappy."

"Really? You didn't mess up my crime scene, did you?

"No, we were careful."

"We? You took Flywheel with you?"

"Of course. He even found new evidence. You'll have to update your priors, Chappy."

"I'll update your priors, alright, if you are messing things up over there. Bring in the evidence."

Fly made a gesture to Harvey to pass the phone over to him.

"Snappy Chappy. It's Fly the Eagle Eye here. Or you could call me Fly the Nosy Guy 'cause my nose can smell metal that even metal-smelling robots can't."

"You guys been drinking? You're not making any sense."

"Well, let me tell it to you this way, Snappy. We found you some serious, I mean very serious, evidence. AND we are following your rule, so we didn't touch it. Look on your phone for a picture of a pile of rocks and something shiny deep in the crevice."

Chappy looked at his message, and sure enough, there was a new picture. "So, it's shiny, Fly. What is it?"

"It's stainless steel, and if you look closely, you might see a blade, like a knife."

"Wow. Good work, Fly. Stay there. I'm sending

somebody from Forensics over to pick it up."

"Make it snappy, Chappy. Almost time for me to feed Bosco. If I don't feed him on time, he becomes nasty, rip-your-leg-off violent."

"I don't want to know what you're talking about," Chappy said. "They'll be right over."

In a matter of minutes, the new SPD Forensics Team leader Raven Sanchez pulled up to the crime scene. Chief Milt Jenkins was in a car behind her.

Harvey extended his hand to Raven, a striking Hispanic woman about 40 years old. "I don't believe we've met. You came to the department after I retired, Ms. Sanchez."

"I feel like I know you, Mr. Hawkshaw. You've had quite a bit of publicity around town."

"Raven!" Fly interrupted. "Still as beautiful as ever. I used to be stark ravin' mad about you in high school."

"I figured you were stark raving mad, too, Fly. Always the comedian."

They hugged. Harvey looked on in amazement. *Is there anyone he doesn't know?*

Milt talked with Harvey while Fly showed Raven his discovery. She took pictures with her high resolution camera from every angle. She stepped back and took pictures of the field in front of the stone wall and the woods behind it.

"How 'bout a picture with you, me, and the evidence, when we dig it out?"

Raven smiled and shook her head. "This is serious business, Fly. Cut the comedy."

Fly made a pouty face.

Sharon Brown, a forensic team member, carefully removed the stones, and Raven took a picture after each one was removed. When the knife sat by itself in the crevice, she took several more shots before holding the knife up by its tip to examine it.

"I don't see much here, but we'll need to test it in

the lab. We might get lucky with a fingerprint or maybe even a trace of blood. I'm not real confident of that, though."

She took out a plastic bag and carefully inserted the knife. "Not sure we'll find much on this, but we might get lucky."

Fly pointed to the intertwined triangles on the hilt of the knife. "What's with the triangles?"

"I don't know yet," Raven said, "but I will before too long. A little internet search should tell us a lot."

"I think it's like some mystical thing. Something to do with some ancient gods. Maybe ancient aliens," Fly said.

"What do you think, Raven?" Milt asked.

"So far, I'm not seeing a connection between the knife and the girl in the grave."

"Wasn't her head cut off?"

"Yes. But we established that the beheading was recent."

"Like when some kids might've hit it with a shovel," Fly interjected.

"Exactly," Raven replied. "I think we might find that this knife is connected to another crime or maybe to no crime at all."

"Complicated," Fly said.

"The more complicated, the better for me. I got in this field to figure out puzzles," Raven said.

"Me too," Fly said.

They all laughed.

"Sorry, I have to leave, guys," Raven said. "Got my team in town checking on a murder. Busy time."

"Murder?" Harvey said. "Who got murdered? Where?"

"I gotta go, bye." Raven and Sharon Brown got in her car and left the scene. Chief Jenkins followed her.

"What's going on, Fly?" Harvey wondered.

"Beats me, but we better get on it. As they say at the reward center, time is money."

MURDER IN THE GAZEBO

Raven and Milt had no sooner left when another car came up to the gravesite. Harvey and Fly walked back over to the wall where they saw the evidence. To their surprise, Chappy got out of the car.

"Are you doing forensics now?" Harvey asked. "You just missed Raven and Milt."

"Yeah, I passed them coming up here. They're heading over to the gazebo. Found a body and had to make sure the forensic team processed the scene correctly."

"The gazebo. Oh no. Who do they think it is?"

"That homeless guy."

"Philip?" Harvey paused. He shook his head and turned his back to the others. His head slumped down. "Oh no." He paused to compose himself. "That's terrible."

"Oh, man," Fly said. "Not Philip. He was a good guy. Knew everything that was going on. Who'd want to kill him?"

"You said he knew everything that was going on, Fly. That's motive enough for someone trying to hide something," Chappy said.

"Are you sure it was murder?"

"I'm not sure yet, Harvey. He'd probably been dead all night."

"Who found him?"

"I think it was a couple of local women who go for a morning walk almost every day and end up at the gazebo. They bring Philip coffee and sometimes food. They called it in right away. Very upset. The dispatcher could hardly understand them. Hysterical."

"Find any evidence?"

"He had some coffee in a paper cup, but we couldn't smell anything strange in it. We need to let Ollie at the medical examiner's office do his thing so we can get a cause of death. Let's get this evidence out of here so I can get back."

"Philip. Man. Horrible," Harvey said to no one in particular.

Fly tried to steer the conversation back to the girl on the mountain. "You're too late, Chappy. The evidence is gone. Milt, Raven, and her assistant documented the new evidence."

They both stared at Fly. "Listen to you, Fly," Harvey noted. "They documented the new evidence."

"I heard that on an NCIS rerun. Sounds pretty good, huh?"

"So, Chappy, how long will the lab work on this evidence take?" Harvey asked.

"About a week, but I'll press them to get it as quickly as possible. Now they've got Philip's case to work on, too."

"If you want, I can sniff around here some more." Fly wrinkled his nose like a bloodhound. "Maybe I'll find more metal."

"You're amazing and kind of creepy, Fly," Chappy said. "Let's see where the evidence we have leads us."

"OK. But I kind of like sniffing out evidence. Maybe I'll come back on my own."

"NO!" Chappy and Harvey yelled in unison.

"Don't do that, Fly. You're not a cop or a licensed PI like Harvey. It could mess up a case against the perpetrator if we find one," Chappy said.

"You guys take all the fun out of being a PI wannabe," Fly said.

Chappy moved toward his car and raised his hand in farewell. "I've got to head to town to see what happened to Philip."

Harvey and Fly went back to their car, sitting silently for a couple of minutes.

"Poor Philip," Harvey said. "A smart guy that got all messed up along the way and ended up on the street."

"I remember him from his Philmont days," Fly said.

"You knew him?"

Fly scowled. "Of course. You know I know everybody."

"But what messed him up?"

"He was over his head in drugs. Bought, sold, used. You name it."

"How did he end up here in Stillwell?"

"Trying to get his act together. Used to have a girlfriend when he was sort of sober. Don't think they ever got married. Don't know about kids."

"Where's she?"

"I think, and I'm only guessing. I think his girlfriend was Archie. That's what they called her in Philmont. Monique Archambeau."

"Why is that name familiar?" Harvey asked.

"Beats me," Fly said. "She was in Stillwell for a while."

"That's it. I think I interrogated her once when we were trying to figure out where Roscoe was."

"Yeah, Boss. She was Roscoe's girlfriend way back."

"Wow. You're saying that Archie was hooked up with Philip and Roscoe? The plot thickens."

"Yup. She lived in Philmont, too. He wasn't so into drugs, maybe just a little. But she got Philip into rehab and got his act cleaned up. At least got him sober for a while."

"So, did Junior know her, too?" Harvey asked.

"Sure. She knew Junior. Just a friendship thing. He was old enough to be her father." Fly smiled. "Maybe he was!"

"Be nice, Fly. So how did Roscoe fit into this picture?"

"Just a guess, but I'm not sure who Roscoe's father is."

"Junior, right?" Harvey asked. "Rumors say he's the father."

"There are plenty of rumors about that, and what

about the mother? Who's she?"

"Felicia. I'm sure of that, Fly."

"But her married name is Savini, and Roscoe's is Savini, right?"

"We're not sure which one is the father."

"And get this, Boss. When Philip was a teenager, Junior hired him to work on the farm."

"What's that got to do with this case?"

"Just another rumor, Harv."

"Geez, Fly. I can't keep all this straight."

Fly took out a piece of paper and a pencil from Harvey's glove compartment and quickly drew a map of the relationship between the players. He showed it to Harvey.

"I think you've got it right," Harvey said. "Philip and Roscoe had the same girlfriend. You said her name was Archie. We don't know for sure who Philip's parents are, and for Roscoe, the only parent we know for sure is Felicia."

Harvey pondered aloud. "When Philip worked on the farm, he probably worked with Noah."

Fly chuckled.

"What's Noah got to do with Philip?"

"Remember, it's a messed up family, Harv."

"Are you saying Philip is related to Noah?"

"Can't prove it, but I think so," Fly smiled. "They have a word for Noah."

"Quit playing games, Fly. Spit it out. What's their connection?"

"Daddy. That's the word. I think Noah is Philip's daddy."

"No way. I can't believe it. Noah? Really?" Harvey scratched his head through his Yankee's cap. "Shocker. Then who's the mommy?"

"Guess."

"Earlene?"

"Too easy. Remember, Noah said they don't have any kids. Well, they don't." Fly paused for effect. "But it doesn't mean he doesn't."

Harvey was wide eyed and listening intently.

"Philip's mother must be the age of Junior, maybe a little younger."

"Duh. Maybe Noah's age?"

Harvey ignored the wise guy's comment. "Roscoe, Three, and Philip are a generation younger than Junior."

"Yup. Nobody's saying who Philip's mother is."

"But you know?"

"Only a guess, but my gut's like my nose." He pointed to his nose. "I can detect metal." He rubbed his stomach. "And I can tell who's telling the truth and who's lying."

"Your gut must be in an uproar around this place."

"I always pop an antacid before I come over here. Okay, Harv. Ready to head out?"

"Wait, wait, wait a minute. I'm not going anywhere until I know who you think Philip's mother is."

"I don't have any proof, so I'm not saying."

"You grew up around here. Who did Philip live with?"

"He moved around. A foster kid."

"Nobody claimed him?"

Fly shook his head. "Nobody talked about who his real parents were."

"Did he know?"

"Hey, he's Philip. He probably found out, but he never said anything to anybody. But somehow, he got money to live for a while. Then he rediscovered drugs and ended up on the street."

"Whoa, Fly. Don't be late for dinner. Tell me, or I'm not leaving here."

"Only thing I'll say is you might get some help from the crazy psychic over on Groveland Street."

"The Clairvoyant Center. Madam Whatshername."

"Marlena, Madam Marlena."

"She's too young to be Philip's mother."

"But she's not the only psychic there."

Harvey smiled. "Whoa! I guess we need a psychic reading. Put it on your to do list, Fly. We've got a lot to do."

"Not going on my list. You know I don't like creepy stuff."

"If you're gonna be a PI, you have to suck it up and just do it."

Fly just shook his head. "Not me. Not doin' it."

COLD CASE REVIEW

Harvey's phone rang.

"We have to talk, Harvey," Chappy said.

"On or off the record?"

"Off. Can you come over to the department?"

"You sure that's the best place to talk? Walls have ears. How 'bout the park?"

"You're right. Meet you there in 10 minutes."

"See you in 20 if you're on time."

"Gettin' to be a wise guy like your partner."

They both arrived at Mershon Park in about 15 minutes. Harvey was fashionably late, and Chappy unfashionably early. Harvey backed in, and Chappy pulled forward so their driver's sides were next to each other, and they could talk easily.

"Reason I wanted to talk is that your old pal Jenkins is getting on my back about this Marlowe case. The media coverage means more people are talking to him, and he's asking why we haven't solved this."

"In other words, the mayor and town council are on his case."

"You got it. I think Philip's murder rattled the town. He's also asking why you and Flywheel are working with me."

"What'd you say about that?"

"I said you were handling the case before you retired and have a lot of information in your head that can help us."

"Wish I did. You and I both know that what looks like a slam dunk is more like a kerplunk."

"See. Another Flywheel comment, Harv."

"Can't help it, Chappy. You hang around with the guy enough, you start talking and thinking like him. But, hey, what can I do to help you? I'll do anything as long as it's a mutual deal."

"Mutual as we can make it, Harvey."

"Deal!" Harvey lifted his arm and gave Chappy a knuckle bump. "Where I ran into a major block was in the most likely place, with the sisters."

"Yeah. They're a real treat. Especially that Eunice."

"But that's not all, Chappy. When I tried to pin it on one or all of them, I kept coming up empty handed. No evidence."

"I know. No blood, no weapons, no nothin' except prints. We had everybody's print except Roscoe's on file. The rest of them lived there, at least parttime. I keep telling Jenkins that. We have lots of suspicions and three men who appear to all be dead."

"That won't get us in a courtroom, Chappy."

"Now we have another murder. Who wanted Philip dead? He knew a lot, but it must have been something big if they had to kill him to keep a secret."

"You think his murder is tied to the Marlowe case?"

"My hunch is yes, but there is no evidence yet. This murderer, if it's the same one in each case, is very careful."

"And look at that girl on the mountain that the kids found. How does all this fit into the puzzle? We don't have any idea who she is yet."

"I think she's a sideline event. She may be tied to one of the people who are suspects, or she could play into this in another way. Finding out who she is may help us backdoor into the Marlowe case."

"Again. No weapon, Chappy. How and where was she murdered? Why did she end up on Marlowe's property? That spot was carefully chosen."

"Murderers like familiar places. They feel more comfortable closer to home. In this case, the perp had to know the property and how to get to the limb maker's house."

"That narrows the suspects but gets us right back to the key players, Chappy. This case feels like a merry-go-round to me... round and round with no end."

"We have all these loose ends, and some of them don't even seem like they go together. We need to think outside the box."

"That's where Fly comes in, Harvey said. "He knows everybody, and he doesn't think like us. He thinks outside the box first and jumps in the box later."

"Yeah, and he's on the edge of the law. Always has been."

"That's why he can help. I'm going to keep working with him, maybe give him some stuff to figure out on his own."

"Livin' dangerously, Harv."

"I know, but he hasn't let me down yet. He might be a little crazy, but he's smart, especially streetsmart. He's already shown me how he can work with people. You know, joke around with them and get the same information that we'd interrogate them about."

"Okay, but that's on you. If he screws up big time, you can bail him out. I'm not getting involved."

"As much as I distrust him, I think he'll pull through. After all, there's money in this for both of us."

Chappy smiled. "I'd be happy to have you guys solve this. It would get Jenkins off my back."

"I can't, and you can't alone, but with Fly, we'll get our guy."

"Or gal," Chappy added.

"Yeah, but it doesn't rhyme."

Chappy shook his head. "So, Fly-like."

They agreed to keep in close contact, and then each went their separate ways.

TOWN ABUZZ

The next day, the stories in the Stillwell Gazette, cable news, and local Internet news services announced that the murder of Philip was the first known murder in Stillwell in the last decade. The stories kept the town abuzz. Everybody had a theory, and nobody knew for sure who would murder Philip.

HOMELESS MAN MURDERED IN GAZEBO

(Stillwell) – The body of a local homeless man known to many as Philip was found around 8:00 a.m. yesterday in the gazebo in the middle of the square. Millie Hunchowder and Alicia Stormer paused to sit in the gazebo during their morning walk. "We thought Philip was sleeping," Ms. Hunchowder said. "He often is when we stop there. Alicia didn't think he was asleep, so she walked over to him. When she saw his tongue hanging out, she screamed so loud that people came out of the stores to see what was going on. There was a coffee cup lying on its side on the gazebo floor."

The murder apparently occurred during the night, and several other residents, like Ms. Hunchowder and Ms. Stormer, thought Philip was sleeping, as usual, yesterday morning and didn't report his condition.

According to local census and police records, Philip's full name was Philip Van Buren Rhinehart, and many believed that he was a descendant of the wealthy Van Buren family that made money trading goods with the Dutch West India Trading Company in the 1600s. He never used his middle or last name.

Local retired police officer Oscar Rhinehart declined to comment about his relationship with Philip, only saying that he was told that their great grandfathers may have been cousins. He also recalled that the last murder in Stillwell was over 10 years ago, when Emile Hudson was killed by his wife, Ambrosia, in a domestic dispute.

Police have not identified any witnesses who saw anyone other than frequent visitors to the gazebo. They are interviewing potential witnesses today and checking nearby surveillance cameras. "Someone knows something," Detective Chapman Chan said following the incident. "It's hard to imagine that this could have happened with no witness. We'll get to the bottom of this senseless murder." Detective Chan declined to comment on any connection between this murder and the missing men from the Marlowe mansion.

~~~

The second story on the first page of the Gazette was just as intriguing for local residents.

SKELETON NOT A MISSING MARLOWE

(Stillwell) –The body found by two local youths as they were building a fort on the mountain last week was thought to be the remains of Asa Marlowe II, who has been missing for 20 years. Authorities today revealed that the DNA did not match Marlowe's. They also said that DNA and other evidence found at the scene would be helpful in identifying the body.

Lead Detective Chapman Chan declined to comment on the matter, stating that it was an ongoing investigation. Local celebrity and private investigator Harvey Hawkshaw also would not comment, saying that he was cooperating with the police department on their search for a killer. Hawkshaw was the lead detective on the missing Marlowe's case until his retirement.

When pressed to find out what was found at the site, Hawkshaw refused to comment but said the police were making progress on the case. When asked about the dismemberment of the body, Hawkshaw said, "The skull was separated from the body, but that could have happened as the body was removed."

When asked about the motivation for someone to

perpetrate such a heinous crime, Hawkshaw said, "They're usually very angry at something or someone. Maybe not the person murdered. The victim could just be an unlucky person in the wrong place at the wrong time."

Similarly, Detective Chan said that people who dismember are seeking control or domination of their victims or their situation. "Either way, the victim has to endure the sadistic actions of the murderer. We hope that this death was swift."

The forensic lab plans to do additional testing on the skull and skeleton as well as the other unidentified evidence they have. The Medical Examiner, Oliver Kingston, said he would have a full report as soon as his examination and the pathology reports were complete. He said that this might take up to four weeks.

~~~

By the time Harvey got to Tootie's, everyone had read the Gazette or seen Harvey and Chappy interviewed on the local streaming news. He was smothered with questions before he could sit down at the counter.

Tootie already had his Joe poured by the time he reached the counter.

"Thanks, Tootie," he said.

"Figured you'd need this. How 'bout your almond croissant?"

"Great idea. You're the best, Tootie. Always looking out for me."

Everybody wanted the inside scoop on Philip and the girl that was found on the mountain. The questions were relentless. "How old was the girl? Has she been there for 20 years? What was she wearing? Did she know Junior?" On and on the questions went.

Finally feeling smothered by the armchair detectives, Harvey said, "Look, my friends. I know you want to know what's going on, but we don't know a lot more than you read in the Gazette or hear on the news."

"I'm not buying that," Rexie said. "Cops always

know a lot more and say a lot less."

"I got to side with Harvey, friends," Oscar said. "Even if he knows more than he's saying, he can't mess up the case. If too much information gets out about this, it will either tip the perpetrator to let her know that they're on to her or give her a chance to get out of town."

"Old cops are like a brotherhood," Rexie said. "I'm not buying your story either."

"That's okay, Rex. We love you," Harvey said. Then he and Oscar gave Rexie a hug.

"Hey, hold on," Alice said. "Oscar, you said the perpetrator is a she. How do you know that?"

"I don't. Just came off the top of my head. Could be he or she or it or they."

"I'm really not buying it now," Rexie said. "Probably a subconscious slip on your part, Oscar. You really think it's one of the sisters in the mansion, don't you?"

"Uh. Geez. No, I don't know."

"I rest my case. I'd bring them all in for questioning," Rexie said.

"Go ahead and add that to your other theories, Rexie," Jeb said. "Maybe it was aliens that escaped from Roswell that did this."

Everyone laughed, and Harvey used this break in the conversation to exit.

"Sorry to leave this party, but I've got work to do," he said as he paid Tootie, leaving her a generous tip.

He planned to meet Fly and go over to Noah's house again to get more information. He knew that it wouldn't be easy getting Fly to visit Noah, but it was something he had to do. He decided it was time to give Fly a job to do, one he could do on his own without further messing up an already messed up situation. He knew they needed information from Junior's first wife and figured it would be an easy assignment for Fly.

VANESSA

"Ok, Fly," Harvey said. "I have an assignment for you." Fly smiled and rubbed his hands together like a little kid learning he was getting ice cream.

"I want you to find out where Junior's first wife is and set up an appointment to meet her."

"Who's going to meet her?"

"You."

The smile left his face. "Me? I don't know anything 'bout her. What am I supposed to meet about?"

Harvey laughed and then reminded him that Vanessa was Junior's first wife and Three's mother. "Get her talking about the past and dredge up some memories of Junior and Three. I want you to record the conversation, too."

"Geez. Anything else for my first assignment, Harv? Pretty intense."

Harvey just smiled.

They parted company, and Fly set about finding Vanessa. He thought she was in a nursing home but didn't know which one. There were two just outside Philmont and one in Stillwell. He figured that Ever Rest Nursing Home up on the mountain was a likely place to find her. Townsfolk called this Mount Ever Rest, and it cared for many of the older residents of Stillwell.

Fly called Ever Rest first.

"Good morning, Ever Rest Nursing Home, Tillie speaking."

"Tillie Fronk. Nice to hear your sweet voice."

"That you, Fly? You creep. How'd you find me?"

"Now, Tillie. By accident. I didn't know you worked at Ever Rest. I'm calling about a resident."

"You stood me up. Broke my heart. I hated you then."

"That was a long time ago, Tillie. Got to let go of that."

99

"Yeah. I let go of that like a hot frying pan years ago. The best thing that ever happened to me. Right after that, I met Bruno. We got married and had kids. Three Brunoettes and a little Bruno."

"Well, you see that, Tillie. It worked out for you."

"And don't try messing around with my kids, who aren't kids anymore, or me. They'll take care of you if you know what I mean."

"Uh, well, er. No messin', trust me. I'm trying to find out if Vanessa Marlowe is living at Ever Rest."

"Only Vanessa we have is a Vanessa Thorndike."

"Hmm. Thorndike. That's interesting. Do you know if she used to be a Marlowe, like maybe the wife of Asa Marlowe?"

"Beats me, but you could come to ask her yourself. She may not recognize you or be able to make much sense of what you ask, but you can try."

Fly made an appointment to see Vanessa that afternoon. Meanwhile, he talked with Harvey again to get some ideas for detective questions. At about 2:00 pm, he drove his battered truck up Amwell Road, the road that crossed the mountain to the north and ended up in Amwell Township. He went into the nursing home and was coolly greeted by Tillie.

"You're looking for Vanessa, right?"

"Hi, Tillie; nice to see you."

"Can't say the same." She pointed to the hallway.

"Room 118 at the end of the hall."

Fly frowned at Tillie and ambled down the hall. He peeked into Room 118 and saw an old, withered woman in a wheelchair looking out the window. He gently knocked, but there was no reaction.

A nurse came up the hallway. "You want to talk to Vanessa?"

Fly nodded.

"She'll never hear you." The nurse went into the room, turned the wheelchair around, and yelled,

"VANESSA, YOU'VE GOT COMPANY."

Fly reached into his coat and turned on his digital recorder

"Junior, is that you?" Vanessa said. "Where have you been?"

"Hello, ma'am. I'm Fly."

"Speak up. Can't hear you without my hearing aids."

Fly yelled. "I'M FLY."

"That's better, but I don't see a fly. It's still cold; no flies now."

"MY NAME IS FLY. I'M HERE TO TALK ABOUT JUNIOR."

"Junior, sure. You know we were married? Had a son. Can't remember his name, but it's a number."

"THREE. HIS NAME IS THREE."

"That's right. I thought it was seven. He disappeared. So did Junior."

"DO YOU KNOW WHAT HAPPENED TO THEM?"

"Heavens no. I figured they went off and had a good time. Drinking, carousing."

"DID JUNIOR HAVE A JOB?"

Vanessa laughed. "No. He didn't like to work. Lots of money."

"DID HE GIVE MONEY TO THREE?"

"Sure. He gave Seven, I mean Three, lots of money. Whatever he wanted. He gave it to that drunken floozy that I guess he ended up marrying, Eunice. Even gave money to Roscoe, his maybe son."

"HIS MAYBE SON?"

"Oh, that was quite a mess. He was out running around. Those party people over in Philmont. I never knew when he'd come home. But I found out that there was this kid born to one of those party girls, and she was claiming Junior was the father. Then all of a sudden, we hear that she married some guy named Savini. The kid was named

Roscoe Savini, but I know Junior sent money to his mother to take care of Roscoe."

Fly looked astonished. "GET OUT. AND WHAT ABOUT YOU? DID HE GIVE YOU MONEY?"

"You kidding? I called him what he was. A loser and a cheapskate. Party, party, party. That's all he did. He ditched me, or maybe I ditched him. Can't remember."

"DO YOU REMEMBER THE LAST TIME YOU SAW HIM?"

"How could I forget? We had a big fight at the mansion. He came back one night with Eunice. Girlfriend, Eunice Gody. Imagine that. He brings his girlfriend home." She tensed up and then sighed. "Three was there. So was his wife, Carmela. She was a real winner, too."

"WHAT WAS SHE LIKE?"

"Smart, devious, controlling. Had Three and Junior wrapped around her finger. She said 'jump,' and they said, 'how high?'"

"SO, YOU WERE SAYING ABOUT THAT LAST TIME YOU SAW HIM."

"Three told Junior he needed money. Junior said he wouldn't give him a cent more. Then Three punched his father. Punched him! Imagine that. Punching your father right in the jaw." She motioned like she was punching Fly in the jaw. "So, I told Junior to get out and take the floozy with him. He left, and Three followed him. I heard yelling outside, and then Junior left in his car, and Three followed him. What a mess."

"SURE, SOUNDS LIKE IT. EVER SEE THE CAR AGAIN?"

"Never saw either one of them again. I think they found the car over in Philmont. Good riddance, that's what I say to Asa Marlowe."

"HE TOOK THE GIRLFRIEND WITH HIM?"

"Are you kidding? She stayed behind and lived with us. That's when I moved out and contacted my lawyer. Bertrand Thorndike."

"THORNDIKE. THAT'S YOUR LAST NAME."

"Ditched the bum and married my lawyer. A great guy. We sued Junior's estate, but we didn't get what we deserved. Money's probably still tied up in the courts."

"SO, EUNICE, IS THE FLOOZY HE BROUGHT HOME?"

"Yes, she is. She still alive?"

"SHE'S STILL ALIVE AND IN THE MANSION. NOT SURE IF THEY GOT MARRIED."

"They would have had to wait until Junior came home to get married. He never came home."

"INTERESTING, VANESSA. THANKS. I'M HAPPY YOU FOUND A GOOD GUY. I WONDER WHAT HAPPENED TO JUNIOR?"

"I think he's long gone. Three could have done him in, or maybe one of his partying friends. I think you'll find him six feet under, and that's fine with me."

Fly thanked Vanessa for talking with him and wished her well. On the way out of the room, Vanessa smiled at him. "Come back anytime, Mr. Cricket."

"FLY. NAME'S FLY. BUT YOU CAN CALL ME WHATEVER YOU WANT."

"What? Have to speak up. Can't hear you."

Fly reached into his coat and turned off his recorder. He waved to Vanessa as he left. She blew him a kiss. As he passed the reception desk, he just waved at Tillie and said nothing more to her. Sometimes nothing is the right thing to say.

FISHING FOR INFORMATION

Harvey and Fly met at their usual spot in Mershon Park. It was a nice day, and Harvey suggested that they walk along the paths in the park and talk about Fly's conversation with Vanessa.

"Oh boy," Fly said. "Walkie talkie."

Harvey ignored him.

Fly told Harvey about the fight, how Junior and Three left in separate cars, and how Eunice remained behind.

"Nice work, Fly. You established that Three could be involved with Junior's disappearance."

"Or the other way around. Maybe Junior was the one who did Three in."

"We've got more to learn. You ready to go see Noah?"

"I'm not goin' there, Harv."

"Why not? He's harmless. Just has a hyper dog."

"You heard me, man. I'm just not."

"Ok. What's going on between you and Noah?"

"Nothin'."

"Money."

"How'd you know?"

"If there's one thing I know as a PI, it's that money causes big problems. Got too little; you're lookin' for more. Got too much; you're lookin' for more. What's your problem with him?"

"Had a deal, but I kinda welched." Fly lowered his head like a puppy about to be reprimanded.

"Oh, man. You cheated him?"

"No, nothin' like that. It was just that I never paid him."

Harvey scowled at him. "So, you broke an agreement, didn't pay him, and you don't call that cheating?"

"Well, I was doin' him a service. I got rid of his

metal scrap, but I was a little short of cash at the time."

"Flywheel! You idiot. He could have you arrested."

"Nah, I made another deal with him."

"I can hardly wait for this one."

"I said I'd either return the metal to him or invest his money and pay him interest on the loan."

"He bought that?"

"Yup. We even shook hands on it. He didn't want the metal back."

Harvey sighed. "Your investment?"

Fly grinned sheepishly. "That didn't work out so well, Harv. I owed him a hundred bucks, which I invested in the eighth race at Saratoga. You know, off track betting."

Harvey shook his head.

"And I was told by my good buddy and parttime bookie, Fast Freddie, that Not Tonight was a sure winner. Ran six races this year, and she won or showed in all of them. Sure shot."

"Guess not, huh?"

"Not Tonight was, well, not tonight. But she came in first! 13-1 odds. Man, I was so excited, all set to pay off my debt and buy some new cigars."

"What went wrong?"

"Ever hear of an objection at a race track?"

"Yeah."

"Seems like the horse in third place, Mango Tango, was ready to crank it up for the final stretch, but Not Tonight cut across two lanes and blocked him."

"A no-no."

"Yup, yup. They had the nerve to disqualify Not Tonight. End of story. End of money."

"You had to tell Noah about this?"

"Well, I never did get around to that."

Harvey shook his head in disgust. "Then you will today. You've gotta fess up, Fly. You also have to pay up."

"Don't have the money. Money's all tied up in investments."

"More losses on horse racing?"

"Nope. There's a casino right next to the track."

Harvey just stared at him and shook his head. The flywheel had nothing more to say. After a prolonged silence that made Flywheel fidgety, Harvey reached into his wallet, took out $100, and handed it to Flywheel.

"Give this to him, understand?"

"No."

"Now you owe me. I'm not going to let you welch, though. Got it?"

Flywheel nodded. "What about the interest?"

Harvey reached back into his wallet, took out a twenty, and sighed. "Bad as my son. He's a money vacuum cleaner. I want all of this back, you hear?"

"Of course, former Detective Hawkshaw," Fly said.

"We need information from Noah, so when we see him, you cough up the money right away."

"What about the interest?"

"That, too. Tell him that's all you have."

"He's not gonna be happy. Been too long."

"How long?"

"Uh, two years, maybe three?"

"Good luck. You made this mess, so talk yourself out of it. Get in my car, and we'll go see Noah."

In a matter of minutes, they were at Noah's house. Harvey gingerly pulled the Mustang up the driveway. "When we get out, watch out for the dog."

"I get along great with dogs, Harv," Flywheel said.

Harvey made sure there were no slurry puddles where he parked. He saw Diesel sitting on the porch, wagging his tail in expectation.

"You get out first and make nice with the dog, Fly."

"What are you, a dog phobic?"

"Go make nice."

Flywheel got out of the car, and Diesel immediately bolted from the porch, came up to Fly, sat down, and made a whimpering sound as he wiggled around, wanting to be

106

petted. Fly made a fuss over him and petted him. He looked at Harvey, who was still in the car, and shrugged his shoulders.

Seeing this, Harvey got out of the car and walked over to them. Diesel immediately started to bark at him and jumped up, pushing his chest with his muddy paws.

Fly shrugged his shoulders again. "I guess some people have it and some people don't, Harv," he said with a smile. "Diesel must know you're an ex-cop."

Fly walked toward the porch, and Diesel followed like a puppy. Harvey brushed himself off and followed at a safe distance.

Noah came out to the porch, signaled Diesel to join him, and scowled at Flywheel. "What are you doing here?"

"Surprise, Noah. I got something for you." Flywheel smiled his biggest toothy smile.

Noah gave him a skeptical glare. "If it's not what you owe me, you can keep it."

Flywheel reached into his jacket, pulled out the money, and handed it to Noah. "It's all there. Count it."

"Interest?"

"You should take a lot of interest in getting your money back," Fly said.

"Don't be a wise guy, Fly. Is the interest included?"

"Well, you see, I invested the money hoping that it would grow and make you some money, but, well, uh, it didn't. That is good news, though. I gave you some interest anyway. You made 20% on your investment. Sorry it took so long, Noah."

Noah glared at him. "Ok. But I'm taking my business elsewhere next time, Flywheel."

"You can try, but I'm the Fly, the only metal guy around. You can always metal with Fly."

Noah sighed and changed the subject. "What brings you guys here?" He paused. "And together? You're like the odd couple."

"Well, Noah, Flywheel is my trainee. He wants to

be a private investigator like me, so I've agreed to tell him all my trade secrets."

Noah looked skeptical. "I believe that line like I believe they found Junior."

"Why wouldn't you believe that they found Junior, Noah?" Harvey asked.

"Because I knew Junior. He had reason to leave Eunice, and I think he did. I just don't think that's his skeleton that they found. Forensics will tell."

"And you know about the skeleton?" Flywheel sounded detective.

"Of course, and everybody else in town, too. I read it in the Stillwell Gazette and heard it on the TV."

Flywheel nodded and stroked his chin. "They think they found a young woman in the grave."

"I heard," Noah replied.

"Been in the ground a long time," Fly said as he fished for more information. "Prob'ly since Three left town."

"Think there's a connection, Noah?" Harvey asked.

"I don't know. You're the private investigator trainee. What do you think, Fly?"

"Could be."

"That's very non-committal of you. You'll go a long way as a PI."

Harvey changed the subject. "We're thinking about going over to see that psychic over there on Groveland Street."

Fly looked intently at Noah.

"You've got to be kidding. You believe in that hocus pocus, Harvey?" Noah asked.

"No, but we felt she might know something about the missing men."

"Really?"

"Well, the three sisters from the mansion visit the Madam from time to time. I see their car over there, and I've seen all of them coming and going."

"Sisters? They aren't sisters."

"I know. It's like sorority sisters. Seems better than calling them ladies."

"You know there are two psychics. Mother and daughter. I wonder why they would go to see the psychics?" Fly added.

"Beats me," Noah said.

Harvey reacted with silence.

"Money," Flywheel finally said.

Harvey elbowed him again.

"Sorry. I retract that last comment."

Noah laughed. "Waste of time paying good money for that psychic mumbo jumbo."

"Don't think they're paying it. They're getting it. Payday, you know?" Fly said.

Noah raised his eyebrows. "A regular Sherlock Holmes you're training, Harvey."

Harvey changed the subject. "Did you say that Junior had reason to leave Eunice, Noah?"

"Sure. She's a real Lulu. Flies off the handle. Sorry, Fly, no pun intended. But she's nasty and was a gold digger for Two's money."

"See, I was right," Fly said.

Harvey just shook his head at Flywheel's comment.

"Just one more question, and then we have to get going," Harvey said. "You said you didn't think the skeleton was Junior. Who do you think it is?"

"If it's a young woman, I don't even have a guess," Noah said. "If I were you, I'd check in some missing person files."

Fly changed the topic deliberately. "Shame about Philip."

Noah nodded but didn't respond. Harvey and Fly made eye contact.

"Thanks, Noah," Harvey said. "And disregard my trainee's comments."

"You don't have to worry about that!"

"Say hello to Earlene for us."

"Will when she gets home."

"She running errands?"

"Oh. Out shopping on the square. She likes it there. Goes there for her weekly get away from me."

"Can't say as I blame her," Fly said.

Harvey glared at Fly. "Don't be rude. A PI has to be polite."

"Does she, I mean, did she visit Philip while she's there?"

Noah was silent for longer than usual. "Uh, I don't know where she goes on the square. Probably just hits the shops. Always brings something home."

"Philip was like an attraction on the square," Fly said. "Especially with the ladies. They like to bring him stuff. You know, coffee, food. They find out about the gossip in town. That guy sure knew what was happenin'. Gonna miss him."

"Is that right? Didn't know he was so popular."

"You know what happened to him, right?" Harvey asked.

"Just what I read in the paper."

"You know him?"

"Not personally. Haven't seen him in years."

"You used to talk to him?"

"Sure. He worked with me at the mansion. A long time ago. Hard worker. Quiet but observant. Knew what was happening."

"Hmm," Fly said as he looked at Harvey. "Wish we could talk with him."

"Too late for that, Fly," Harvey replied. "I think we need to go. Thanks, Noah."

"So long, Noah, sir," Fly said.

Noah just shook his head. Fly patted Diesel as they left the house, got in the car, and drove back to Fly's truck in Mershon Park. They planned to meet at the park the next morning.

110

MORE INFORMATION

It was a warm early spring day, and Harvey and Fly sat at a picnic table in Mershon Park.

"No walkie-talkie today, Harvey?"

"Leg's sore, shoulder's sore."

"You sound like an old man. Old service injury from saving cats?"

Harvey scowled at Fly and moved on with the conversation. "So, let's figure things out. What did we learn?"

"I think Noah knows more about Earlene's visits to town, a lot more. Especially seeing Philip. He or Earlene probably know something about Philip's murder."

"You're leaping to a lot of conclusions, Fly. Any evidence?"

Fly pointed to his gut.

"What about the girl on the mountain, Fly?"

"Noah had a good idea. We should check the missing person files."

"You have to wonder how a girl could be missing from this small town, and the newspaper back then didn't make a big deal about it," Harvey said.

"I can't remember a missing girl 20 years ago. Do you, Harv?"

He shook his head. "That seems like something we'd remember."

Fly paused. "The girl must be from another town. Maybe another state."

"Seems like you'd need to know something about the mountain and Marlowe property to bury someone in that location," Harvey said.

"So, who she is might lead us to who might have killed her."

"Brilliant, Fly. You're thinking like a detective."

"Pretty scary, huh?"

They agreed to concentrate on finding out who the

woman was before they drew too many conclusions. There were enough possible suspects around who knew the Marlowe property. Almost everyone in town knew about the limb maker's house and how it was one of the oldest remnants of buildings in Stillwell.

"I have a friend at the library who can help us figure out if the girl was local," Harvey said.

"Library?" Fly looked surprised. "You going old school on me, Harv?"

"Libraries aren't so old school anymore. Anyway, this is an old case. There would be something in the old newspapers."

"What about the Internet?" Flywheel held up his cell phone. "You can find everything there."

"Not everything. I need to read old copies of the Stillwell Gazette and other papers. The library still has all those old papers on microfilm. Old technology, but at least they have the papers."

"Who's your contact?"

"She's an old high school friend."

"Hmm. She? Girlfriend?"

"I'm married, Flywheel."

"You weren't then."

"Ancient history. She'll help me. What are you going to do to help solve this, Fly? I mean, besides humming and staring."

"How 'bout I start with Roscoe? He had a bunch of friends around the area. Most of them overdosed, but I know a few guys who got straightened out. They may remember something."

"Give me a few days in the library, and let's connect on Friday."

"Where?"

"Your place. Maybe you can tell me what upcycling is or at least something about Roscoe."

They parted ways and agreed to contact each other when they found a clue or on Friday, whichever came first.

Flywheel got in his truck and rambled down the street. Harvey headed toward the library.

Harvey entered the library and headed to the information desk. Theola Parks was on duty.

"Morning, Harvey," she said. "Lookin' for Millie?"

Harvey nodded. "She working today?"

"I'll check." Theola picked up the phone and dialed 321. "Hey, Millie. We're checking to see if you're up for your favorite visitor." Theola laughed. "Ok. I'll send him right up."

Stillwell Library was the central library for Jefferson County and had many more resources than the satellite libraries. Harvey took the stairs to the second floor and headed toward the large Research sign.

Millie was all smiles and gave him a hug when Harvey came up to her desk. "Always good to see you, Harvey."

"Likewise, Millie. Don't say anything about you know what."

"The prom? That's old news, Harv. Decades-old! But I still remember that Kool Aid punch. Or should I say, I still remember how you tripped on your own feet and dumped a cup of punch down the front of my dress?"

"So much for not saying anything," Harvey said. "Guess I was clumsy as a kid."

Millie laughed. "I can laugh now. But I wasn't handling the spill too well, or when you stuck me with a pin trying to put on my corsage."

Harvey shook his head. "I'm just glad you didn't mention my recent exposure in the paper and on TV."

"Oh, you were exposed, alright. I figured that was over now. I didn't want to embarrass my prom date any more than I already did." She smiled at Harvey. "So, what can I find for you this time, Harvey? Missing poodles? A plot to catch candy thieves at the market? What are you up to?"

"Serious stuff, Millie. I need to find information

about a missing woman from about 20 years ago. We don't have any idea who she might be, but we have a locket that was buried with her. I need the names of some missing people from that time. They don't have to be from Stillwell. Could be from anywhere."

"I don't recall any big story about a missing person other than the Marlowes. We have a ton of stuff on the Marlowes, a filing cabinet full. I can point you to some places to look, Harvey, but I can't look for you."

"You did at the prom!"

"I couldn't find you. By the time I got YOUR punch off my dress, you were off with the guys."

They both laughed, and Millie proceeded to show Harvey the microfilm archives, books by Asa Sr., and real estate transactions for the Marlowe properties.

Harvey spent the next three hours combing the articles that had anything to do with any missing women from 20 years ago. He took pictures with his cellphone and made some audio notes that his phone converted to text. Finally, he went back to thank Millie.

"So, Millie, if you could keep this off your radar, I'd appreciate it."

"That skeleton is on everybody's radar, Harvey. I have one suggestion." She paused. "That locket. Was there something inside it?"

"I think so, but I need to find out."

"If it's a picture, you can post it on social media asking if anyone recognizes it or post it on several of the missing person's sites. You might get a bite."

"Great idea, Millie. I'm putting my trainee on it."

"Trainee?"

"Yeah, a guy named Flywheel."

"Fly, of course. Everybody knows Fly. Picks up our scrap metal all the time. A metal hound. Always checking out the dumpster behind the library."

She smiled, gave a goodbye hug, and noticed that Harvey was still limping a bit as he left.

Harvey pulled out his phone and called Flywheel as soon as he left the building. "Fly. Harv here. I found some good stuff. Can you meet me in the park?"

Flywheel responded. "I'm working, Harv. I thought we were supposed to talk on Friday."

"Too complicated. Can you stop by the park? Just take that stupid pizza sign off the roof of your truck and go over there."

"I got another job. I have a nice car."

"So come over anyway."

"Got somebody with me."

"Bring 'im along. Just don't let 'im hear anything."

"Guaranteed. I'll be there, and my passenger will be silent."

"You the man, Fly. Great."

THE LOCKET

Forty-five minutes later, Harvey pulled his Mustang into Mershon Park and drove back 200 yards to the parking area. Before long, Flywheel drove in and parked next to him.

"What's this?" Harvey asked, looking incredulously at his vehicle.

"So, what's the big news? Found Three?"

"No. I mean, what is this you're driving?"

"What's it look like?"

"A hearse."

"You're pretty sharp today, Harvey. You on pain medication?"

"No, but do you have a body in the back?"

"Of course. She wouldn't fit in the front seat. I told you my passenger wouldn't say a word, so whatcha wanna tell me?"

"Uh. You're creeping me out, Fly."

"I'm usually creepy, but I like being the creeper. Oh, and the name is Flywheel, not Fly when I'm working as a professional carter of the deceased."

"You're going to need a funeral home if you don't get serious. Now think like a detective for a minute, will you?"

"Ok, Boss. Whatcha got in mind?"

"I heard from the Medical Examiner by way of Chappy on the QT, if you know what I mean."

"No, I don't. What's QT, quitting time?"

"It's an old saying. This means it's a secret or it's to be kept quiet. Quiet. QT. Got it?"

"You're telling me the ME told Chappy the secret, and he told you who told me. I don't call that much of a secret."

"Do you want to know this or not? I think you might have an idea about this in that pea-sized brain of yours."

"Fire away, Boss."

Harvey pointed to his own eyes with his index and middle fingers and then to Fly's eyes. "Focus. The ME said that the locket was pretty old, but it could have been given to the victim by an older relative. It was 18-karat gold, and there was a picture of a man and woman inside it. They were older, so they could be the victim's parents. Okay, so far?"

Fly shook his head up and down. "Could be grandparents. Or aunt and uncle. Or?"

"Ok, enough."

Harvey took out his cell phone and opened the Photos app. The picture of an African-American couple appeared. They looked like they were in their 60s and dressed in their finest clothes. It was a formal picture, but thumbnail size to fit in the locket.

"Cool. They look like me."

"So, if these are the woman's parents, she is likely African American, too. What I need help with is identifying them. If we can figure out who they are, we might be able to figure out who the skull belongs to."

"No problemo, Harv. I'm also Fly, the social media guy." Fly put his finger to his temple and looked upward. "Here's what we do. We share the pictures on Twitter, Facebook, Instagram, and a bunch of other social media and ask if anyone can identify them. Okay, so far?"

"Don't be a wisenheimer."

"Don't know what that is either."

"A wise guy."

"Cool. I'm wise to the ways of social media. Now you focus. So, we give the picture a hashtag so people can feed information from various social media. You know what a hashtag is, right?"

"No, sounds like something to do with marijuana like hashish."

Fly laughed and slapped his knee. "You crack me up, Boss. A hashtag looks like the pound symbol, like a slanted tic-tac-toe board. You put it in front of a subject that you want to link to on one of the social media sites. Like in a tweet, you put #missingperson. You run the words together. This will link to other people on social media who are interested in finding a missing person. Got that, Boss?"

"Not bad for a wiseacre," Harvey said. "You know how to do all this, too?"

"Are you kidding, Harvey? This stuff is a breeze. Easy peasy."

"Noah said there are missing person databases on the Internet. We can post it there, too."

"We'll go there if we have to, but I think somebody will know these two people. We will be more likely to find them on social media than old missing person files. More people are on social media. Better chance of hits. If we can find who the people in the locket are, we can find out who the woman in the grave is. I'm going to start working on this after I get rid of my quiet guest, of course. What are you going to do, Harv?"

"I've got plenty of people to check on." Harvey pointed to the back of the hearse. "You worry about her, and I'll worry about other people."

They went their separate ways.

Fly dropped off his passenger at the Smythe Funeral Home and then headed back to the Upcycle Center, where he was greeted like a long-lost relative by Bosco. "Sorry little guy," Fly said. "Doin' some serious business so I can buy you some biscuits." Bosco bounced around, wanting some attention, and got out his chewed-up hunk of rope to play tug of war with Fly.

After a few minutes, Fly fed Bosco and got down to business on his laptop. He had scanned pictures of the couple in the locket that Chappy had reluctantly sent him. He posted a tweet and the pictures on Twitter. "@Flywheel. Recognize these people? People linked to #missingperson. Let me know. Share. Thx."

From Twitter, Fly went on to link his tweet to Instagram, Facebook, and Pinterest. Finally, he went to Pipl, Zabasearch, and YoName and a half dozen sites he didn't use and barely knew about. These sites aggregate information from many social networking sites, blogs, and other places on the internet where people may be found. He figured the more people who saw the picture and could identify them, the more likely he'd be to find the people.

While he used his name as the contact, he tagged each post with keywords that might lead people back to him without using the word murder. He wanted people to think that these people were missing. He could get more specific if he could pin down a name for the couple.

When he sent all the missing person requests, Fly called Harvey.

"This better be good, Fly," Harvey said.

"Of course, Harv. Did the deed. Pictures are flying through cyberspace as we speak." Fly ducked as if to avoid a flying object. "Ooh. That one just went through your window."

"I don't know about you. I think you're flying through space. You didn't take anything, did you?"

"I'm Fly, the sober guy. No booze, no drugs, not even catnip. It wasn't always like that, but it is now. That's all that matters."

"So, what can we expect from your trip to space?"

"If we hit paydirt, somebody, maybe several somebodies, will contact me. Won't take long."

"Ok, let me know when you hit paydirt, space cadet."

"Space cadet. I like that, Harv. Detective mentee, space cadet, super gumshoe." Fly smiled as Harvey hung up.

Fly knew that he might find more information by talking to the locals in Philmont, so he got in his truck and drove into town. "No sense wasting time," he said. "Time's money, and I need that reward!"

NEW INFORMATION

Two days later, Fly called Harvey to report on his search for the people pictured in the locket on social media.

"Got some news, Harvey," Fly said.

"I'm all ears."

"That's good 'cause this isn't a video chat. Here's the good news." Fly paused for dramatic effect. "I got a lot of hits, and a lot of people think it's their relatives or old friends or someone they know from their town."

"How many hits?"

"A few hundred."

"Hundred? Geez, Fly, it will take us weeks to track all these people down."

"Get with the program, Harv. This is social media. We can get to a lot of people at once. And I did."

"Find any good leads?"

Fly laughed. "Might say that. Tossed out the leads that were obviously false, like the guy who said it was his wealthy parents who promised him millions of dollars. I asked the ones that sounded legit to tell me who the people are, how they know them, and where they live."

Harvey pressed him to skip the process details and get to who was in the locket.

"Harvey, you're the one who always says not to skip the details. Remember what you said? 'The devil is in the details.'"

"Memory like an elephant," Harvey mumbled. "Yeah, sure, keep going, Sherlock."

"I got the hundred or so hits down to 13, and then I asked them more questions." Fly paused again just to frustrate Harvey.

"Come on, Fly. What questions?"

"Like the names of the people in the picture. Where they live, how old the picture is, and anything else they wanted to tell me about the locket people."

"And, of course, you asked if they had a missing

daughter or other female relative?"

"No way, Harv. That's the clincher. You hope one of them tells us that without us asking."

"Good thinking, Fly. Where'd you learn that trick?"

"Reruns of Columbo on the oldies TV channel."

"Did you get any info to whittle the 13 down to people we can talk with directly?"

"I have been whittling alright. Three people came up with the same name for the people, and two of them mentioned a missing daughter."

"Holy Cannoli, Sherlock. Who? I'm dying to know."

"Good one, Harv. Dying to know!"

Fly continued to tell him what he found. The people in the locket looked to be around 60 years old. Their names were Precious and Terrell Washington. They lived in Atlanta, Georgia. They had a granddaughter named Ebony Jackson, who left home when she was 18 and was last known to be visiting a cousin someplace in the northeast.

Harvey looked intently at Fly, impressed with his sleuthing. "Who told you all this?"

"Ebony's younger sister, Daniela. Another one of the Washingtons' grandkids."

"When did she tell you the girl went missing?"

"Right around the time Junior disappeared, so about 20 years ago."

"This is good stuff, Fly. I wonder how she ended up around here?"

"That's where the second source came in handy."

"Who?"

"The dead girl's cousin. The one she came north to see."

"Whoa. You know who the cousin is?"

Fly couldn't help smiling. "Ready for this, Harv? She lives in Philmont."

"Get out of town!"

"It gets better, Harv. I know her!"

"But you know everybody, Fly."

"I really know her. Kiana, Kiana Jones. A special friend, if you know what I mean."

"Not sure I want to know, but why didn't you know about the missing cousin, then?"

"Haven't seen Kiana for at least 20 years. We split up before this thing with her cousin would have happened."

"We have to talk with her. She must have reported her cousin missing."

"Call the police? Doubt it, Harv. If they got something to hide, they definitely wouldn't be callin' the police."

"Ok. Enough of this phone talk. I'm coming out to see you at your place."

Harvey's Mustang rolled up to the Upcycle Center in less than 20 minutes.

"Pedal to the metal, Harv?" Fly greeted.

"Light traffic and a slight disregard for speed limits."

"Ok. So, what's the plan?"

"Philmont. Let's head to Philmont."

"Ok, Harv, but I don't know about you going where I'd be going."

"Do I look like a cop?"

"Looks don't matter. They can smell that you're a cop like I can smell metal in a dirt pile."

"How about if I just go along for the ride? When we get there, if it looks like I might be a problem. I'll stay in the car."

Fly pointed to his truck. "Better go with me."

"I'm not riding in that junkyard refugee."

"Watch what you say about junkyards and old trucks. I'm sensitive."

Harvey reluctantly agreed to go with Fly, so he pushed a worn-out muffler off the front seat so he could sit down. They clanked and rattled for eight miles until they got to Philmont.

"You have an address for this Kiana lady?"

Fly looked insulted. "You can't go into these things unprepared, Harvey. You told me that yourself. Sure. I know that she works at Burger King on the evening shift, so we can talk to her until about 4:00 p.m. We're good to go if she's home."

They pulled up to a large house that had once been home to a wealthy member of the community back in the day when industry flourished in Philmont. It had been divided into apartments many years ago. Fly took out his phone, found her name in his contact list, put it on speakerphone, and pressed her number.

She recognized his name right away. "Hello, Sly Fly. Where have you been?"

"Hey, K. Been around. You okay?"

"Sure, now that I'm talking to you."

Harvey whispered. "I don't want to hear about your love life."

"Say, K, I have a friend with me, and we'd like to talk with you. We're right out in front of your place."

"A cop?"

"Not anymore. Friend of mine. He's cool."

"Sorry, Fly, but I'm not talkin' to cops."

"It's about Ebony."

"What do you know about Ebony?"

"That's why we want to talk to you."

She paused on the line, taken aback by a reference to her long-lost cousin.

"You there?"

She sighed. "Yeah. I'll talk with you but just for a little bit. Got to go to work soon."

They entered the foyer of the house and saw on a mailbox that she was in apartment four. Third floor in the

123

back of the building.

"No elevator?" Harvey asked.

"Suck it up, old man. You can walk it."

"My gimpy leg hurts already." Harvey lagged behind, but he made it to the third-floor landing, huffing and puffing and groaning about his leg and shoulder. Fly knocked on the door, and a beautiful, forty-something black woman opened the door, opened her arms, and gave Fly a big, prolonged hug.

After what Harvey felt was sufficient hug time, he said, "ahem," as if he was clearing his throat.

They ended the embrace, and Fly said. "This is my friend, Harvey. Harvey, Kiana. Kiana, Harvey." They each nodded without shaking hands.

"Say, Harvey," Kiana said. "You look familiar. Like I know you from TV. Are you a celebrity or something?"

"No, I'm just a retired cop turned private investigator."

"Wait. I did see you on TV. Not long ago. You were the guy that fell in front of his house and thought there was a bomb about to go off." She started to laugh.

"It really wasn't that funny, Kiana."

"It was, Harv," Fly chimed in. "You're there with your...."

Harvey cut him off. "Enough already."

"You should've been a plumber," Kiana said as she doubled over in laughter.

Harvey let them get the tearful laugh out of their system before he called their visit to order. "So, Kiana, we'd like to talk with you about your cousin, Ebony Jones."

She calmed down and tried to compose herself. "Haven't seen her for years. I'm about the same age as her, and she left, let me see, about 20 years ago. Haven't seen or heard from her since."

"Was she visiting you for very long?" Harvey asked.

"A month or so. Came up from Atlanta. Said she was moving around the country and wanted to crash here for a while. I think she was escaping from a bad scene in Atlanta. She never did give me the nasty details."

"Did we know each other than, K?" Fly wondered.

"Of course, we did. Don't you remember partying? Oh, maybe you don't. You were a little out of it then."

"Uh, I think we don't need to hear this," Fly said.

"And no, I don't remember Ebony."

"She stayed here and partied a lot. Got to know a bunch of locals and then just left one day."

"Did she take her things with her?"

"Didn't have many things. A couple of changes of clothes which are enough to fit in a backpack. That's about it."

"Did she take the backpack with her, K?"

"Hard to remember, Fly, but I don't think so. She was a free spirit. Traveled light, traveled fast."

Harvey jumped into the conversation. "Do you remember some of the people she hung out with?"

"Man, that was 20 years ago. Let me see. Some of them are dead, like Deshawn, Tyrese, and Marquis. Drugs, big time."

"Any living people you can remember?" Harvey asked.

"Some white guys. There was Roscoe. I guess he's alive, but I haven't seen him in years, either. And another white guy with a number for a name. What was it?"

"Let me say some numbers. One, two, three, four, five."

She looked at Harvey. "Three, that was it. Three. Looked like a rich guy, with fancy clothes and all. But he got to know Ebony. Then when she took off, he took off too."

"With her?"

"I have no clue, Mr. Harvey. Both were here, and both were gone."

Fly and Harvey looked at each other, nodded, thanked Kiana for her information, and started to leave.

"Oh," Harvey said, turning back toward Kiana. "You mentioned another guy, Roscoe. Was he involved with Ebony?"

"Oh, yeah. That was quite a mess. Three liked Ebony, and Roscoe did too. She was a good looker. I tried to keep both of them away from here. They really went at it like she was a trophy. Some rivalry they had."

"I could see that," Fly said.

"Wait," she said. "Why are you asking about Ebony?"

"We're trying to figure some things out about missing people, and her name came up," Harvey said.

"Is she alive?"

"We don't know, but your information will help us."

"She's dead, isn't she?"

"We honestly don't know, Kiana."

"Don't worry, K," Fly said. "If she's alive and we find her, I'll let you know. If she isn't, well, I'll let you know that, too. She hasn't been here, and she hasn't been home in over 20 years. If you ask around, maybe someone who was here then can give us a clue."

"What about the Roscoe and Three I told you about?"

"Well, unfortunately, they're missing, too," Harvey said.

"Oh," was the only comment Kiana could muster.

Harvey thanked her. Fly gave her a hug and said goodbye.

REPORTING TO THE ME

Harvey called his old buddy, Oliver Kingston, the Medical Examiner.

"Hey, Ollie. Hawkshaw here."

"Hawkster. How you doin', man?"

"Ok. Had a rough time, but I retired and got back in the game on my own terms."

"Yeah, saw you on TV. I heard you were snoopin' round the murders and missing guys. Just like when you were on the clock here."

"Yeah. I know you're still on the case, and you have that body of the girl figured out."

"Wouldn't say that. I can tell you she was a female who had been in the ground a long time. Maybe 20 years."

"That would be my guess, too. That's when Junior and the other guys disappeared. How old would you say she was?"

"Well, when you look at her clavicles, her collarbones, the bones aren't fully developed. That usually happens at age 23 or 24. Her pelvis was adult-size, so she wasn't a kid. If I had to make a guess, which I do, I'd say she was around 20 or 21."

"Interesting. What else can you tell me about her? You said she was female."

"African American."

"How did she die?"

"From what I can tell, it looks like several vertebrae in her neck were broken, but the kids accidentally decapitated her with their shovel. Makes it a little harder to tell, but I'm sure the vertebrae injuries happened a couple of decades ago."

"Any signs of blood in the grave after all these years?"

"We tried. Used Luminol. It reacts with blood and shows up under blue light. Makes it glow, but you know that, Harv."

"But if she had a broken neck, there wouldn't be

127

any blood anyway. Right, Ollie?"

"Right."

"So, the young lady met a nasty end by an unknown perp. She was hauled up the hill to a place the killer figured she'd never be found."

"Until those kids came along."

"Yeah. I asked them why they dug the hole where they did. They said the ground sunk a little at that spot, and they figured it would be easier to dig there."

"I'm sure it was. It sunk because the body decomposed and caused the ground to sink."

"I'm not sure I want to process that picture. Anything else, Ollie?"

"Not unless we can get an ID on the body, and that will be tough."

"I've got my ace assistant, Fly, working on it. I think he's on to something."

"Fly? Really? Guess he's on our side of the law now. When you know anything else, let me know, and we can proceed with the search for the killer."

"Let me ask you one more thing, Ollie. What do you think about the choice of that grave site?"

Ollie paused before he replied. "We have a dead girl on the property where there are three missing men. I'd bet money that somebody on the property knows something."

"On the property now or was on the property then and is missing now."

"Good point," Ollie said. "You're on the right track, Harv. Good luck, and please try to stay out of the news."

"Trying, but sometimes the news finds me. I'll let you know when we find more info."

PLANNING THE MANSION VISIT

Harvey's phone rang as he drove home. Chappy wanted to meet with Fly and him in Mershon Park so he could bring them up to date. It was another beautiful spring day, and Harvey was right on time. He sat impatiently in his car with his window down, waiting for Fly and Chappy to arrive. Finally, Chappy pulled up, late by his usual 20 minutes.

"Sorry, Harv," Chappy said. "Got a lot going on, and then I got a call from forensics."

"Anything interesting?" Harvey wondered.

"I'm not sure how helpful this is, but ... oh, wait a minute. Your buddy is clanking up the lane in that heap of junk he calls a truck. I'll wait till he gets here. I hate repeating stuff."

By the time Harvey and Chappy left their cars and moved to the picnic table, Fly had pulled into a parking space, his truck coughing a final volley of greenhouse gasses. He got out and walked to the picnic table to meet the other men. "Sorry, I'm late, guys," he said. "Got a lot going on, and then I got a call."

Chappy gave him a weird look.

"That's a Chappy excuse," Harvey said.

"I know. Thought I'd use it just to get a rise out of Detective Snappy Chappy!"

Chappy frowned and looked at Harvey. "Can't you do something with him?"

Harvey just shrugged his shoulders. "Information isn't free, so sometimes you have to put up with him."

Fly just smiled at both of them. "What do we have, guys?"

"Nothing new on the forensics front," Chappy said.

"Don't be so sure about that. I just talked with Ollie, and he can pin down some things like sex, age, and ethnicity." Harvey then went on to explain what he learned from Ollie.

Chappy looked angry. "How come I didn't get a report from Ollie?"

"We got a lot more than a report, Snappy," Fly said. "We know who the victim is. How's that for rookie detecting?"

"Get out of town," Chappy said. "Really?"

Fly told Chappy about Kiana and her missing cousin, Ebony. Chappy was astounded that they were able to come up with the name of the victim so quickly.

"Of course, we need to confirm the identity," Harvey said. Ollie's going to try to get some dental records from Atlanta. I hope the grandparents are still alive or that someone knows how to get the records. He's also checking out the DNA link with Atlanta."

"You guys were pretty successful," Chappy reluctantly said. "Let me tell you about my unsuccessful visit yesterday. I drove up to see Eunice hoping that I'd also get to speak with the other ladies, the sisters as you call them. What a treat. Eunice was out of it. Whatever she said was like venom coming out of her mouth. She wouldn't answer a question or cooperate in any way. When I suggested getting a sample of her DNA, she told me what I could do with my DNA sample. Not nice."

"You can always get a court order to search the property or get the DNA," Harvey said.

"Only if you can show a reason," Chappy replied. "We're better off if we can get her DNA off something of hers like a toothbrush."

"I could act like a toothbrush salesman and get her to trade in her old toothbrush for a new one," Fly said with his wise guy glint in his eye.

"Ignore him," Harvey said.

"But he may be on to something, Harv. We could send him to see Eunice, and he could try to get a DNA sample from her and the sisters in the mansion."

"I think you can pull this off, Fly," Harvey said.

"And how would I do this? I'm not a bad salesman,

but getting toothbrushes from three possible widows? Fuhgeddaboudit!" Fly made it clear that he didn't want to be in that mansion.

"Whose idea was the toothbrush, wingnut?" Harvey said.

Chappy just shook his head. "I'm not even supposed to be talking to you guys, let alone figuring out ways to illegally get DNA. I have to get going and have a few words with Ollie. Gotta go."

Harvey and Fly remained at the park after Chappy left. Harvey picked up a handful of last season's acorns from the ground and causally flicked them nowhere in particular as they talked.

"Think this will work, Harv?"

"I have no clue, but you have to think it will work or it won't."

"Great, Harv. Nice to know you have no clue, and you're the guy who's my mentor."

"Some of my best cases were solved when I had no clue. I relied on my gut, and things worked out. You do that all the time. You know, your gut feeling."

"You got a lot to rely on, Harv," Fly said.

Harvey threw the handful of acorn scraps at him. Fly ducked and laughed.

"I'm supposed to go up there and get this lady talking? She knows me as the metal guy. Doubt she'll talk when I start asking cop questions."

"Nope. You'll get the same reaction as Chappy."

"So, I'm supposed to act like a metal guy? What's that going to get us?"

"Metal!"

"Very funny, Harv. We need the big E, evidence. Something that ties her to the missing guys or even Ebony."

"Remember your conversation with Vanessa? You

came away with lots of information."

"Yeah, but she was happy to have a visitor. And she thought my name was Cricket! Don't think Eunice wants a visitor. Probably not Felicia or Carmela either."

"See those shoes you're wearing?"

"Yeah, so?"

"Nike, right?"

"Where you going with this, Harv?"

"Their motto."

"Just do it," Fly said. A big smile came on his face.

"Ok, boss, but if something happens to me, I want you to take care of Bosco."

"You'll be fine. You can talk your way out of anything."

The look on Fly's face said he wasn't so sure about that. They talked awhile and came up with a plan for Fly to get what he needed at the mansion.

"So, let me see if I've got this plan right," Fly said.

"Step 1 - I contact Noah and find out where their trash is located so I can get a DNA sample even though I don't know who the sample belongs to. Geez!

Step 2 - I ask if I can collect some metal. No problem.

Step 3 - I casually mention that I saw something on TV about the 20th anniversary of the disappearance of the men. I try to get her to say something about it. Maybe I'll get lucky on this one.

Step 4 - I collect some trash. I can do this.

Step 5 - I take some pictures of what I find or anything else that's interesting. I don't think it will be a family portrait."

"Sounds good to me, Fly. You can do it. Just do it."

"But I'm not sure when to go there to meet her, Harv. She might not even be there."

"That would be great if she's not there. You have a better chance of getting evidence from the other sisters. They should be easier to talk to than the witch."

Fly shivered and crossed his forearms. "Don't call her that, Harv. I have this thing about witches, you know. Wizard of Oz thing. Call her something else."

"Well, my little pretty," Harvey cackled.

"Shut up, Harv. I have bad memories. Mama used to make me watch that show every year. Threatened to send me off to Oz."

Harvey chuckled. "How are you going to talk to these people if you have bad memories from an ancient movie?"

"Not a problem. I can shift gears and go into my salesman mode. Then I'm cool."

"You'll need to be. This is dangerous stuff you're getting' yourself into."

GATHERING EVIDENCE

Harvey and Fly went over the plan again without the use of the word witches. Harvey agreed to stay in his car out of sight in the field off Quarry Road in case the plan had to be scuttled and rescue was needed. They didn't tell Chappy about the plan so he wouldn't get in more trouble with Chief Jenkins.

At about 9:30 the next morning, Fly's truck clanked and sputtered up the gravel driveway toward the mansion. He wasn't sure if his truck would make it up the hill since the clutch had been slipping the past few days. The old mansion was nestled in a grove of oak trees that were probably planted when it was built over a century ago. There wasn't much of a lawn around the mansion, just natural plants that survived well in the oaks' understory.

The driveway split just before the mansion, with one lane going north to an old barn several hundred yards straight up the hill. Fly knew that the metal would be near the barn, but that wasn't his mission today. He drove up the driveway on the right to the mansion.

The mansion was built in the Victorian era and was large—three stories with a turret in the front on the north side. The brick and wooden structure had a sweeping porch that encompassed the front and south sides.

Fly pulled into the circular driveway and parked in front of the house. He gingerly walked up the five steps to get up to the porch, carefully looking all around to see if there was a clue anywhere to be found. *Nothin' too interesting outside*, he thought.

He looked at the old mechanical doorbell. *How the heck does this work*, he wondered. He turned the knob in its center, and it made a surprisingly loud ring. He jumped back.

No one came to the door initially, so he turned it again. The door opened, and a woman in a dark dress appeared.

Creepy, he thought. But Fly was able to muster a greeting. "Hello, Ms. Marlowe."

"Who are you? What do you want?"

"I'm Flywheel. Remember me? I've been here before with Noah to pick up scrap metal."

"No. I don't remember. I didn't call for a metal pickup."

She stumbled a bit and grabbed the edge of the door to stay upright. Flywheel detected the smell of alcohol.

"You sure you don't have some metal that you want to get rid of? I can remove it for free."

"I'll tell you what I'd like, Mr. Flywheel. I'd like to be left alone and for you to be out of here. This is private property, and you're trespassing."

"I understand, ma'am. With all the problems you've had with the missing people, I feel bad for you."

"Long time ago. Never heard from any of them. They're all dead. I just know it."

Fly put on his sad face. "If there's anything else I can do to help, like take out your trash or help you clean up. I'd be happy to."

"I have lots of trash, but Noah's supposed to take care of that. I don't know about any metal. You can go look for yourself."

"Can I take some trash out for you?"

"Dumpster's up by the barn. Recycling's there, too. Wait a second."

Fly waited, but she didn't return. After several minutes, he poked his head in the open door. "Ms. Marlowe?" He still got no answer and didn't hear her. He walked through the wide foyer that led into a hallway with the staircase on his right that led to the second floor. "Ms. Marlowe?" he said in a louder voice. Then he walked up the hallway to the kitchen. "Ms. Marlowe!" He saw her slumped over at the kitchen table, a can of recyclables tipped over on the floor next to her.

Fly walked over to her and gingerly pushed her arm. She didn't move, but he could hear her snoring in her drunken stupor. There was an ashtray loaded with cigarette butts on the table and empty bottles of whiskey and vodka strewed around the room. Trash everywhere.

Payday, he thought.

There was so much trash and so many bottles that he didn't know where to begin. He found some plastic shopping bags and was starting to comb through the debris, hoping to find something that might have fingerprints or DNA on it, when he heard someone coming down the stairs. He quickly put several cigarette filters in the bag along with some bottles and other containers.

"Who's there? That you, Eunice?" a woman's voice asked.

Now, what do I do? Fly's heart was racing.

"Eunice?"

"No. It's me, Flywheel."

"Flywheel? We don't know any Flywheel."

"I came to help get rid of your trash and recycling, ma'am."

The woman appeared in the kitchen doorway and pointed a long rifle at him. She looked to be a generation younger than Eunice. "What do you really want?"

"I collect metal sc … scr … scrap metal from people. Why don't you put that gun down?"

"She let you in?"

"Sure. I'm helping her with the recycling and trash while I'm here. See?" Fly pointed to the recycle bin next to Eunice. "But she kind of decided to take a nap."

"She's a nasty, drunken old fool."

"And your name is?"

"None of your business. Now we've got three choices. You can leave, I can call the cops, or I can shoot you."

"Uh, now let's not get crazy, Ms. None of Your Business. I can leave, but I'd like to help you with this mess. You could call the cops, but they might have some questions about the missing men that Ms. Eunice was telling me about. And shooting me, well, that would really be bad because you could end up with a life sentence."

"I already have a life sentence living with this witch."

Fly shook. "Oh no. Don't call her a witch. I have some issues with witches. You know, the Wizard of Oz and stuff."

The lady laughed. "The Wizard of Oz? Oh my God. You're a real wimp."

"Well, you see. I was very young when my mother made me watch that movie. And we watched it all the time. And I got freaked out all the time when I saw the wicked lady in black. I can't say what she was. Very scary."

She put the gun down. "Well, we don't see many people here. Like never, so it's kind of nice to see a real human being."

"So, who are you?"

"Carmela."

"How do you fit in here?"

"I don't, but I live here."

"You related to somebody here?"

"Eunice, sort of. She was Junior's second wife. Asa, or Three, as he was called, was Junior's son by his first wife. And I was married to Three."

"He's missing, right?" Fly asked.

"Beats me. He was always missing, as far as I'm concerned. A rich playboy that I regretted marrying from the day I said 'I do.'"

"Too bad."

"For me. He could be somewhere living it up, or more likely, he's six feet under."

"What makes you say that he might be dead?"

"He was here one day, 20 years ago, and then he was gone without a trace. Never heard from him again, just like his father. And then there was Roscoe. Same thing."

"What did the police say about all this?"

"I'm not sure. I left when the men vanished. Moved on with my life."

"But you're here now."

"Moved back a year or two ago. Needed a place to stay."

"Where were you all those years?"

"Here and there. You know. Living with people, then on my own."

Just then, there was a groan coming from the kitchen table. Eunice lifted her head. "Who are you?"

"You met me before, Eunice," Fly said.

"What are you doing in my kitchen?" Eunice asked.

"I said I'd take your trash up to the dumpster, remember?"

Fly looked at Carmela and whispered. "This happens a lot?"

"All the time. Like I said, a nasty, drunken fool."

Fly looked down at Eunice. "So, Eunice, you want me to take the trash out? I can do that, and you won't have such a mess here." He was talking in a louder-than-usual voice, the way he talked to Vanessa. He gave her no chance to respond before he picked up his bag of evidence.

"Get out of here," Eunice yelled. "Get out of here, or I'll call the cops."

"Doubt that," Carmela said. "You better get going, though, Mr. Flywheel. When she's like this, she can get violent."

"Move that gun so she doesn't get it."

"That's alright. It isn't loaded."

Fly smiled and grabbed his bag of newfound evidence. He nodded to Carmela and then quickly left the house. He thought that he might have a chance to find something else, so he headed up to the barn.

Fly dictated a text to Harvey. "Survived the house, Harv. Eunice was drunk, but I got the stuff I needed. Met Carmela. She didn't shoot me. Good thing. Checking out

138

the dumpster and barn."

The dumpster in front of the barn looked like it was hardly used. The sisters just left stuff in the house until Noah came to clean up. The area around the dumpster suggested that raccoons and other vermin had many a meal there. Fly decided not to take any of it. My luck, I'd get rabies, he thought.

Metal was another story. He was the only one who recycled metal from their property, and he hadn't been there in many years. Old wheels, worn-out parts of farm equipment, dented metal containers, and more were stacked beside the barn. He had a field day loading his pickup with other people's junk that would become his income. It was a "kid in a candy store" moment for Fly.

When he finished and was ready to leave, his curiosity got the best of him. He opened the old barn door just enough to squeeze inside. He used the flashlight in his cell phone to scan the barn. Nothing seemed out of place. Dust and grime covered everything except near one area that looked like a door in the floor with a pull-up metal handle on it. It seemed to be an access point to a cellar. Fly pulled up the handle and saw a stairwell leading to a very dark lower level below.

Should I go down? He wondered.

He started down the ancient wooden stairs before he answered his own question. As he shined the light around, he could see many bottles containing liquid, old jars containing food, and containers that looked like they might have the powder in them. Across the storage room was a stone wall that looked like it was part of the foundation supporting the barn. It had an old door made of wooden planks, and it was locked with a rusted padlock. As he took a step toward the door, he heard his name called from above.

"Flywheel. Where are you? You okay?" Harvey was looking for his partner.

"Yeah. I'm down here," Fly yelled.

"Get up here. We gotta get outta here," Harvey yelled back.

"I'm on to something," Fly yelled.

"Cops think something's going on here. Somebody must have called them. You gotta get out."

Reluctantly, Fly turned his light back toward the stairs and headed up to meet Harvey. He started to tell Harvey about the door in the barn basement, but Harvey cut him off.

"The police heard that something was going on at the mansion, and they dispatched a car to check it out. Now hurry up. Let's get out of here."

They got in their separate vehicles and quickly headed down the driveway, and when they reached Quarry Road, they turned right to head farther up the mountain toward the old quarry. Behind them, they heard sirens as police cars took a right off Quarry Road into the mansion driveway.

Harvey was already waiting when Fly and his struggling truck made it to the gravesite.

Fly showed Harvey the bags of evidence he collected from the sisters.

"How'd you get all this stuff?" Harvey asked.

"Man, you should see that place. What a mess. That kitchen was cattywampus. Stuff is scattered everywhere. Booze bottles, overflowing trash, full ashtrays."

"Cattywampus?"

"Messed up, scattered. My word of the day on my computer vocabulary program."

"Get out, Fly. You have a vocabulary program?"

"Yeah. What's so crazy about that?"

"Just surprising. I'll have to remember that word."

"I got the evidence surreptitiously."

"When did you learn that word?"

"Yesterday. But I was pretty clever in getting this stuff without them realizing that I was taking it. Eunice was out of it. Boozed to the gills. Carmela was just happy to see someone and didn't care what I took after she put the gun down."

"Gun down?"

"Wasn't loaded. But she had my knees knocking for a few minutes."

Fly transferred the evidence to Harvey's car, and they agreed that Harvey should take it to Chappy. Fly recommended that they continue up Quarry Road to the top of the mountain and take Church Road back to Stillwell to avoid the police. They could hear a second siren as more police approached Quarry Road.

Harvey called Chappy on his way back to town.

"Chappy. What's happening? I heard sirens going up toward the mansion."

"A lot of nothing. We got a call from somebody there saying there was an intruder. She didn't give her name, so it could have been any of the sisters."

Felicia, Harvey thought. Fly was with Eunice and Carmela.

"Whoever it was left before we got there," Chappy said. "May not have been anything. They call all the time. What was going on with Fly up there?"

"Nothing. Fly said Eunice was drunk, and Carmela pointed a rifle at him. Felicia didn't show her face. But he got the stuff."

"Could have been a crank call."

"I think it was Felicia that called," Harvey said.

"What makes you say that?"

"Because Fly was with Eunice and Carmela."

"In the house? Geez, Harvey. That's breaking and entering. A misdemeanor, maybe a felony, if there was damage done. That's jail time, Harvey."

"No B&E. He was let in, sort of, by Eunice and permitted to help clean up the kitchen. It was cattywampus."

"What? What are you talking about, Harv? Cattywampus?"

141

"Fly's word of the day. The place was a mess, just like that family. Filled with trash and bottles of booze."

"He took evidence from the scene? That's not admissible."

"They let him do it. He got some cigarette buts, drink cups, and bottles with prints on them. Good stuff."

Chappy was silent for a few minutes.

"Ok. I'm not sure it's admissible, but it might give us some DNA or fingerprints," Chappy replied. "We already have the sisters' prints, at least Felicia and Eunice. Not sure we have Carmela's."

"Well, you might compare these with what you have on file. Might get a lead. I'll bring the bags over to you later today, Chappy. Anything else I should know about the case?"

"We've got the forensics back from Philip's murder."

"Poison?"

"Good guess."

"Ricin?"

"No, ricin would be too slow."

"Cyanide. Nasty stuff and quick."

"Nope."

"Geez. What's left?"

"Something you'd find on an old farm."

"Oh yeah. Arsenic. Used in pesticides."

"You got it, Harv."

"Somebody knew what they were doing. Get it done quickly."

"Yeah. This stuff moves into your organs quickly if you take in a large amount."

They talked for a while about Philip's murder and speculated about who might have done it.

"Philip's wake is tonight," Harvey said. "You going?"

"Not sure yet. I've been putting in a lot of overtime, and the wife isn't happy."

"We'll be there. My wife's out of town, and Fly doesn't have a wife. Or at least I don't think so."

"Keep him under control."

Harvey laughed.

THE WAKE

Philip's wake was held at the Smythe Funeral Home on Brant Street in Stillwell. It had recently been remodeled, as their motto says, to become "the best funeral parlor in town." Of course, most were quick to state that it was also the only funeral parlor in town.

Many people in Stillwell and surrounding areas knew Philip, so his wake was attended by a large, eclectic collection of locals and a few people from out of town. Some came out of sorrow for the homeless, murdered man, others out of curiosity, and still others in hopes of learning something new about how Philip died. He had few true friends but many acquaintances.

Chappy changed his mind, and he and some of his detectives were in the stateroom to observe the mourners. Flywheel and Harvey were there as well. As they entered the room, they joined the line of people moving to the open casket. Some people marveled at how good Philip looked. "Much better than in real life," Alice Gemmel said. "Handsome when he's cleaned up."

Others commented on how sad his life must have been with no home and being dependent on others for food. Still, others mentioned how he was able to learn the town's "dirt" just from sitting in the gazebo.

"Heard a lady say he looks good," Fly whispered to Harvey. "Doesn't look good to me. Looks dead. You know, like a doornail. Looks like he's been to a taxidermist."

Harvey elbowed Fly, gave him a dirty look, and pushed him past the casket toward two empty seats. As they went to their chairs, Fly nudged Harvey, cocked his head, and motioned toward the back of the room, where he saw several familiar faces. Chappy was sitting in the back row, trying to look invisible. Ollie sat next to him. Noah Zark sat nearby with Earlene.

"Pretend you don't see them. Don't look their

way," Harvey whispered. "You see the sisters?"

Fly turned again, panning the room. "Nope."

Soon, Rosie Harbock, the town gossip, passed by the casket, touched Philip's folded hands, and then came over to them. She was in her 50s and always wore flamboyant dresses and hats. Her funeral attire was no exception, a light blue dress with large pink and white hibiscus flowers all over it. Her wide-brimmed hat had matching flowers on its band. She looked ready for the Kentucky Derby.

As she headed toward them, Harvey said, "Don't say anything."

Rosie became flirty when she saw Harvey. "Hi there, Harvey. What do you think about this? Wasn't this awful? Poor Philip."

"Very sad. Don't have a clue, Rosie."

"Come on, Harv. We've known each other for years. You know you can trust me." She fluttered her eyelashes.

"Ha. I can trust you until you can get on your cell phone. You know I can't talk about this case, and that's what you want to know about. Good try, though."

"Who's this handsome dude that's with you?"

Fly extended his hand, which Rosie latched onto and didn't let go. "Flywheel, but you can call me Fly."

"Ooh. You give me your number, and I can call you very soon."

Fly yanked his hand away from her and moved back.

Harvey knew how to flip the discussion with Rosie. "How 'bout you, Rosie? If Philip was murdered, who do you think did it?"

"I have my suspicions based on pretty good evidence from someone who knew the lay of the land."

"Who has this good evidence?"

"Had. Philip had some evidence, but you can see where it got him."

"And now you have it?"

"I wouldn't want anyone to know what he told me."

"You can trust me, Rosie," Fly interjected.

"Ha! I don't know who you are, big boy, and I certainly don't want to talk here in the funeral parlor."

"Fly is my trustworthy assistant, Rosie," Harvey said. "You can talk with him, and he won't talk to anyone but me."

"We'll see," she said as she walked away.

As the crowd continued to pay their respects or satisfy their curiosity, two women in flowing dresses came in.

"Know them, Harvey?"

"Not sure. The older one looks kind of familiar."

"Psycho ladies," Fly said. "The younger one runs Madam Marlena's Clairvoyance Center over on Groveland Street. You know the place. It has a sign next to the door that says they do readings and stuff. Last time I picked up metal refuse from them ..."

"Junk. Don't get fancy with me, Fly."

"Well, I took a picture of the sign. Look at this," Fly said as he showed him his phone. The sign said Madam Marlena, Spiritualist, Readings, Metaphysical Advice, Esoteric Classes, and Online Seminars.

"That's the place we're going for a reading. We need to know how Noah's connected with them."

"Low on my To Do list, remember Harv?"

"Got to figure out the connection, though."

"Pretty obvious, don't you think, Harv?"

"Speculation. You've got a rumor about Philip's father, and you think the old lady is his mother. You think, but you don't know for sure. Right?"

"Yeah. Speculation. Haven't had that vocabulary word yet."

"Mama Psychic looks familiar. I've seen her coming into Tootie's to buy takeout. Wait. I remember her mentioning something about Philip to Tootie. I guess the older woman is her mother."

"Now you're speculating, Harv. Think she was feeding Philip?"

"Sure thing, Fly. I've seen her in the gazebo talking to him."

They looked closely at them as they slowly walked around the room, nodding at people. When Madam Marlena's mother got in front of the casket, she looked at Philip, then turned slightly and looked at Noah. She started to wobble. She put the back of her hand against her forehead, her eyes rolled, and in a dramatic sweeping motion, fell to the floor.

"Mother," Marlena yelled. "Someone help. Please!"

A nurse in the room came right over to her and stretched her out on the floor in front of the casket. "Get a wet cloth."

Fly jumped up. He took out a rag that he always carried in case he had to touch some toxic metal, dipped it in a vase that held funeral flowers, and brought it to the nurse. She made a face but lifted it up to put it on Marlena's mother's forehead.

Smelling the old rag, Mother opened her eyes, scowled, and tried to get up. "Don't put that dirty thing on me," she said.

Fly and the nurse picked her up and put her in the seat that a woman offered in the front row next to Harvey. When Fly returned to his seat, he asked Harvey what that was all about.

"Guess she was taken aback by Philip's appearance. Or Noah's presence. Or maybe she needed some attention. But she sure didn't like your cruddy rag."

Fly just smiled. "You know, Harv, with acting like that, maybe she knows a few things. Better expedite that reading."

"You've got that right, Fly. I'll expedite it. Nice word!"

THE PSYCHICS

Fly and Harvey met at the park the next day to debrief the wake.

"Here's what I'm thinking, Fly," Harvey said.

Fly put his hands to his head like he was receiving brain waves. "Wait. Wait. I'm having a telepathic experience. I'm thinking what you're thinking."

"Right. Here we go with the Fly guy wise guy stuff again."

"No. Seriously, Harv. I'm thinking that you want us to go have a visit with the psychic. Like we're really there for a reading. Not like a cop interview."

Harvey smiled. "A reading, not an interrogation."

Harvey gave him a knuckle bump. Fly beamed.

"Let's just go over there and see if we can find out something."

"Like what?"

"You're the trainee; what do you think we might find out?"

"Hmm. I think there is a connection between the swami and the three ladies."

"What makes you say that?"

"Remember, I see a lot, Harv. When I'm cruisin' 'round to pick up recyclable refuse, I see who's where when."

"You know something? You been holding out information on the sisters?"

"Yeah. Never thought about it 'til now, but they come to see the swami a lot. At least the last couple years. Maybe once a month, maybe more. I see them there near the beginning of the month."

"All three?"

"Sometimes, or only two or just one."

"Very cool. We often know a lot more than we think we do, but we don't dig it out of our subconscious until we have some kind of trigger. The ladies visiting came to you because mentioning swami was a trigger to remind you of their visit."

"A trigger, huh? I'll have to remember that."

"It's Roy Rogers' horse, too, Fly."

"Who's Roy Rogers?"

"Never mind. That's my generation."

They decided that now was as good a time as ever, so they headed to see the psychic.

Harvey drove down Groveland Street and pulled up in front of Madam Marlena's Clairvoyance Center. Before long, Flywheel came clanking up the street in his dilapidated pickup truck, got out, and came over to see Harvey.

"Not glad to be here, Harvey," Flywheel said.

"You didn't have to show up."

"Didn't have to make a gob of money either. What's the plan?"

"If we're going to find out what happened to Philip, we have to think outside the box. Try all kinds of leads."

"Here? With Looney Marlena and her loonier mother? You're so far outside the box that I can't see the box. You're goin' weird on me, Harv."

"Nah. Nothin' weird about this. I did my homework and talked to Noah again. Found that Madam Marlena's mother used to be a psychic and operated in this house at the time when the Marlowe men disappeared. He used to visit her once a week to read cards, palms, and crystal balls. She must know something, so let's go see."

"Noah came here? Probably more than readings. How do you know she's there?"

"Undercover work. Surveillance." He paused. "So, you in or out, Flywheel?"

Flywheel hesitated.

"You win. I'm in," Flywheel said.

"Good. 'Cause if you're not in, you're out a lot of money. I heard the reward has been gathering a lot of interest. That's how it got to $150K."

"Okay. Okay. I don't like it, but I'm in."

They walked up to the small, sky-blue ranch house and saw a yellow triangular sign on the door. "Clairvoyant Crossing" with the silhouette of a woman with her hands on a crystal ball. Below the picture, it said, "Madam Marlena, Psychic."

"Oh man," Flywheel wrung his hands. "I'm already creeped out." He started breathing heavily.

"Here." Harvey took a rumpled-up paper bag from his pocket and gave it to Fly.

"What's this for?"

"Cover your mouth and nose and then breathe into the bag. You're hyperventilating."

Fly did as directed, and his breathing came under control quickly.

"You a medic, Harv?"

"Nope. Had a bad experience, so now I always carry a bag. I'll tell you about it sometime."

Harvey rang the doorbell, which played a few bars of the spooky Toccata and Fugue in D minor by Bach. Flywheel turned and started to go back to the car, muttering something about creepy Halloween music.

"Get back here, wimp," Harvey said. "I'm cutting you out of the reward if you leave."

Flywheel abruptly pivoted and started back. A voice from behind the door said, "Who's there?"

Flywheel looked perplexed. "If she's a psychic, she should know who's here."

Harvey shook his head. "You're hopeless, Fly."

The door opened, and a short, older woman appeared, catching them both by surprise.

"Uh, Madam Marlena?" Harvey said.

"Say, I know you," Fly interrupted. "You passed out at Philip's wake."

"Oh, my knight in shining armor," she replied. "You saved my life."

"Well, I wouldn't go so far as to say that. You just needed a little reviving. The nurse, she's the hero."

She looked at Harvey. "No. I'm her mother, but I'm a medium and palmist. May I help you?"

"Well, I hope so."

Flywheel smiled. "Cool. You're a short medium, and I'm large. We'll get along just fine."

"Good. I can use a few extra bucks. I mean, I'd be happy to assist you."

"You sure you're a clair-a-majiggy?" Flywheel asked.

"Clairvoyant. Of course, I taught Madam Marlena to use her psychic gifts. She used to call me swami mommy. Now her kids call me swami grandmommy. Cute, eh?"

Harvey and Flywheel gave each other a wide-eyed glance.

"Addams family," Fly whispered.

She invited them into the waiting room and disappeared behind curtains covering the doorway while organ music droned on. In a few minutes, she returned wearing a pink and yellow robe and purple turban with a large, fake diamond embedded in it. She motioned for them to join her behind the curtain in the spiritual reading room.

Flywheel pushed Harvey ahead of him. "You get the prize behind the curtain."

Harvey entered the room and then grabbed Flywheel by the shirt to pull him in.

The room was decorated to look like it was from the 19th century. It was dark, illuminated by a low-wattage lamp. Walls had textile hangings with strange symbols on them – circles, starbursts, and triangles. A couch was covered with a multi-squared, multi-colored Afghan. There was a table, two overstuffed chairs, and smaller Afghans on the seats. A middle-eastern rug with elaborate floral designs covered the floor. The window curtains matched the colors of the Afghans, adorned with strings of small light bulbs of various colors.

Swami grand mommy suddenly had a much more serious look and silently gestured for them to sit down on one side of the circular table while she sat on the other side. "My name is Madam DuBois, Mia DuBois, and I am here to help you uncover secrets locked deep in your subconscious."

"So, how much is this costing us?" Flywheel asked.

Harvey swung his foot over and kicked Flywheel in the shin. "Please ignore my partner, Madam DuBois. He says strange things when he's nervous."

As the lights dimmed, the crystal ball illuminated, growing slowly in intensity. Madam DuBois began talking in a soft tone as she massaged the crystal ball. A black cat jumped on her lap.

"Try to visualize what you want to know. Stare into the crystal ball."

She paused for what seemed like an eternity. "Relax and let your eyes go out of focus. Don't force your thoughts. Keep thinking of your questions. You may see images in the crystal ball, or the ball may cause you to have a memory, a deep memory you've long forgotten."

She paused again. "Eventually, the images will fade away, and your subconscious will give you the information you need. Maybe not today, but in the future when you need it."

Madam DuBois told Fly to rest his hands gently on the crystal ball. He did as she directed, and the ball began to glow brighter. "You ... you take it, Harvey," Flywheel said. "You're better at this stuff. I'll just look at the ball."

The ball dimmed, and when Harvey put both hands on it, the ball brightened again. The room was silent, and Harvey stared at the ball. In a couple of minutes, he heard a low humming sound. "What's that?" he asked.

He quickly realized that the sound was coming from Flywheel. A low-humming mantra.

The usually cool Harvey looked at Flywheel, who

was deep in a meditative trance. His head began to shake. He began to talk. "I see him … in a white robe. I see Philip. He's calling out. 'Mommy, mommy, where are you?' I see a man on a farm. Philip calls out again. 'Daddy, daddy, where are you?'"

Madam Dubois, visibly shaken, pushed Harvey's hands off the crystal ball and called Flywheel's name to interrupt his thoughts.

"What? Where am I? Who were those people?" Flywheel said.

Madam DuBois stood up. "Well, er, I think that's all we can do for today, gentlemen. You may want to return when my daughter is here. She might help you have other visions. Thank you. This is only an introduction to the crystal ball reading, so we won't charge you. Goodbye."

Before they could say anything, they were ushered out, and the door slammed behind them.

Flywheel smiled at Harvey, and they gave each other high fives.

"Sweet," Flywheel said.

"We were pretty sure who Philip's parents were going in, but I didn't expect that reaction."

"Guilty. Let's nail her and get on with the reward."

"No, you turkey. Forget the reward. We have no evidence. She might be his mother, but that doesn't make her his murderer. No evidence means no conviction means no money. And the reward isn't for Philip's death; it's for finding Junior. Focus, Flywheel."

Flywheel started humming again. Harvey swatted him on the back of the head as they headed to the street.

"Ok. So far, we have no evidence, only missing people, one skeleton that we think is Ebony, one body—Philip, and one swami grand mommy who obviously knows something. We need to keep talking to people."

"You're always thinkin' ahead, Harv."

"Got to. If you don't think ahead, you'll be a step behind."

"Now what?"

"We need to find out more about the missing men, like Roscoe. We know he's been missing almost as long as the other two guys. Your girlfriend in Philmont hasn't seen him."

"First of all, she's not my girlfriend."

"Ok. Acquaintance. What about Roscoe, though? Who else would know about him?"

"He used to come around with junk all the time. Always needed money. High most of the time."

"Stolen junk?"

"I don't ask a lot of questions."

"When did he stop coming by?"

"Let's see." Fly looked up and scratched his head. "I'd say 15, 20 years ago. Maybe longer. Said he was going to visit his mother."

"We know where she is. Living in the mansion with Two's wife and maybe Three's wife from time to time. Sisters with missing relatives."

"I don't know, Harv. Have you ever seen Felicia? We've only heard she's there."

Harv tugged on his chin. "Hmm. You have a point, Fly."

"But we have some evidence about who is there in the mansion."

"You're sounding more like a PI every day."

"PI? Partial idiot?"

"Don't insult me or you, Fly. Private investigator. We need to find out if Felicia is still there."

"They said she was upstairs when I was there."

"Did you see her?"

"Nope."

"You don't think she's there, huh?"

Fly made a gesture like he was slitting his throat.

Harvey shrugged. "Nothing surprises me in this game, Fly."

PUTTING PIECES TOGETHER

They drove back to Harvey's house and met in the Situation Room.

Fly looked around the room at the clippings and notes on the boards. "Nice digs, Harv."

"Something to drink?"

"Sure. How about H_2O on the rocks? Good for my dehydration. Visiting swamis always makes me thirsty."

Harvey got him some water and continued the discussion. "So, what do you think the swami knows?"

"Well, I think she knows we're suspicious of her."

"Agreed. And?"

"She's Philip's mother."

"What's your evidence?"

"You're always wanting evidence, Harv. You make my job hard!"

Harvey laughed and moved on. "What else did you find out?"

"The sisters are coming to her to pay her off. She knows something about Junior or Three or Roscoe or someone."

"The only thing you can say for sure is that the sisters are coming over to visit."

"Yeah, but you know they're probably extorting her, Harv."

"Possibly, but no clues lead to that. Only your gut and metal head."

"Hey. Be nice." Fly made a gesture like he was primping the hair on his metal head. "You have to admit. I know a lot about this case. You can call me sleuth." He took a deep breath and puffed up his chest.

"Good trainee," Harvey said as he patted him on the head like a puppy. "When you summarize what you know, you usually more than you think you know."

"Funny thing, though," Fly said. "We only know that we have missing people and dead people. Hardly any evidence or suspects."

"This is when cases get fun; Fly. You've got to talk to people and use some science to find suspects. Then you have to be able to pin the crime on the suspect or suspects."

"Checkmate."

"You play chess, Fly? That's what it's like, checkmate."

"Nah, I heard LL Cool J or somebody say that on a TV show."

"Sounds good, though. Keep that line."

"What now, Boss?"

"I'm not your boss, but we've got work to do. Got to do a little crowdsourcing. We talk to a lot of people. No one knows everything, or maybe not very much, but you put it all together, and you've got a magic solution."

"Checkmate. You got me on that one, Harvey. I don't have a clue what you mean."

"You will."

Harvey's phone rang, and Chappy's face appeared on the screen.

"Chappy. How ya doin'? Got some good stuff for us?"

"Not as good as the stuff you gave me. But we did have a good hit on the trash that Crazy Fly gave us."

"Scuze me," Fly said. "Just 'cause I call you Snappy Chappy, which by the way, is a serious compliment in my world, doesn't mean you can call me crazy."

"Whoops! Sorry, Fly. How about wackadoodle? Is that better?"

"Not really, but it sounds classier, Snappy."

"Okay, you two, enough," Harvey said.

"That's okay, Harv. Snappy and I go way back, and I think he forgets that he owes me something really big. Right, Snappy?"

"Ancient history. Not worth talking about."

Fly ignored Snappy's comment and went on. "So,

Harv, Snappy was working a case involving these twin crooks, the Stitzell brothers, Harley and Harold. I knew these guys when they were young. They used to do B & Es on expensive cars to take electronics and whatever else they could fence from whoever left their car doors open."

"Ok. Fly. I think that's enough," Chappy interrupted.

"Oh no. There's more. So, these guys graduated to stealing cars and taking them to chop shops. Made a ton of money. Then they got so good, or bad, at this that they opened what they called their auto repair business. This turned out to be their own chop shop. They came to me and wanted me to take their scrap metal and parts they couldn't fence."

"Enough," Chappy said.

"Now we get to the good part," Fly continued. "Being a good citizen, I reported this attempt to do business with me to a young detective known as Detective Chan."

Harvey could see Chappy shaking his head and scowling.

"Now you'd think they'd give me a big reward, right? No. They didn't do that 'cause they didn't know who tipped off the detective. And that detective, Mr. Snappy Chappy, got all the credit ... AND a promotion ... AND probably a raise."

"True, Chappy?" Harvey asked.

Chappy didn't say anything.

"I rest my case," Fly said. "So Snappy Chappy owes me big time. No money, although he's been making more money from his promotion for years. All I want is a little R-E-S-P-E-C-T."

After more silence, Chappy spoke up. "Fly, I'm really sorry. I've been sorry for years, and I haven't said that to you. You helped me out, and I took advantage of you."

"We'll, I guess we cleared that up," Harvey said.

"I wouldn't go that far, Harv, but I'll accept

Chappy's confession and apology."

"Great. Let's move on. We have cases to solve."

"At least I know the Stitzell twins didn't do in Ebony or Philip," Fly said. "Those guys are still in the slammer. Murdered somebody before they took his car. In for life without parole."

Harvey wanted to get back to business. "Whatcha got for us, Chappy?" he asked.

"Got a lead on Philip's murder. Seems like the cup he drank the coffee from wasn't from a local store. Came from one of those big box stores–Frugal's Discount Center or Cheapy's. We're checking it out. It was the Hotright brand. Coffee was one of those home brands you can make a cup at a time."

"Not Tootie's?" Harvey wondered.

"No. Somebody probably made the coffee at home and laced it with arsenic."

"So, where do you get arsenic?" Fly asked. "Been illegal for years."

"Good question. You're right. It is illegal in the US, but like a lot of illegal things, there's an underground market for it."

"Not your usual thing you can buy in a hardware store," Harvey commented.

"But wouldn't Philip know he was being poisoned?" Fly wondered.

Chappy went on to explain that arsenic has no color, taste, or odor. "Philip knew he didn't feel well, but he probably didn't know why. He probably got doses of coffee over a few days. When you're homeless, you can't afford to go to the doctor."

"No motive yet? He must have some serious goods on someone for them to kill him."

"If we can figure out what he knew that got him killed, we'd be on the right track. Might lead us to a perpetrator, Harv."

Fly perked up. "Like who?"

"I learned long ago that you can have a lot of suspicions, but they may not prove a case. You need a clear link to evidence."

"Come on, Snappy. Who do you think did this?"

"I also learned a long time ago that I shouldn't mention the names of suspicious people. Most suspicions are wrong."

Harvey changed the subject. "So, we know how Philip died. Where are we with Ebony?"

"We have more on that one, but still no suspects."

"So, what's new?"

"Forensics checked with the dental records on file with the missing person's bureau in Atlanta and got a hit. The records matched Ebony Jones."

"You're confirming the skeleton is Ebony Jones?" Harvey asked.

"Yup."

"Anything on the choice of burial places, Chappy?"

"You'd think it was someone who knew the property and knew about the limb maker's house. But that's not as easy as it seems. People that lived and worked on the property could be involved. But half the people in Stillwell, and who knows where else, knew about the old guy that made prosthetics for people from the Civil War until the 1940s. He lived until he was over 100 and made limbs right to the end."

"Fly, tell him about Kiana," Harvey said.

"Isn't that our investigation? Why should we tell him?"

"We're all in this game. Chappy's giving us information, and we have to reciprocate if we have anything."

"I tried that once. See where it got me?"

Chappy interrupted. "History, Fly, I screwed up, but I apologized, and we have to move on. Who's Kiana?"

Fly sighed. "Ebony's cousin. Lives in Philmont."

Chappy was excited. "Great, Fly. Do you know

Kiana?"

"Yeah, from a long time ago. Before she had a kid, she was kind of wild. Party girl. Not into drugs much, but she knew all about who was."

"So, Ebony just showed up at Kiana's house?"

"I guess. She was there for about a month, then she disappeared. We know where she ended up."

"Whoever murdered her had some connection to this property or at least knew about it," Chappy said.

"Kinda looks that way," Fly said.

"Who from here would have known Kiana and Ebony?"

"Some party guy or girl, Snappy," Fly said. "Hey, Harv, did you catch how I included a girl as a suspect? You taught me that. Be inclusive, not exclusive, early in the investigation."

"What do you think, Harv?" Chappy wondered.

"I don't think Kiana had much to do with Ebony or her murder. She seems like she's been clean for a long time, and she didn't know too much about her cousin except she was running away from her life in Atlanta."

Chappy countered. "Ebony's been dead a long time, too. Can't rule anything out."

Fly shook his head. "Man, this detective stuff is confusing."

"We can't rule out Kiana, but we also can't rule out anybody who knew this property," Harvey said.

"Like?" Chappy asked.

Fly quickly replied. "Can't be Asa One. He's long dead. Not likely to be Two. He was pretty old to be partying, although Sweet Eunice said he'd disappear for a while like his son. Then there are the other two. Three and Roscoe."

"Both were in Philmont getting their drugs," Harvey added.

"Kiana probably knew both of them," Chappy said.

"And both knew where the limb maker lived and

160

how unlikely it would be for somebody to find a body there," Harvey said.

"Until the Hopper kids came along," Fly said. "Cool kids. Liked to dig in the dirt. My kinda kids."

"So, we've got two missing suspects and a skeleton," Chappy stated the obvious.

Harvey asked Chappy for more details about the condition of the body when it was found. Was she clothed? If so, were there stains on the clothing? What color were the bones? Chappy reported that she, indeed, was fully clothed, but the clothing was falling apart. There weren't any apparent bloodstains, but bones also picked up the reddish stain from the soil.

Hearing this, Fly chimed in. "I got an idea."

Snappy made a weird face.

"Listen, Chappy," Fly quickly replied. "S'pose this isn't the only body buried up there? What if one of the suspects is there, too?"

"So, how are you going to find out?" Chappy asked.

"Might not be me finding out. You got more high-tech stuff than I do."

"Like?"

"Old metal detectors, for one. We might have found Ebony if her locket had come up on a metal detector. I've got a few of them at the Upcycle Center."

"Ok."

"Even better, a GPR scanner. You know Ground Penetrating Radar?"

"We don't have that at the headquarters. We'd have to job that out."

"Snappy, Snappy, you're so old school. Even I have one of them. I've found some great antique metal stuff with it. You guys should buy one."

"You must have some deep pockets, Fly. Those things start at about $15,000."

"Not if you have friends who owe you a lot of money. When I barter, I win."

"I'm not going to ask how you could have friends that owe you that much."

"Good. 'Cause I'm not going to tell you. But you could rent a GPR for a day for around $1K. Good investment."

"I'll keep that in mind, Fly. I gotta go. Too many crimes, not enough time. Bye, guys."

The screen on Harvey's phone went dark.

"What now, Boss?"

"Lot of stuff to deal with, Fly. Lots of people who know something but aren't saying anything."

"We can't talk to them all."

"We can try to, and we can do other things that might help."

"Like?"

"Check out the mountain near the limb maker's house with some of your equipment."

"You're thinking there might be another body buried up there?"

Harvey nodded. "People follow patterns, and if you can figure out their pattern, you have a better chance of finding them."

"Not so easy, though."

"It is easier if you use your ..." Harvey pointed to his head and winked.

"I know where I need to go," Fly said. "I think my friend knows more than she's saying."

PHILMONT

Fly drove into Philmont the next day to talk with Kiana. He called her before he arrived to let her know he was stopping by her apartment.

"Hey, K."

"Fly! I don't hear from you for 20 years, and now you're contacting me a second time. What's up?"

"I'm almost at your apartment, so I'll be right up."

"Oh, wait!"

Before she could say anything, Fly hung up the call.

Fly went straight up to Apartment 4. He knocked once, and the door immediately opened. Fly could see a man who looked to be around 20 years old sitting on the couch watching a late-morning TV game show.

"Uh, let me introduce you to my son, Fly. I think you'll like him. We can talk in the kitchen if this is a private conversation."

She turned to face the tall, lean young black man. "Son, come meet a friend of mine."

The young man came over, smiled at Fly, and extended his hand.

"Fly, I'd like you to meet … Fly."

Fly's eyes opened wide. "What? You're Fly, too?"

"It's really Flywheel, but my friends call me Fly."

Kiana responded. "I liked your name. Thought it was kind of cute, so I named my boy after you."

Fly was speechless. Kiana didn't expect such a reaction from Fly. Young Fly, feeling awkward, excused himself and headed to his bedroom.

"I know what you're thinking, Fly. Fly Sr., but he isn't Fly Jr. He's Flywheel Jones."

The usually loquacious Fly still couldn't find words to express his shock.

"It's a long story, Fly. I'll tell you sometime, but not right now."

"Sure, K. Uh, I'm, uh, okay. We can talk about it at

another time."

They adjourned to the kitchen, sat at the table, and silently looked at each other.

"You telling me the truth, K?"

"Well, sort of."

"Sort of?"

"You know I was kind of wild when I was young."

"Like Ebony."

"Not that wild. She was reckless. Crazy wild."

"What about the sort of?"

"Well, I found myself pregnant."

"And you think I'm the daddy?"

"I don't know. I just know you meant a lot to me despite my being wild. My Fly is the best thing that ever happened to me. And, well, you know. I chose to think you were the father."

"But you don't know."

She shook her head. "No, Fly, I don't know, and I'm choosing not to find out."

"This is a heavy hit. I came here to talk about Ebony, and you're telling me this. Seems like a nice kid, but I'm not sure what to say to him or you."

"You don't need to say anything, Fly. Just know that he's a great kid. He is going to the community college and will transfer to finish his degree in criminal justice at State next year. Wants to be a detective."

"Funny. So, do I."

They laughed. Fly composed himself, took a deep breath, and they got down to business.

"I came to tell you about Ebony and ask you some questions."

"She's dead, isn't she?"

Fly nodded.

"I knew it. She was hanging with those guys, those druggies, and God knows what they were getting into."

"Do you remember the guys she hung out with?"

"The usual crowd from around here. Most of them

are in prison or dead. But she also liked to party with this guy from Stillwell. I told you about him. Richie Rich, if you know what I mean."

"What do you mean Richie Rich?"

"You know. Nice car, nice clothes. You just knew he had a lot of money."

"White guy, right?"

She nodded.

"What was going down at that time?"

"You should know. He was into Nose Candy. Coke."

"Sure. Cocaine. Expensive stuff."

"Then jelly beans came along. Cheap crack cocaine and everybody could be wasted cheaper. But this guy never seemed to have a shortage of money. He'd buy whatever the other stoners wanted—meth, marijuana, alcohol, you name it, he'd buy it."

"Guess he got really popular around here."

"Like the Pied Piper. He'd blow into town, and there'd be five guys sucking up to him to get their drugs."

"Three, right?"

"That was him. Never used a last name, but everybody knew Three."

"Whatever happened to him?"

"Well, he was Ebony's BFF. They saw something in each other. If they were ever sober, maybe they'd have been a match."

"She was a druggie, too?"

"Understatement. She was high as a kite, and Three kept her that way. He was like a puppy around her. Bought her clothes, booze, and lots of drugs."

"What was her problem?"

"Memory. The memory of her time with her abusive father in Atlanta. Never talked much about it, but it must have been bad. Wanted to forget her past."

"And then she disappeared."

"Well, not right away. That's when this other guy

came into the picture. I think he was the guy you went to school with. Another druggie, but not part of Three's crowd."

"Let me guess. The other guy hits on Ebony."

"You're so smart, Fly." She looks at Fly with a warm smile.

Fly looked down and pretended to be embarrassed by the compliment. "Let me guess again. This guy's name was Roscoe."

"Brilliant," she said.

"If that's Roscoe, those two men are still missing. And then there's Ebony, too. We didn't even know that Ebony was a part of this. When did Ebony go missing, Kiana?"

"Hard to remember 20 years back. I think Roscoe came to town and made a play for Ebony. Roscoe seemed to know Three. Didn't get along."

"But Ebony left town?"

"From what you're telling me, I don't think she left on her own. Sounds like she was killed and buried before she had a chance to leave town."

"We have to prove that, though, before we can arrest someone."

"Look at you, Fly. You sound like a detective already."

"By the way, Kiana. You know where they found Ebony?"

"No clue."

"On the Marlowe property in Stillwell. Some kids were digging a fort and found her."

"That was Three's last name, wasn't it?"

"Yup. He lived at the mansion off and on. Must have spent plenty of time in town here."

"Yeah, way too much time. What about Roscoe?"

"Know where he lived?"

"No clue, Fly."

"At the Marlowe mansion."

"You've gotta be kidding, Fly. Same place as Three?"

"Yup. Sounds like there was something going on between them before Three came into town, doesn't it?"

"Maybe one of them killed Ebony. But both of them are missing. How are you going to prove anything if you can't talk to them? I can't believe this, Fly. Poor Ebony."

"I know, Kiana," Fly said as he hugged her to console her. "Thanks, Kiana. You were a big help. Let's get together sometime."

"You know where to find me."

They hugged again, and Fly left.

It had been a long time since Fly had been to his old territory in Philmont. He still picked up metal around town, but he stayed away from the areas where the stoners hung out. The sober Fly couldn't afford to repeat his checkered past. For old time's sake, he drove through his old territory, but he didn't see too many familiar faces. He rode around and saw some kids trying to make a buck selling pot on corners. Some had packets that they gave customers in exchange for money.

Dealing, Fly thought. Stupid kids are wasting their lives. Man, I'm getting old.

ANOTHER BODY

Fly called Harvey to fill him in on his conversation with Kiana.

"Interesting stuff," Fly said. "Kiana didn't think she knew much. The more she talked, the more she could remember."

"Like what?" Harvey wanted to know.

"Like Three and Ebony. Roscoe came along, and that made three."

"You're saying Three plus two makes three?"

"Don't confuse me, Harvey. Now you're being the wisenheimer."

"How does Kiana know this?"

"She saw a lot in the short time Ebony lived with her."

"So, these guys were fighting for Ebony."

"More than fighting, Harv. Ebony ended up dead."

"Who do you think did it, Fly? They both lived on the Marlowe property, sometimes together. One of them prob'ly killed Ebony. That got the other one mad."

"Raging mad. Killing mad," Fly's voice sounded angry.

"But we don't know where either one is. We've got a motive and the victim. We don't know where the perp is."

"Perp? Come on, Harv. That's cop talk gives me the willies."

"Better get used to cop talk if you want to be a PI. This isn't getting us anywhere, so let's figure out how we can find another body."

"You know I can bring the GPR when we need it," Fly said." Came with a drone, so it's an airborne GPR."

"You know how to operate a drone and the GPR?"

Fly boasted. "Quick learner, Harv. Whiz kid in shop class in school. Got the golden hammer award."

"A digital hammer?"

"Would be today, whatever a digital hammer is!"

"That's how you keep your truck in such good shape?"

"Don't pick on my truck. She's rustic. Gets more valuable with age."

"Right. I can hardly wait to see how you fly the airborne contraption."

"You'll be surprised, big guy. Give me a couple of days to brush up, and I'll be finding all kinds of things up on that hill."

Harvey laughed. "See you in a couple of days, whiz kid."

———————

Two days later, they met in Mershon Park. Fly had the payload carefully packaged in a crate in the back of his truck.

"So, whiz kid, did you figure this out?"

Fly smirked at Harvey. "Of course. It was easy after I got a little help from my friends."

"Like the song? Drugs?"

"Harvey, that's the old me. I'm clean as a whistle and ready to bristle!"

"Ok, then, show me how this thing works."

Fly pulled the cover off the crate so Harvey could take a peek at the GPR and the drone.

"They aren't hooked together, Fly. How are you going to fly it like that?"

"Duh. Right after I put them together, Harv. Trust me. Okay?"

Harvey looked skeptical.

"When it comes to this stuff, I'm the mentor, and you're the mentee, Harv. Just tell me where we're flying this baby."

"I don't know. I'm just the mentee for this operation," Harvey said. "You're the PI. Where do you think the body or bodies are?"

"Up on the slope, someplace near the limb maker's house."

"It's obvious, Fly. Criminals are creatures of habit. They aren't necessarily creative when it comes to disposing of bodies. If they have a good spot one time, they use it again."

"Brilliant for a mentee."

Harvey shook his head and ignored the comment. "Just follow me up Quarry Road and use the back road we used before. I'll meet you at the limb maker's house unless that heap of junk you're driving won't make it through the potholes and gullies."

"I almost wrecked it when we went up to the limb makers the first time. If you wreck my truck leading me up some beat-up road, you're paying. Understand?"

"Don't worry. I won't wreck it, Fly. If you notice, I'm not driving your truck."

"Oh, yeah." They both laughed.

The unpaved road to the field, which was called Limbmaker Road, was as bad as Fly remembered. He grumbled and complained with every bump he hit, and even though Harvey was not in his truck, he told him more than once that he was going to fire him as a mentee. They finally got to the crumbling old house and saw that Ebony's grave had been filled in, probably for safety reasons. The yellow police tape had been removed.

"Looks like nothing happened here," Fly observed.

"They collected all they needed. Removed the body, took plenty of soil samples, and combed the area for any other evidence."

"So where do you want to scan, big guy?" Fly said.

"First, how's this thing work?"

"You want the official Fly technical explanation or the kindergarten version."

"Let's start with kindergarten, so you can get it right."

"Ooh. Be nice. I know how to operate this, and you

don't, so here's the kindergarten version. This is a red rectangle. A rectangle has four straight sides. You okay so far, Harv?"

"That's more like fourth grade, but I know what a rectangle is. Skip ahead to the hard stuff."

"The rectangular piece contains the Ground Penetrating Radar or GPR."

Fly looked to see if Harvey was with him. Harvey smirked and shook his head.

"We attach it to the bottom of the drone."

Fly attached the GPR.

"Next, we need a laptop, which I just happen to have in this case." With a sweeping motion, he pulled the laptop out of the case like a magician pulling a rabbit out of a hat. "The laptop will control the GPR and receive pictures from it. The drone will fly a pattern so it won't miss any spot in the field. We'll fly low and slow in a grid pattern. It sends radar signals from the GPR into the ground below. The signals bounce back to the GPR and show you whatever the signal hits. It can show stuff way underground, like a yard or two or maybe just a few inches underground, depending on the soil. It goes farther through sand than it does through rock. Okay, so far, Harv?"

Harvey nodded that he understood, but his face told another story.

Fly attached the GPR to the base of the drone. "What we get is a picture on the laptop of what the radar hits. Objects will look different than the other ground around them. You got it, big guy? It may not be clear like a picture, but the GPR can detect metal and non-metal, like a body."

Harvey nodded.

"So, let's start right here next to Ebony's grave. I'll program it to follow the stone wall north to the woods, then west over the field. We'll scootch it in a bit and fly it east back to us. We'll keep doing it until we fly over the whole field. Got that, Harv?"

"I'm a 'show me' kind of guy, Fly, so just start flying, and I'll catch on."

Fly set the computer on the tailgate of the truck and set up the fly pattern for the drone. He made sure he was receiving an image from the ground, and then he sent the drone up.

"Cool," Harvey said as he saw the images that came into the computer.

The computer flew its pattern over the field in narrow strips to be sure every inch of the field was covered. After about 15 minutes, Harvey's attention span was waning.

"Is this going to get us anything, Fly?"

"Be patient. Isn't that what you always say, Harv? Be patient if you want to be a PI. Sometimes you don't find anything for quite a while, and then, wham, you hit the payload. Remember saying that?"

"No, but I'm sure I did because it's the truth."
They went silent as they continued to look at the computer screen.

"Wait. Stop." Harvey yelled.

Fly paused the drone, and a shadowy image came up on the screen. It was only a few feet underground.

"Told you, Harv!" Fly said.

"Go really slow, Fly." Harvey was getting excited. Fly slowly moved the drone back over the shadow. As he did, the shape of a man, still clothed, appeared on the screen.

"It's a body!" Fly yelled. "My first body." Fly got out his phone and took a picture of his computer screen.

"Where is that?" Harvey started jumping up and down like a second grader, being told it was recess time.

"Let me lock in the location coordinates, and I'll set her down as close as possible to it. Grab a shovel."

The drone gently glided down and sat on the far end of the field near the tree line. The field hadn't been farmed in the past few years, so there were remnants of weeds, small trees, and shrubs starting the succession of the field.

They used a hand-held GPS unit to match the coordinates of the GPR. When they were sure where the body was located, Harvey handed the shovel to Fly. "You're younger than me, Fly, and I want you to have full credit for finding this body. Just don't go crazy and chop the head off."

Fly didn't complain one bit as he began digging in the soil. At around two feet, he found the sheath of a knife.

"Looks like a buck knife sheath," Harvey said. "No knife, though."

Fly reached in to pull it out.

"Don't touch it, Fly."

"Why not? Finders keepers."

"You want your prints on this? Losers weepers." Harvey took out his cell phone and took a picture of the sheath. "What kind of knife did you find in the wall near where Ebony was buried?"

"Buck knife," Fly replied.

"Bingo."

"Got to share that with Snappy?" Fly said.

"We've got a bigger catch than this," Harvey said as he pointed to the ground where Fly was standing. "Nice day to go fishing."

Fly gingerly dug in the soil, whose top layer was woven with roots from the nearby trees.

"Who do you think it is, Fly?"

"I'd bet on Three. He was a rich boy, not much of a fighter."

"I'd bet on Roscoe," Harvey said. "He's streetwise and probably got into fights all the time."

"How much you putting on this, Harv?"

"Five bucks."

"Could be Junior."

They looked at each other, and both said, "Nah."

They shook hands on the deal, and Fly resumed digging. In a few minutes, he hit something soft, but it had a different texture than the soil.

"Stop," Harvey said. "We don't want to destroy the evidence."

"You mean we can't see who it is? How are we going to know who wins the bet?"

"Patience. Ollie Kingston will tell us."

"Can't we peek at the clothing to see who it might be?"

"NO!" Harvey yelled. "If you want this reward, you don't mess up the evidence. That's another reason to have patience. Patience equals money."

"Yes, sir, Boss. We'll follow the money."

They brushed some soil over the knife sheath and put most of the dirt back in the hole where the body was found.

"Why do we have to cover this body up so much?" Fly said.

"We don't want to attract wild animals like lions and tigers and bears."

"Oh, my!" Fly shivered as he realized that he was quoting lines from that terrifying Oz movie.

They went back to the drone.

"We ready to pack it up and call Snappy?"

"Not yet," Harvey said. "What if there's more evidence to find?"

"You're right."

They started up the drone from the location of the body and spent the next hour scanning the rest of the field. They found nothing else, but that was okay with them since they had already made the catch of the day.

SHARING THE NEWS

It was around 5:00 pm when Harvey called Chappy to set up a meeting to visit the field off Limbmaker Road the next day. He didn't tell him what he had found, just that he wanted to show him something. Chappy was curious and got mad when Harvey refused to tell him what he had found or where it was. He only told Chappy to meet Fly and him at the usual location in Mershon Park at 9:00 am.

Harvey and Fly agreed to meet there at 8:45. Fly kept the shovel in his truck and added a second one to it. He also left the GPR and drone in the back of his truck just in case it was needed.

Nine o'clock came and went, and no Chappy. Finally, at 9:20, Chappy pulled up.

"Sorry, guys," he said.

"We know something came up, and you had to take care of it," Fly said. "We got your number. Better wipe that donut dust off your face."

Chappy wiped his face and then realized that he hadn't had a donut. "Wise guy."

"Gotcha!"

"Okay, you guys. This better be good."

"Guaranteed," Harvey said. "Better than good."

They went on to tell Chappy about what Fly learned from Kiana and how they figured it was either Three or Roscoe who murdered Ebony.

"Not bad," Chappy said. "Is that it?"

"We're just getting warmed up," Fly said. "You tell him, Harv."

"No, you tell him, Fly. You did the hard work."

"No, I'm the mentee."

Chappy interrupted. "Stop. Just tell me."

Harvey went on to tell Chappy about Fly's drone and GPR unit. He then told him about the visit to the field next to the limb maker's house. He deliberately dragged out their find as long as possible.

"Tell me already," Chappy said. "Give me the short version."

"You tell him, Fly," Harvey said.'

"Sure. Well, we flew the GPR over the field, and after a while, we saw a shadow underground. We lightly dug in the area. Lightly, not too deep. We first found a knife sheath. Looked like a hunter's knife, maybe a buck knife. Could be the sheath for the knife I found in the wall with my superior metal detecting nose."

"The short version," Chappy said.

"We didn't touch the knife sheath. You or Ollie have the knife we found on the wall. It could be the one that goes with the sheath. Next, we looked back at the shadow picture and zoomed in a little closer. Guess what we found?"

"Just tell me." Chappy was growing impatient.

"A body. Dead, of course. Probably underground a long time."

Chappy stared at Fly. "Really? You're saying there's another body right here in this field?"

"Yup," Fly replied like a kid that finally did what he was supposed to do.

"Who do you think it is?"

"Not sure, Chappy. But, hey, we have a pool. For just five bucks, you can choose who it is. You can choose Three or Roscoe. They both had the motive to kill each other. One of them killed Ebony."

"You seem pretty sure about that," Chappy said.

"I bet you one of them killed Ebony. Then the other one killed the guy who killed Ebony." Fly said.

"Don't be so sure, Fly," Chappy said. "Better keep your options open awhile longer. Junior's missing, too. These cold cases can take some wild twists and turns."

"My bet's still on, and my pool is still open."

"Sorry, Fly. The bets are off for me. I could get in deep trouble at headquarters for betting on unsolved cases."

"Oh, man, you're no fun. I say if you're going to solve a murder, make it fun. Like we say at the Smythe Funeral Home, the first part of the funeral is fun."

"You're a sick pup, Fly," Harvey chimed in. "We won't remember that you said that. Now, let's get back to what we're going to do."

Chappy agreed. "This is a big deal. Let's go check it out."

They made the trek up to the field near Limbmaker Road. Harvey and Fly were in Fly's truck, with Chappy following behind. Everything was as they left it when they arrived at the crime scene. Fly pointed out where the sheath was buried, and Harvey explained how they found the grave.

"Before we dig further into this," Fly said with a laugh and a knee slap. "Get it. Dig into this."
Neither Chappy nor Harvey laughed.

Fly continued. "I think we need to see the GPR pictures. Kind of like seeing the pictures of Egypt before you go see the mummies."

"You're insufferable," Chappy said as Fly set up his laptop.

As they viewed the pictures, it was clear that there was a body in the grave. Chappy drew a quick conclusion. "I think this requires the forensic team. I'm glad you guys didn't touch anything."

"Man, I wanted to," Fly said. "Sheath's pretty old. I start frothing at the mouth when I see cool stuff like that."

"I think you caught rabies from that hound of yours," Harvey said.

"Be nice. Bosco's a healthy watchdog."

"He's a watchdog, alright. He just sits and watches while you go crazy over your wrecked cars and old hot water tanks."

Chappy told them to cut their banter and find something else to do. He said that the forensic team needed to process the area to see if there was other evidence and then carefully remove the corpse.

"Don't look too hard for other stuff, especially underground. We covered this whole field, and all we found was the sheath and Roscoe or Three." Fly sounded like a proud father telling how his daughter was on the honor roll.

"Check this out," Fly said. They walked over to his truck and lifted the tarp from the crate holding the GPR and the drone.

"Impressive," Chappy said. "Wish we had this in the department."

"You can, for a modest fee. You know I like to give customers a bargain."

"I don't think our budget can handle this. How much?"

"Cheap. Only $298 a day, down from $1K or only $1,600 to rent it for a week. It's probably better to buy it from me for only $15,000. Like new. Only used once by a little old lady before I got it."

Chappy mumbled something, ignoring Fly's sales pitch. Then he asked to see the results of the field survey again. Harvey showed him the saved video on the laptop.

"Can we borrow this?"

Before Harvey could answer, Fly interjected. "We have a special today on evidence. I could lease this laptop for only $200 per day, which gives you full rights to the evidence."

"Shut up, Fly," Harvey said. "You can't win this one."

"I have a counteroffer," Chappy said. "How about if we borrow this evidence from you and copy it onto our computer? That way, we won't have to charge you with withholding evidence, which, by the way, is a violation of state and federal law. It could lead to a fine or possible incarceration."

Fly took the laptop out of the truck and a flash

drive from his pocket. He copied the video file to the flash drive and handed it to Chappy without saying a word.

"A great decision, Fly. I'll let you know who's in the grave as soon we find out."

"Deal. Information beats jail any day," Fly said.
Fly and Harvey took off and headed back to the park to get Harvey's Mustang.

THE WORD IS OUT

The Channel 8 News team caught wind of the second body. You never knew who was related to whom or who was friends with each other in Stillwell. The news team seemed to know things before they happened, and Heather Compton was on the scene with a live report from Quarry Road.

The 6:00 p.m. newscast led off with a large red banner saying Breaking News and a crawler across the bottom saying, "Second body found on Marlowe property." Ominous-sounding background music played.

Heather Compton began. "The Stillwell Police have made a discovery that may bring them closer to finding another missing person in the decades-old Marlowe family cold case. Detective Chapman Chan of the Stillwell Police Department reportedly called in the forensic team when two unidentified people located a body beneath the field near the limb maker's house on the Marlowe estate. According to a reliable source, there was a body and another piece of evidence, perhaps a murder weapon, located using sophisticated high-tech equipment.

The grave is in the same field where the remains of Ebony Jackson were discovered by local children in recent weeks. The roadway and field behind me have been blocked off pending the removal of the body and other evidence.

"Stay tuned to Channel 8 News for more details. Channel 8 is your place for the latest local news 24 hours a day."

Within a minute, Harvey's phone rang.

"Did you see the news, Harv?" Fly spoke rapidly; his heart was racing as if he was running at full tilt on a treadmill. "How'd they know we found the body?"

"Hey, man, calm down. They don't know it was us."

"They knew everything else. Did Chappy rat us

out?"

"Don't think so, but we can't rule him out. You know those reporters monitor police calls. Somebody could have been talking, and it got picked up by reporters."

"They're gonna know who we are. Matter of time. There goes the reward."

"Relax, Fly. Chill out. Chappy knows we found this grave, and that's all that matters."

"I'm not liking this," Fly persisted.

"I'll catch up with you tomorrow. If anyone from the paper calls, don't say anything. Nothing. And be careful. Reporters will keep asking you questions until they get something out of you. They're looking for sound bites that they can use on the evening news. Go throw Bosco some tennis balls; he'll like it. I'll catch up with you tomorrow sometime."

The whole crew was at Tootie's Cafe and already jabbering about finding the second body in the field when Harvey walked in.

"Here he comes," Rexie said. "Where you been, Harv? You must have been pushing that case pretty hard."

"Been around. Busy, you know."

"No, we don't know, Harv," Alice Gemmel said. "We like to be informed, and you haven't been here lately, as missing as the Marlowes."

"I can't tell you anything about the case. Proprietary information."

"Proprietary, Harv?" Jeb Wheeler was looking down at his phone. "According to Merriam-Webster, proprietary can refer to 'a business secretly owned by and run as a cover for an intelligence organization.'"

"Who are you getting involved with, Harv, the CIA or one of those militias?" Rexie asked.

"You guys are too much. Why would I want to get involved with them?"

"Five letters, Harv," Oscar said. "M O N E Y, moola, greenbacks. You don't have us fooled."

"And your buddy is up to his eyeballs in this, too," Alice said.

"Which buddy?"

"Come on, Harv," Tootie said. "Your buddy Flywheel as much told us you guys were working together. Even called himself your mentee."

"He hasn't learned how to keep his mouth shut yet," Harvey replied.

The crew talked amongst themselves and shook their heads. Harvey was a regular, and they felt he needed to keep them informed.

"Yes, I'm working on the case we're talking about, but I'm also working on Philip's murder. When this started out, it was all about the money. Now, it's all about justice for the dead."

"How dramatic," Rosie said. "I should feed that line to Heather Compton. I can hear her on the cable news. 'Cop turned private investigator Harvey Hawkshaw says he's searching for killers to get justice for the dead.'"

Harvey shook his head.

"Ok. Harv," Oscar said. "All we want is for you to come clean with us. Glad to hear you're still working on my distant cousin Philip's case."

"Anything we can do to help?" Alice asked.

"Keep your eyes open and your ears peeled. You could pick up something that no one else sees or hears."

"I like my bananas peeled," a familiar voice from the back said.

The group turned and saw Fly walking in from the back door of the café.

"Fly," Harvey said. "We were just talking about you, how you need to keep your lips sealed."

"What? That's no way to speak to your favorite mentee."

"You're my default mentee, unofficial and loose-lipped."

Tootie interrupted. "Hi, Fly; what's it like working for this guy?"

"First, I'd like to say that I don't work FOR him; I work WITH him. I learned early on that we're partners."

"That's right. 50-50," Harvey added.

"Whatever you say, Boss!"

The whole crew laughed. They went on to discuss the possibilities of who murdered Philip and when that could have happened. Alice promoted her theory that it was someone who he trusted, or he would never have accepted the coffee.

"That could be half the town, Alice," Jeb said. "He was a quintessential homeless person."

"You mean like a well-known homeless guy?" Fly asked.

"Thank you, Fly," Alice said. "Jeb has a way with words—far, far away."

"But you must know more about Philip, Oscar," Rexie said. "I mean, being his cousin and living right here in town."

"You'd think," Oscar said. "But Philip was put in foster care at birth. My mother's sister fostered him and gave him her last name, Rhinehart. She gave him up when he became unmanageable when he was three or four. He was in a series of foster homes before and after that."

"You're not his biological cousin," Harvey said.

"Probably not. I saw him around town. Even booked him a couple of times for vagrancy and drug possession. He almost died a couple of times, and it really messed up his head. You saw where he ended up."

"Didn't his biological mother try to help?"

"I have no idea. Remember, this was all hush-hush back then. I think it was a teenage pregnancy."

"He was the same age as Junior's son," Tootie chimed in. "They hung out together. I remember them from school."

"Does his mother even know he's dead?"

"Oh yeah," Tootie said. "She made quite a scene at his wake."

"Whoa!" Fly yelled as he held his hands up, pretending that this was news to him. "Stop the music. Lightbulb moment. You're saying that Philip's mother is the lady that passed out at the wake?"

"Yes," Tootie said. "I don't think that's such a big secret."

"News to me," Alice said.

"Me, too," said Rexie.

"Swami grandmommy," Fly blurted.

"Never heard her called that," Tootie said. "Maybe that's what her grandkids call her. She's Madam DuBois, the psychic."

"You've got it. That's her," Fly said, shaking his head up and down.

Almost everyone in the crew knew who Madam DuBois was. They knew she was a psychic, but no one admitted to having a reading at the Clairvoyant Center.

The crew members started up the chatter again as they began to leave Tootie's, continuing to talk in front of the café.

"What do you think, Harv," Fly asked. "How'd I do?"

"Good job, Fly. You ferreted out some great info. I loved the way you faked that surprise about the swami grandmommy. Now we can say it's widely known that the swami is Philip's mother."

"And we're pretty sure Noah is the father, but I can't see either one of them murdering Philip."

"We still don't have a motive, Fly, but this is starting to make sense."

Fly looked at Harvey like he was crazy. "Maybe for you, but for me, it's still messed up."

"Stay tuned, Fly. It's like dominos. You push one tile, and all the others fall down."

GO FIGURE

Harvey and Fly walked out the front door of Tootie's and waved to the crew, still conducting their armchair detective discussion on the sidewalk. When they looked across the square at the gazebo, they could see that the police tape was still blocking access to the crime scene. Philip's belongings and his food and drink residue had been removed as evidence.

"I think we need to give Ollie Kingston a call," Harvey said. "He's probably got the toxicology report back from the lab, and he might have other insight into how Philip died."

"Chappy already told us it was poison. He said it was in coffee, but it wasn't in a takeout container like you'd get at Tootie's. Prob'ly homemade," Fly said.

"That was the prelim, Fly. But they could have found something else in his system."

"Like drugs. He could have just OD'd."

"That's why we need to talk with Ollie."

With the gazebo blocked off, they sat on a bench along the brick sidewalk that wove through the island. Harvey called the medical examiner's office and tapped the speakerphone icon, so Fly could hear the conversation.

"Hey, Ollie. Harvey Hawkshaw. How 'ya doin'?"

"Busy, Harv. You guys keep finding bodies, and that makes a lot of work for us."

"Consider our job security, Ollie."

He laughed. "So, what can I help you with, my friend?"

"I'm here with my associate, Flywheel."

"Flywheel. Gosh, I haven't seen Flywheel since he helped get rid of my metal after it got destroyed in that tropical storm a few years back. What was that storm?"

"Erma. Yeah, it was Erma. A great storm for metal pickup." Fly said. "How you doin', Ollie? Got any metal you want to get rid of?"

"Ignore him, Ollie. Always hustling for a buck. I called because we're wondering if you figured out how Philip died and what the pathology report showed."

"Well, you aren't in the Stillwell PD anymore, but you're still one of us. I guess I can tell you the general details, maybe not all the small ones."

"Just tell us what you can. Chappy told us about the prelim. We just want to confirm it and find out if there is something new."

"For one, the main cause of death was poisoning. It was quick, probably painless. Hope so, anyway. The poison that we picked up from a few drops left in the coffee cup was arsenic. A lot of it. We looked at the amount of arsenic in just a few drops. If you project that out to a cup, poor Philip ingested enough to kill several people."

"Wouldn't he know the coffee was bad?" Fly asked.

"Well, the victim also had recently ingested some drugs, opioids. We found them in his stomach. Opioids cause dehydration, among other things, and this would make him eager to drink anything. There were a couple of empty water bottles lying near him."

"But he still must have known something wasn't right," Harvey said.

"Colorless, tasteless, odorless. The perfect poison to kill someone."

"And the killer knew him because he accepted the coffee from him." Harvey deduced.

"Or her. We can't rule anyone out in this case. Philip knew a lot of people and took handouts from many."

"So where would the killer get arsenic? I thought it was illegal."

"You're right, Harv. They stopped producing it in the US in 1985 and eliminated it from pesticides in 1993. It is still produced and sold in other parts of the world."

"Did you find any of the poison in his hair or fingernails?"

"No. He died before the poison could get to his hair or fingernails. That's how we know it was a hefty dose. About 180 milligrams or three-hundredths of a teaspoon can kill an adult, and this person must have used at least a full teaspoon. It wasn't administered over time but in one big dose. It hadn't infiltrated all his organs yet. It was enough to stop his heart. Of course, those opioids helped this process along."

"Yikes. I'm stayin' away from that stuff," Fly said. "Nasty."

"No other evidence of foul play, Ollie?"

"No. We did an autopsy, and the victim was definitely done in by the poison."

"You've been a big help, Ollie. Thanks."

"You ruined my appetite," Fly said. "I'm skipping coffee, tea, and water from now on."

Ollie laughed. "I guess I'll see you in here for death by dehydration."

"That's sick, Ollie," Fly said.

"Just a little ME humor, my friend."

"See what I have to work with, Ollie," Harvey said.

Fly just stared at Harvey. Finally, he said, "We've got to find who did this, Harv."

"Yup," Harvey agreed. "Philip died a horrible death, so let's get on with figuring out why. Keep in touch, Ollie."

"You, too, Harv. Bye."

"That's a good idea, big guy," Fly said. "How we gonna do that?"

"Talk to people."

"Like?"

"Hey, who's the mentee here? I'm supposed to ask you questions to help you figure out how to figure out."

"Go figure!" Fly slapped his knee and laughed.

Harvey switched to asking questions. "So, if you were the detective on the case, who would you want to talk with, Fly?"

"I'd really like to talk with the missing people, but if I could do that, they wouldn't be missing anymore."

"Next?"

"The sisters in the mansion again, but really grill them. And I'd like to talk with the swami grand mommy again, but with her daughter there, too. That's enough for now."

"Which is first?"

"The psychics, for sure. They're Philip's relatives. But getting information from them would be like getting you to pay me for my detective services."

"The reward is at the end, my friend. Don't kid yourself about getting rich quickly. Detective work is long, often boring, and sometimes not rewarding."

"Geez, Harv, I'm glad I'm doing this!"

"No, you don't see it. You just made a logical decision. Instead of wallowing around in the muck of possibilities, you figured out that we needed to focus on the people who knew Philip and would likely give us more information. Good job, Fly."

Fly scratched his head, unsure of what had just happened but glad Harvey felt he was on the right track.

Harvey suggested that they take the time to plan some questions they wanted answers to from the swamis. They drew up a list of just the key questions:

1. How are you related to Philip? They knew, but they wanted to hear what the swamis said.

2. How do you think he died?

3. Why do you think he was killed?

4. If you were an investigator, who would you want to talk with about his death?

"So how do they sound, Fly?"

"Cop questions. But if they can answer these, we're cool."

"It's not IF they can answer them, it's WILL they answer them at all, and WILL they will answer them honestly."

"Think they'll be honest?"

"Doubt it," Harvey said.

Fly reached over and gave Harvey a knuckle bump. They agreed to drive separately past Madam Marlena's Clairvoyance Center on Groveland Street every few hours to see when the swamis' cars were there and when they were gone. After a couple of days of surveillance, they concluded that early afternoon was a good time to visit. Both cars were usually there.

ANOTHER SWAMI VISIT

They left Fly's truck in the park and drove to Groveland Street in Harvey's Mustang.

"Did you shower this morning?" Fly asked before they got out of the car.

"Why would you ask that? That's insulting."

"In my old business, we used to say, 'Nobody buys a mattress from a stinky salesman.' Just saying."

"Yes, I took a shower, and I'll always remember that great advice whenever I'm buying a mattress." Harvey grimaced and shook his head.

They parked on the street in front of the Clairvoyant Center.

"You ready?" Harvey asked.

"Ready, Teddy." Fly was bopping his head up and down as he listened to music.

"Nervous?"

"Nope. Nope. Nope. Not nervous. Not me." Fly held his hand out to show he was calm, but when it started to shake, he quickly pulled it back.

"Yes, you are. Better take a couple of deep breaths and take those things out of your ears. I don't want you hyperventilating when you're supposed to be cool and calm."

Fly took a couple of breaths and took out his earbuds. "There. Like a cucumber. Let's go meet the swamis."

Harvey rang the doorbell, and the mysterious organ music played.

"I forgot to go to the bathroom," Fly said.

"Too late. Put it on hold!"

The door opened, and Madam Marlena appeared in her flowing fluorescent-green gown with ruby trim on it. She had an air of aloofness that added mystery to her presence.

"Gentlemen." She paused for dramatic effect.

"How may I help you?"

"Ooh," Fly groaned, looking pained with his legs crossed."

"Yes," Harvey replied. "I'm Harvey Hawkshaw, and this is my associate, Flywheel. We'd like a word with you."

Fly groaned again.

"Is he alright?"

"I gotta use the bathroom," Fly blurted out.

"Come in," she beckoned. "The bathroom's down the hallway on the right side."

Fly flew to the bathroom while Harvey told Madam that they would like to talk with her about a recent incident involving her family. He explained that they had been here before and met with Madam DuBois.

"Are you a cop?"

"No, I'm not, but I'm trying to figure out how my friend Philip Reinhart died. It was so sudden. It caught us off guard."

Fly quickly returned. "Thank you. Now I'm ready."

"Perhaps if we had a session," Madam Marlena suggested, "You could speak with him and get an answer."

"Wait. Did I miss something? You're talking about talking to a dead guy?"

"Yes, of course," she replied.

"That's a little too high on my freak-o-meter. Maybe I should excuse myself."

Harvey put his hand on Fly's shoulder as he tried to turn and leave. "My friend Fly is a bit sensitive, Madam. I think we should try to connect with Philip, and I'll keep Fly calm and under control. Won't I, Fly?" Harvey squeezed Fly's shoulder.

Fly was breathing heavily. Words were not an option, so he just nodded.

"Fine. Let's go into the next room so we can find Philip."

Madam Marlena led the way, and Fly made gestures

to Harvey behind her back to end this and leave. He groaned again, and Harvey pushed him ahead. As they entered, swami's grandmommy was seated on the couch with her eyes closed. She might have been meditating or maybe just taking a nap.

"She's setting the tone for us to reach Philip."

"How'd she knows that?" Fly said aloud.

"Where are you, Fly?" Harvey said. "They know about stuff like this. It's a clairvoyant center."

"I had a girlfriend in high school named Claire Voyant. She always knew what I was thinking before I did anything."

"Gentlemen, have a seat and calm yourselves."

As Fly sat down, swami grand mommy opened her eyes. She immediately recognized Fly from the funeral home and his previous visit. "I don't have anything to say to these men. They've been here before."

"Mother," Madam Marlena said. "I think you should join us."

Reluctantly, Madam DuBois sat at the table with the men and her daughter.

Fly mustered the strength to say, "Nice to see you again, swami grandmommy."

"Mother, these men wish to contact Philip. Would you like to help us?"

Madam DuBois glared at her daughter. Of course, she didn't want anything to do with these men. Nevertheless, they sat around the table as if they were about to start a pinochle game. As lights dimmed, the colorful bulbs surrounding the couch came on, casting an eerie palate of colors throughout the room.

The table started to jiggle. Fly had a sheepish look on his face. "Sorry. Jimmy's knees. Can't help it."

Madam DuBois started humming a low mournful sound. No tune in particular, just low and sad.

"I'm summoning the spirit of Philip," Madam Marlena said. "Come to us, Philip. Show your presence."

On cue, a book fell off the bookshelf. "Will you get that for us, Mr. Hawkshaw?"

Harvey walked over and picked up the red-covered book from the floor, and brought it back to the table.

Marlena picked it up. "Secrets of the Dead," she read aloud from the cover. "A sure sign from Philip that he took secrets to the grave with him."

"Like what?" Fly asked. "I want to know who killed him."

"He can't speak with us, but I will try to reach him." She paused for what seemed like several minutes and then said. "Philip, Philip, share a secret with me."

Another book fell off the shelf, and Marlena picked it up. "The Haunted Mansion," she read.

"What about the mansion?" Fly asked excitedly.

"We must use the crystal ball to learn more," Marlena said.

The ball was in the center of the table, and Marlena directed Fly and Harvey to put their hands on it. When they did, it began to glow and increase in warmth. Marlena put her hands on it, and she began to shake. "I can feel Philip's energy. He says that he is alright and that his murderer is still alive and nearby. He sees a new grave that we haven't found."

As suddenly as it illuminated, the ball darkened, and Marlena slumped over on the table, exhausted from her contact with the other world. She recovered quickly and sat up.

"You're some creepy lady," Fly said.

"I'll take that as a compliment, Mr. Flywheel," she said.

"So, Madam Marlena," Harvey said. "We don't know much about Philip's murder, but we know that he knew the murderer."

She nodded.

"And he's saying that there's a grave that we haven't found yet?"

She nodded again.

"And this all has something to do with the mansion?"

"That's the way I read it," she said.

"What else do you think Philip is saying?"

"I guess he's pointing to people who live in the mansion."

"Hmm." Harvey hummed as he massaged his chin. "That gives us some people to talk with."

"Good," Marlena said.

"Say, I have one last question, if it's okay," Harvey said.

"Sure."

"I happened to be going by the other day on my way to an appointment, and I just happened to see the three women who live in the mansion. You know, Junior's wife, Three's wife, and Roscoe's mother. They were coming out of your house and heading to their car."

Marlena didn't say anything and tried her best to act nonchalant.

"You must know them, right?" Harvey asked.

"I know the women you speak of, but you must be confused. They weren't here the other day."

"Are they clients of yours?"

"No."

"How 'bout you, swami grand mommy?" Fly asked.

"They are your clients?"

"I'm not at liberty to say. Client/clairvoyant privilege."

"Well, if you can't say anything, it sounds like you might be hiding something from us."

"Now, Mr. Flywheel. Don't draw any conclusions when you don't have any facts," Madam Marlena interjected.

"We're just trying to understand all these relationships. Like with you and your brother."

"What do you mean, my brother?"

194

"Philip. He was your brother, right?"

"Where did you get that information, Mr. Flywheel?" Madam Marlena had a fearful, angry look.

"Maybe you should ask your mother," Fly said as he looked at Madam DuBois.

Marlena scowled at her mother. "Do you know what they're talking about, Mother?"

"Well, uh, he may be some distant cousin. Never knew him well."

"Better tell the truth, Madam DuBois. If you don't, we will," Fly said.

Madam Marlena was confused and getting increasingly upset. "Mother. Tell the truth. What are they talking about?"

After a moment of silence, she spoke up. "The truth is that Philip was my son, your half-brother, who was born when I was young, in high school."

Madam Marlena was ashen. "You never told me this. Why?"

"I figured that you didn't need to know about Philip. I gave him up for adoption when he was born, but no one wanted him, so he was put in foster care."

"All his life? He was in foster care all his life? How could you, mother?"

Madam DuBois was silent, blotting her eyes with her hankie.

"That's enough, Mother. I think it's time for this session to be over."

Sensing Madam DuBois's vulnerability, Harvey asked another question. "In our session, you mentioned the ladies in the mansion. We saw them here not just the other day but often, about once a month. "

Before Marlena could answer, her mother spoke. "Oh, they know a lot. A real lot about their husbands and maybe that girl that was buried up on the hill. They could tell you a whole lot."

"Mother, stop!"

195

Marlena stood up and again started to usher the men from the house.

"I do have one more question," Harvey said. "If you were going to poison your son, where would you get the poison?"

"Oh my God," Madam DuBois said.

"Shut up, Mother." Madam Marlena pointed at the men and then toward the door. "That's it. You can't talk to us like this. Leave now."

Harvey and Fly sauntered from the house like warriors celebrating a victory.

"Good show, Harvey," Fly said as they walked down the sidewalk to Harvey's car. "You really got them showing their cards."

"Strategy 98. When you want to trip up the person you are interviewing, ask them an 'if or what if' question. If they know something, they'll usually lie about the answer or say something helpful."

"Or throw us out. That poison question did it. So good. Home run," Fly said. "Freaked out, swami grandmommy. Madam Marlena, too. I say 'guilty as charged.'"

"Yeah, but we still need some evidence that associates them with the poison."

"Like?"

Harvey just looked at Fly. "Like poison, ding-dong. If they have arsenic around, then we have some evidence and enough to get them in for a chat with Chappy."

"We need to see about the third grave, too," Fly said.

"These ladies are wrapped up in this case like a mummy."

"Maybe a grand mummy!"

"Good one, Harv. You're starting to loosen up."

FORENSICS

After they left the swamis, Harvey pulled into the lot behind the police station. He put the phone on speaker, so Fly could hear, and then he called Chappy.

"Hey, Chappy, it's your favorite former cop."

"Hi, Harv. You got you-know-who with you?"

"I'm here, Snappy," Fly said. "Your favorite mentee detective with his favorite mentor."

"Harvey, rescue me from this guy."

"I'd like to, Chappy, but Fly is Fly, and I can't change him. We're in your parking lot, but we're not coming in. Fly freaks out near too many uniforms."

"Man, Fly sure has issues."

"I do," Fly chimed in. "I even have the final issue of Mad Magazine. Collector's item."

"I'll be right out."

Chappy knew better than to bring Harvey inside the department. He'd be too social with his old buddies, and before long, everyone would know what they were talking about. He was much better as an informant and remote assistant.

Fly moved to the back seat so Chappy could sit up front.

"The reason I called … " Harvey continued.

Chappy interrupted. "I know, you want to find out about the stuff Fly 'borrowed' from the Marlowe trashcan."

"How did you know that?"

"I'm psychic."

"Like the swami grandmommy." Fly chimed in. "You oughta check her out, Chappy. She knows a lot and isn't saying much."

"Ignore him," Harvey said. "I want to know about the forensics."

"Well, they were interesting. We have fingerprints and DNA. They likely belong to the sisters, but we don't know who each sample belongs to. And strangely, there is a fourth set of prints and DNA, too."

"What can you tell from this?" Harvey asked.

"Again, we have four sets of prints with three people living there."

"May not all match," Fly added. "Could be some other prints or DNA there. Like from the murderer."

"Fly's right. Any chance of identifying the DNA through the national database?"

"We tried the national database, called CODIS, Combined DNA Index System, but found nothing. I guess whoever they are, they haven't been in much trouble," Chappy replied.

"Fingerprint database?"

"NGI, Next Generation Identification. We tried that, too. Nothing there either. Coming up with dead ends."

"And dead bodies," Fly said.

"Can we at least tell the genders from what you have?"

"Yes, Harvey," Chappy said. "We can, and we did."

"And," Harvey said.

"Drumroll, please. Da-da-da-da-da-da-da-da-tish. How'd you like that cymbal at the end?"

Chappy ignored Fly and talked about the prints they found. "On the prints, you count the ridges. You know, those lines that make up the print. Males have more ridges than females. They also have larger fingertips, so we count the ridges and measure the fingertips. Then we go to a handy-dandy chart, find the matching numbers, and you can tell if the prints are made by a male or female."

"Can you get prints off a 20-year-old body?" Harvey asked.

"It's very unlikely," Chappy said. "After 20 years, you usually only have a skeleton, but these prints are from people in the Marlowe house."

"Wait," Fly said. "I saw on a TV show where they got the prints off a 2000-year-old mummy."

"Come on, Fly," Harvey said. "That must have been some 1950s movie like Abbot and Costello."

"How'd you know?"

Both Harvey and Chappy groaned.

"But DNA must be easier," Fly said. "I remember from high school biology. All those Xs and Ys. I paid attention some of the time, but I liked playing tic-tac-toe with Herbie Rodriguez. We used X and Y instead of X and O, so we were learning genetics, right?"

"Thank you for sharing that, Fly. It's important that you sort of studied biology. I won't let you do any testing on me," Chappy responded.

"Now, boys," Harvey said. "Continue, Detective."

"Say nothing, Fly. Take notes. I was about to say that you just need to know the chromosome makeup of the DNA in the cells. Males have XY chromosomes, and females have XX chromosomes."

"I was right," Fly blurted. "It's Xs and Ys."

"You'd be wise to shut up, Fly."

"C'mon, tell us the results of the fingerprint and DNA analyses." Harvey was growing impatient.

"Wait, wait," Fly interrupted. "I bet $5 that it's four females."

"Just tell us, for crying out loud." Harvey glared at Fly.

"You lose, Fly. Three females, who we can guess are the three women in the mansion, and one unidentified male."

"Hmm." Fly looked confused.

Chappy went on to explain that they could only match the data if the people had given samples at some time. He said there was nothing in the national databases matching the fingerprints or DNA of the people in the mansion.

"Say, I know we took prints of the women in the mansion when I was on the case. Way back when only two women were there."

"Any idea where you kept those prints, Harv?"

"Sure. In the evidence room with the Marlowe case files. I think I can find what we need."

"Geez, Harvey. Do you know how much material we have from this case?"

"Let me look at the boxes. I bet I can pin those prints down in 10 minutes."

"I'll bet $5 he can do it in eight minutes," Fly chimed in.

Chappy glared at Fly. "You'll need permission to get in the evidence room."

"Call Milt. He'll let me in."

"Doubt it. If he says okay, you'll need a credible observer with you."

Fly raised his hand.

"What do you want?" Chappy asked.

"I can be an observer."

"Credible. I said a credible observable."

Fly frowned and looked insulted. Then he smiled. "I guess that makes me incredible!"

"We'd have to get permission for me to look at my old evidence. I might have a better chance at getting approved because I worked here."

"Let me see what I can do," Chappy said. He left the car and went inside to talk with Milt. It seemed like an eternity, but 20 minutes later, Harvey's phone rang.

"Chappy. What did you find out?"

"You can come in, and I can observe you locating the evidence."

"Fly?"

"They said the evidence room is a no-fly zone."

Harvey laughed. "I have to take him back to his car; then I'll come back. Okay?"

"I'll be here. Just ask for me at reception."

———————

When Harvey went into the station and checked in,

Chappy came right out and led him to the evidence room. There were boxes everywhere labeled on the outside with the name of the case, the date the evidence was put there, and a general idea of what was inside. The boxes went back many years and contained things like written reports and fingerprints. Today, most reports and DNA are stored on computer servers.

"Here you go, Harvey," Chappy said. "This section has a lot of Marlowe boxes in it. Good luck."

Harvey carefully looked at the lower-level boxes and used the step ladder to look more closely at the ones on the upper shelves. "Brings back memories," he said.

"Where would you put the print files?"

"Can't remember how I would have tagged the box."

He continued looking and stopped at one box. "Says that it's pictures, etc. I think this might be it. The prints were the etcetera part."

They pulled down the box, opened it, and became distracted by the pictures of Three, Roscoe, Junior, and Eunice. Felicia was in there, but Carmela was not. They kept rooting like they were at a flea market, and near the bottom of the box, they struck gold.

Harvey stood up like a victor at a bowling tournament holding his trophy in the air. "Here they are. Just two sets of prints, but that might give you something to go on. Look at this. They're labeled Eunice and Felicia. We can check them with forensics. Two down, two to go."

"Eight minutes, Harvey," Chappy said. "Tell Fly he nailed it. On second thought, don't tell him. We don't need to humor him."

"I won't unless I want to brag to him about my memory."

"Don't, please."

Chappy took the prints and said he would ask the forensics team to immediately compare the old prints to the recent ones taken from the Marlowe trash. "I'll let you know as soon as we have a match."

They shook hands, and Harvey left smiling.

WHO'S WHERE?

The next morning, Harvey and Fly were sitting in Harvey's Situation Room, drinking coffee and noshing on donuts that Fly had brought with him. They eagerly awaited Chappy's 9:00 a.m. call.

At 9:20, Harvey's phone rang, and he quickly answered. "Don't even say it, Chappy. We know you're sorry you're late, and we know you were busy."

"This time, I was. Whoops. I mean, I'm always busy, but I had to wait for the forensics team to give me the scoop on what they found."

"Just tell us. We're sitting here dying to find out."

Fly made a groaning noise in the background.

"So, they had to make your old prints digital and then clean them up a bit so they could overlay them on the new digital prints."

"And?"

"They could only match one of the old prints to the new prints Fly found."

"You're saying there was one known person there, and the other three are unknown?"

"Let me guess," Fly said. Before anyone could say anything, he blurted, "Eunice."

"Pretty good, Fly," Chappy said. "It was Eunice, all right. In fact, her prints were all over the materials you brought back."

Harvey spoke up. "You mean to tell me that Felicia's prints weren't on any of that stuff?"

"Nope," Chappy replied. "So, we have two unidentified female prints and one unidentified male."

"Sounds like we're heading to Fulton Street again," Fly said.

"What on earth are you talking about, Fly?" Chappy asked.

"Fulton Street. A street near me in Philmont. No outlet. Dead end."

"How am I supposed to know that, Fly? Geez. Speak in terms I understand, please."

Harvey got the conversation back on track. "Ok. I think they found something we needed to know, but I'm disappointed that it didn't lead us too far. Thanks for trying, Chappy."

That ended the conversation, and Harvey and Fly sat silently for a couple of minutes.

"Thought we'd have somethin'," Fly said.

"We do. Every little bit of information is helpful."

"How's this helpful?"

"You tell me what we just found out, Fly."

"That Eunice drinks a lot and touches stuff in the kitchen a lot."

"Yep. What's that tell you about the other two in the house?"

"They must not be hanging out with Eunice or at least very little," Fly replied.

"Could be Carmela, Fly. We don't have her prints."

"Well, it's not Felicia, Harv. Maybe Earlene? Swami grand mommy? Marlena?"

"No, Fly. A male."

Harvey wrote the possibilities on his whiteboard, and Fly sat there thinking.

Fly finally broke the silence. "Know what we need, Harv?"

Harvey shrugged.

"A snitch."

Harvey agreed. "But the only snitch we had is dead. If I'd known that Philip was going to be killed, I'd have pressed him for more information."

Fly nodded in agreement. "Those prints were from a male. Aren't too many males left around in that wacky family? It can't be Philip or Junior. It could be Roscoe or Three. One of them could be alive."

"Could be Noah," Harvey said. "I'm not saying he's a murderer, just that he might have been there talking to one or all the women. After all, he's worked for them for years. He said he still does from time to time. We ought to check that out."

The men drove over to Noah's house in search of a fingerprint. When they arrived, they got the usual greeting from Diesel, with Fly leading the way and Harvey keeping a safe distance behind.

Earlene, Noah's wife, opened the door partway. "What do you want?" she snapped.

"We'd like to speak with Noah. Is he around?" Harvey smiled at Earlene.

"He's not here." Earlene didn't look at them.

Fly asked, "So, Ms. Zark, you know where he is?"

"None of your business. Uh… probably running an errand."

"When will he be back?" Fly pressed for more information.

She paused. "Don't know, and you don't need to know."

"Could you tell him we have some information on Philip that might interest him?"

"Like what?"

Fly spoke up. "Proprietary information. We can only speak with him. Have him call Harvey."

She slammed the door.

As they were walking away from the house, Fly turned and looked back. They could see Earlene through the glass panel on the front door, looking very serious. She was talking on her cell phone as she watched them leave.

"Check her out, Harv. It must be an important call. Bet she's calling Noah."

"Probably."

"You hear that 'uh' pause when she was talking about where Noah was, Harv?"

"Pauses, hesitations, and uhs can say a lot. She knew where he was and wasn't about to tell us. We'll try again."

They drove back to Harvey's house to get Fly's truck. They pulled up behind it and sat for a minute, reconstructing what they knew.

"How many times do we have to keep going over this?" Fly was annoyed.

"Have we solved the case? No. So we keep trying to tie what we know together until we figure out who did what? Get it?"

Fly sighed like a little kid who had just found out that the ride to grandma's house would take two hours.

"OK, let's just focus on one piece of this. The most recent thing."

"Philip?"

"Well, we need to figure out who killed him, but I'm thinking about the second body we found up on the mountain."

"Oh yeah. It wasn't Three, so who is it, Harv?"

"I didn't say it wasn't Three. Could be him."

Fly scratched his head. "That leaves us nowhere. Roscoe, Three, and Junior. Could be any of them."

Harvey took out his cell phone and called Chappy again.

"You again?" Chappy answered. "What now?"

"You know I wouldn't bother you unless it was important."

"Cut the bull, Harv."

"Did I hear you right, Chappy? I think you said that the second body on the mountain wasn't Three, right?"

"That's news to me, Harv. You dreaming or drinking?"

"Well, do you think it's Three?"

"Can't tell you, Harv. We're keeping a tight wrap on this. Don't want it out just yet, or the media will be all over us. We won't have answers."

"It's Junior, isn't it?"

The phone was silent for a few seconds, which seemed like hours.

"I told you, Harv. I can't officially tell you."

"Now that's really confusing," Fly said in the background. "He told us that he can't tell us!"

"I heard that, Fly," Chappy said.

"How about unofficially, Chappy? You can trust me," Harvey said.

"You, yeah. Your numbskull partner, no."

"I'll get him to keep it under wraps. It's Junior, isn't it?" Harvey repeated.

"I just can't say, Harv. If I see this in the paper or on TV tomorrow or any time before I release it, I'm done, and you're done. No more leads or help with your investigation. No reward. Understand?"

"So, it is Junior."

"I never said that, and you don't know if it's Junior or somebody else. I know you're listening, Fly. You promise to keep your mouth shut about this?"

"Of course," Fly said. "You can trust me, and I'm telling you I told you so."

"I guess I'll know that soon enough."

After the phone call, Harvey had a long talk with Fly about the importance of trust in an investigation. Fly just listened without any wise guy comments.

"So, we know that Junior drove away from the mansion the night he went missing. How would he get killed, brought back, and buried in that field?"

"Roscoe or Three," Fly said. "One of them killed Junior to get his money."

Harvey continued. "Eunice could have poisoned him in at the house, and then one or both of the guys could have put him in the car, taken him up the hill, and buried him."

"What if it isn't Junior they found in the second grave, Harv?"

"Did Chappy say it was?"

"Nope, Boss. He didn't say who it was."

"Then we need more information."

"Let's at least try to figure out Ebony," Harvey said. "Somebody buried Ebony up there, and possibly the same somebody buried Junior or whoever in the same field," Fly noted. "Could be Three or Roscoe or both."

"What makes you think that?"

"Well, Three and Roscoe both loved Ebony."

Harvey nodded.

"They could have fought over her. You know, a real fight, maybe with fists or guns or knives. And then something could have happened, you know, out of anger or maybe by accident, and Ebony ends up dead."

"Good thinking, Fly. Keep going."

"These guys have a body on their hands and have to do something about it."

Harvey adds to the theory. "Three and Roscoe both are familiar with the Marlowe property. They know the limb maker's house is in the upper field, but nobody goes there except people farming the land."

"How's this, Harv," Fly continued. "One or both of them followed Junior, killed him, put him in his car, and drove to the Marlowe estate. They stopped by the barn long enough to get a shovel and then went up the back road to the field and buried him."

"Good, Fly. So, you think they did this together?"

"Good question, Harv. It's a lot of digging for one person. Ebony was down about four or five feet."

"I don't know about that," Harvey said. "The kids said the ground was sunken. That's why they were digging there."

Fly continued his questioning. "Do you think Roscoe would help Three?"

"Nope," Harvey replied. "Three would rather see Roscoe dead if he killed Ebony. But if is a big word."

"How did Ebony die?" Fly wondered.

"Good point. We don't know, but that's important. Might give us more info."

Harvey called Oliver Kingston again.

"Hi, Ollie, Harvey here."

"Hey, Harv. Catch the bad guy yet?"

"Ha. Always the comedian, Ollie. You can help me, though."

Harvey explained that they were piecing the Ebony Jackson case together and wanted to get a cause of death.

"Well, you know that this information is part of an ongoing investigation, and ..."

Harvey interrupted him. "Just cut to the chase, Ollie. How'd she die?"

"Oh, alright, Harv. She had a broken neck, the kind of injury that you get from a fall, like falling down a flight of stairs."

"Accidental or deliberate?"

"Wish I knew. Most of these fall injuries are accidental. That's a good question for your perp if you have one."

"We have perps in mind, but the ones that knew Ebony are missing. Thanks, as usual, Ollie. Oh, one more thing. Do you have a cause of death on Junior?"

"You think Junior is here?"

"Sure."

"I'm afraid to ask how you found out."

"You know who found the body, Ollie?"

Before Ollie could answer, Fly chimed in. "The Hawkshaw and Flywheel team, supersleuths!"

"Is that right?"

"So, what's your prelim?" Harvey asked.

"Prelim is that it wasn't Junior."

"What?" Harvey was astonished. "Looks like the team needs to rethink its information."

"I can confirm that it was a homicide. Probably a knife."

"How 'bout that," Fly said. "That explains it."

"What?" Ollie asked.

"I don't think we should tell you, Ollie," Harvey said. "We have standards in our field."

"You've got dead bodies in your field, too. Fess up. I was straight with you."

"We found a knife," Fly blurted out. "In the stone wall. Took a real metal detector to find it."

"You had a metal detector up there?"

"Yeah. Me. Fly the human detectorist."

"Chappy knows this, right?"

"Of course, Ollie. Who are we to withhold information?" Harvey said. "We gave the knife to the forensics team. Better check with them. Thanks again, my man. Catch you later." Harvey quickly hung up.

Harvey and Fly debriefed their conversation with Ollie.

"Ebony might not have been murdered after all, Harv. Could have been an accident."

"We might not ever know that. The victim, of course, was there, and we assume that Three and Roscoe were there, but we can't ask them until we find them."

"Alive. Need somebody undead to give us some answers." Fly said.

A TANGLED WEB

Harvey and Fly met in Mershon Park the next morning.

"You know, Harv," Fly said. "Something's rotten in Denmark."

"Ah, Hamlet. You like Shakespeare?"

"He's alright, but I prefer Pabst beer."

Harvey groaned. "Things are rotten in Stillwell, too," Harvey replied. "Didn't know you were into literature."

"That's the only thing I remember from reading Hamlet in high school, but it's cool."

"We've got too much going on," Harvey said. "We need to find more evidence."

"Like Three and Roscoe."

"And the gravedigger, if it isn't them."

"We need to talk to Noah again, Harv. My gut's telling me that he knows something. Maybe a lot."

"I'm not feeling the same way you are, Fly, but when I have a gut feeling, it's usually telling me something. Let's go with your gut. Maybe he's home now."

They went to Noah's house, but Diesel wasn't there to greet them. They knocked, and Earlene came to the door.

"Hi, Earlene," Harvey said. "Noah here?"

"No, he's not. I told you that before."

"Where's Diesel? I like that pup," Fly said.

"With Noah."

"We wanted to talk with Noah. Do you know where he is?"

"He doesn't want to talk to you. Leave."

Earlene seemed colder than she was on the previous visit. Harvey was not about to give up.

"When do you think he will be home?"

"Don't know."

"You don't seem too forthcoming with

211

information," Harvey said.

Earlene shrugged her shoulders and said nothing.

"Well, if you don't suggest a time to talk with Noah, we'll just come back when we think he's here."

"Don't bother coming back," she said. "We don't want to talk with you."

"Really?" Fly said. "Noah always talked with us before. Sounds kind of suspicious to me."

"I have nothing more to say, and Noah doesn't either. We're done with you and Detective Chan nosing into our business."

"So Chappy's been around here, too," Fly noted.

"Leave now, or I'll call the police and file trespassing charges against you."

Harvey raised his arms as if to surrender.

"I think we aren't wanted here," Fly said.

At that, the two walked back to Harvey's car.

"Look at what she's doing, Fly."

Fly turned and looked back at the bungalow. "She's looking at us and talking on her cell again. Just like last time. I guess we know who she's talking to."

"Maybe it's Noah or maybe someone else who's tied into this mess."

Harvey said he needed a break, so he could collect his thoughts. Fly thought that was a good idea. Harvey needed to see his homies at Tootie's, and Fly said that he should go back to the Upcycle Center to catch up on business.

"Got to make some money somewhere. You could go broke trying to make money as a PI," Fly said.

"You'll love it when you get the reward," Harvey said. "Like a savings plan. You keep putting a little money away, and then one day, you have a lot."

When Harvey walked into Tootie's, the gang was just about wrapping up their "meeting," as they called the morning gathering. They wanted to pump him for more information about the Marlowe case.

"You on the case?" Oscar asked.

"Which case? We have more cases than they do over at the brewery."

"Yeah," Alice said. "Poor Philip. And that Ebony girl. Now Junior."

Harvey sat up straight. "Junior? What do you know about Junior?"

She looked at him incredulously. "Come on, Harv. Surely you know that they found Junior in another grave up on the Marlowe property. Not too far from the limb maker's house where the Hopper kids found that girl."

"How do you know that, Alice?"

She pointed to the front page of the Stillwell Gazette, where the headline said, "Another Body Found on Mountain."

"Oh no," he said aloud.

"How could you have missed it, Harv? Old age setting in?" Rexie said and then chuckled.

"Let me see that." Harvey pointed to the newspaper, and Alice passed it to him.

There was an article by Donald Gilpain about finding Junior. It even suggested the cause of death.

"You don't even have to read it, Harv," Alice said. "It'll be on Breaking News again soon. That Compton girl has been giving live reports from the Marlowe property all morning."

"Don't believe everything you hear in the media," Harvey said. He was in shock. Who could have leaked this? He thought. And wrong information, too. I know who will think I leaked it!

Without saying anything else, Harvey got up and left Tootie's.

"What's wrong with him?" Oscar asked after he left. "We must have hit a nerve."

When he got to the parking lot, he called Fly and asked if he'd heard misinformation had been leaked saying the body was Junior. He had not heard it and was shaken

213

by the news. "There go our tips from Chappy."

"And Ollie."

The next call was to Chappy, who answered on the first ring.

"I've been waiting for your call."

"What's going on?"

"I don't know, you tell me. I confided in you, and you made promises. The next thing I know, promises are broken, and information is in the paper and on TV. Wrong information at that. Explain yourself, Harvey."

"I can't because I don't know. I didn't see the news or the paper until I got to Tootie's. It wasn't me, Chappy. I told no one."

"Fly?"

"Nope. He said he told no one, and I trusted him. You might not, but I do."

"Who else did you talk to?"

"Only Ollie."

"Loose lips, Ollie?"

"I don't know that about him. I guess I need to talk with him."

"If it's not him, then we have an inside snitch who wants to mess with the investigation."

Harvey called Ollie.

"Hi, my friend," Ollie said in his usual chipper tone.

"So, Ollie, when we talked yesterday, you gave me good information about Junior."

"That's right; if you call saying the body wasn't Junior good information."

"Did you tell anyone else that the body was or wasn't Junior?"

"Well, let's see. I talked about it with my wife at dinner, and my assistant, Joline, knew about it. She needs to know what's going on. In each case, I think I said the body was somebody other than Junior."

"Somebody must have misheard you. Do you think either of them would contact the Stillwell Gazette or the

214

Channel 8 News about it?"

"I don't think so."

"What's Joline's last name, Ollie?"

"Gilpain. Joline Gilpain."

"That's it, Ollie. She's the leak."

"Huh?"

"Joline must have misunderstood you and told her brother, Bob Gilpain, the reporter for the Stillwell Gazette, that the body was Junior. The Channel 8 News is owned by the same company as the Gazette, Boxlight Media." Harvey said. "Did you tell her the body was Junior, Ollie?"

"No. I told her just the opposite. Somehow, she got it wrong. The media is saying it's Junior that was found. We know that's not true. She must have heard part of the discussion and drawn a wrong conclusion, Harv. I need to have a long talk with her. She's good, but she was really careless this time."

"Please call Chappy and tell him that I didn't leak any information."

"Will do, my friend. Sorry."

———————

It was a matter of minutes until Chappy called Harvey.

"That was quick," Harvey began. "I just talked with Ollie."

"Yeah, Ollie was pretty upset. I guess he learned a lesson, but now the cat's out of the bag. I have to go talk with Eunice to inform her it wasn't Junior you guys found. Thought I had some time, but I better go there right away."

"Good luck. Think she'll be surprised or upset?"

"Neither. It's been at least 20 years, and I'm not so sure she'd have been upset 20 years ago. You know that was a bad relationship."

"That's what I figure, too."

"At least we have a weapon on this murder. That knife you found seems to be the likely weapon. The only thing we can check it against is what's left of whoever you found up there. But there are probably some scrapes or breaks in the bones that we can link to the knife. Forensics will rule it in or out."

"Prints? Can you get prints off a knife after 20 years?"

"They'll try. Latent prints can last on metal for up to 40 years. The knife was under a rock in the wall, so we'll find out quickly if we can get prints. I know they're working on it now."

"Good. What did you hear about Philip, Chappy?"

"Nada. No local chatter. Gone silent."

"Maybe we can help, Chappy."

"Just keep you-know-who under control."

"I don't know about that. Some of our best leads have come when you-know-who is a little whacky."

"Then don't break the law."

When he finished talking with Chappy, Harvey called Fly and told him to meet him in the parking lot behind Tootie's. They needed to help Chappy by looking more closely at the scene of Philip's death.

OTHER EYES

Harvey expected to meet Fly in half an hour, so he waited 40 minutes and then left home. As he pulled into the parking lot behind Tootie's, he could hear Fly's truck clanking a half block away.

"You're like an ice cream truck, Fly," he said as Fly got out of his truck. "You can tell you're coming before you get here. Don't bill yourself as a stealth sleuth."

"My signature, Boss. Keeps me out of trouble. Can't get away with anything without people hearing Minerva."

"We need to go look over the crime scene again."

"Cops have done that already."

"It needs PI eyes."

They walked to the sidewalk and around Tootie's to the square. "Now look around and see where you see security cameras. Some will be obvious, some pretty well hidden."

"Didn't the cops already check this stuff out?"

"They haven't solved the murder yet, so we just go there and look. Time is money."

They started with the area near the gazebo, and Harvey spotted two cameras on the posts that supported its roof, each focusing on the area near the gazebo from a different angle. They were white to blend in with the paint on the posts.

"Look at this, Fly," Harvey said. "Tiny mini cameras. It must only be a centimeter wide. I know this camera. Used this type all the time. HD and night vision. Check it on your cellphone. Very cool."

"Where'd you use them, Harv?"

"On a couple of surveillance jobs."

"Cops use these?"

"Sure, but they hook them up to a receiver nearby so the video can be streamed to the station or wherever."

"Who do you think put these here?"

"I'm guessing the city installed them to keep an eye on things at night, but they tied the stores around into the network. Tootie could keep files on her server."

"Let's see what they found."

"Not from these cameras. Look real closely at the center, Fly."

Fly looked at them. "Who'd do a thing like that?"

There was white paint over the lens of the camera, so the only thing that could be seen was darkness.

"I'd say a murderer might want to block the camera's vision."

"But there are other cameras around, right?"

They went on a tour of the square on the same side as Tootie's Café. With every camera, they found paint on the lens, rendering them useless in identifying a perpetrator.

"But, Boss. There must be a video of whoever painted the cameras. Didn't the cops see that? They must have noticed the cameras didn't have pictures. Must be some dude or dudette walking right up to the camera and plopping a drop right on it."

Harvey texted Chappy. "Have you guys looked at all the videos from the businesses near the gazebo?

Within a minute, he replied. "Not yet. Plan to do that soon. Very busy."

"Busy. Can you believe that, Boss?"

"Unfortunately, yes, Fly. Too much crime and not enough detectives to keep up with it."

"We can look at it."

"Ha. Think they'll let us do that. Think again."

"Worth askin'. But wait. They control the cameras at the square and maybe others around there, but who controls Tootie's cameras?"

"Tootie! Good thinking, Fly."

They immediately went to see Tootie and explained that they wanted to check her digital files to help solve Philip's murder.

"You can try. The cops took copies of my files

from around that time, but you can still see them on my server. Knock yourselves out, guys."

Tootie led them to a back room where her server was located and showed them how to access the video from when Philip was murdered. They started at the date of the murder and went backward in time.

"Well planned," Fly said. "We're a couple of days before the murder, and the screen's still dark. Like midnight with no moon and no lights on."

He no sooner said that when the screen lit up, revealing the gazebo in the distance and a person with a small paint brush walking backward away from Tootie's. The person walked backward to a camera in another store, and you could see the person painting on the lens of the security camera there. Fly moved the recording back in time and saw the same figure dressed in dark clothing wearing a hoodie go to other stores whose cameras may have been aimed at the gazebo. The time stamp on the video said 3:00 a.m.

Harvey and Fly continued the reverse time travel to the previous day and saw the same figure go backward from the camera across the street to the gazebo and hand Philip a paper cup. It looked like the same kind of cup that you would buy in quantity. They had a clear picture of the person except for the face.

"Man or woman, Boss?"

"Tough. Kind of short, maybe 5' 5". Completely covered, gloves and all. Never looks at the camera."

"Woman." Fly sounded confident. "Run it forward. Look how she walks."

Harvey ran the video back to where the perp was walking across the street, then ran it forward.

"Just a little wiggle. See that, Boss?"

"Might be right, Fly."

"Run it again and check the shoes."

Harvey ran it again and zoomed in on the shoes.

"Running shoes. Don't think it's Eunice."

They both laughed.

"Look at the logo, Fly."

"Brooks. Good running shoes. Brooks logo. Sideways V."

"What about the color, Fly?"

"Shoes are black, logo's pink."

"Woman?"

"Boss, you can't judge a shoe by its color. Get with the program. Pink doesn't mean girlie anymore."

"Guess I'm old fashioned. But remember that pink logo. We might see it again."

They spent time looking at the video and determined that the perp parked somewhere out of the view of security cameras and walked to the square.

"Seen enough?" Harvey asked.

Fly nodded.

"Many a mickle makes a muckle."

"There you go again, Boss."

"Small bits of information add up to evidence," Harvey said.

"Why didn't you say that?"

"More fun to say the Scottish version."

They thanked Tootie for letting them look at the video and assured her that they had reset it. They also told her that the video might play a big role in the case later on.

They left Tootie's and walked out to their vehicles to plan their next move.

THE CHASE

Harvey and Fly drove over to Noah's house in hopes of finding Noah, but no one was home. "Next best stop is the mansion. Noah might be there," Harvey said.

"Let's call. Might figure out where they are," Fly said.

"I have Earlene's number but not Noah's. Here." Harvey handed Fly the phone. "If she stonewalls, hang up."

Fly called Earlene with the speakerphone on.

"Hello, Earlene?"

"Who's this?"

"Fly. Fly the metal guy."

"Fly the thief," she replied.

He wanted to come back at her in the worst way, but he could see Harvey shaking his head. Instead, he said, "Noah there?"

"I told you before," she said. "He's not here. He has things to do."

Harvey signaled for Fly to mute the speakerphone, and he whispered to Fly. "Do you hear that background noise?"

Fly nodded his head and whispered. "Truck. They're in a truck. Going fast."

Harvey put the speaker back on. "Excuse me; I had a brief interruption. Do you know where he is?"

"If I did, I wouldn't tell you," she replied.

"When can we see him?" Fly asked.

"Never. He doesn't want to talk with you."

"Doesn't sound like the Noah I know," Fly replied to no one. The phone went dead.

Fly looked at Harvey. "I don't think she likes us, Harv."

They talked about where Noah and Earlene might be and narrowed it down to two places. They were near the Marlowe estate or possibly the Clairvoyant Center.

Whichever it was, they were in a hurry.

"We're almost at the mansion. Let's go there," Harvey said.

"Why not the swami shop? Not that I want to be creeped out again."

"Truck's going too fast for that part of town. But that's a likely choice for another day. Remember how swami's grandmommy reacted when we mentioned the Marlowe estate?"

"Yeah," Fly said. "She sure got upset. She knew what was going on."

"Both at the estate and Philip's death."

"Well, if she's Philip's mommy and Noah's the daddy, I guess that's a big connection."

Harvey nodded in agreement.

"Family connections. Messed up family connections."

"So, you think Noah is related to the Marlowes and the swamis, Fly?"

Fly nodded his head up and down. "I'd bet money on it, and you know I'm a careful bettor."

"You mean like with Noah's money at the track?"

Fly scowled at Harvey. "Exception. I'm saying that either Noah or Earlene is related to the Marlowes."

"You mean a blood relative like a sister or cousin?"

"Yeah. I'll even go further, Harv. With that nasty attitude, I'd say it's Earlene. Sounds just like Eunice." Fly puffed out his chest and moved his head up and down like a proud rooster.

"Another reason to visit the mansion," Harvey said.

As they drove up Quarry Road, they saw a cloud of dust coming from the Marlowe driveway. They drove toward the cloud and saw two vehicles. Noah's truck was chasing a red sports car.

"Get your phone out, Fly. Get your camera ready," Harvey yelled. "Start recording video. See if you can catch the plate on the red car." He slowed his Mustang down and pulled to the side of the road. Fly did as directed and set the camera on video. The dust settled as soon as the cars left the gravel driveway. He let the camera run until the car and truck drove past.

Fly looked at his video and made the picture larger. "Got it," he announced. "I caught the plate."

"Great. What's it say?"

"Pennsylvania plate. A little blurry, but I think I can read it. NXP-ULV9."

"Double-check it. Read it again, just to be sure."

"Yup. NXP-ULV9. For sure."

"Call that into Chappy and describe the car. By the way, did you catch what that car was?"

"Looked like a red Dodge Charger. Recent, like new."

"That will help. Now give Chappy a call and tell him."

"Me. You sure?"

"It's about time you two got along."

Fly reluctantly found Chappy in his contact list and pressed the number. Chappy took the call immediately.

"Fly?"

"Yup. That's me."

"Strange. You never called me before."

"Yeah, but I got some information for you."

"Spit it out fast," Harvey said. "Don't waste time."

Fly quickly told Chappy the whole story of the cars coming down the driveway at rapid speed as if they were trying to get away from something or Noah was chasing the red Charger.

"Where are you now," Chappy asked.

"Just below the mansion off to the side of Quarry Road near the driveway. I'm sending you the video I got."

"Get the plate?"

"Yeah. Pennsy plate. NXP-ULV9."

"I'll look it up. You said a red Charger, right?"

"Roger, Snappy."

"I'm on it right now, Fly. Here we go. From the Philadelphia area." Chappy paused. Fly could hear computer keyboard clicks. "Oh, man. Bummer."

"What's wrong?"

"Rental car. Enterprise."

"Can you get who rented it?"

"No," Chappy replied. "They won't give you the name. Privacy rights. And besides, the person who rented it may not be the driver of the car. Could even be stolen for all we know."

"Let me look at this video again. No surprise. Male," Fly said.

"Either of you recognizes him?"

"Looks to be in his 40s. Hard to tell. Wearing a baseball cap and sunglasses," Fly said as he held the phone up for Harvey to see. "Don't know the dude."

"Me neither," Harvey added. "We're going up to the mansion and snooping around."

"I'll look at the video," Chappy said. "I'll see if we can come up with something. That rental in Philly has me confused. Who would live that far away yet have an interest in the Marlowes? And why was Noah in that chase?"

Harvey and Fly went back and forth on whether to go to the mansion or to follow the two cars. Chappy could hear their dialogue.

"You two are right at the mansion. Go there and see what's going on. I'll send a couple of cars out to track down the two drivers. Shouldn't be hard to find them in this small town."

Harvey and Fly did as directed and continued up the drive to the mansion. Everything appeared quiet as they approached the front door. They cranked the old doorbell and waited. No one came to the door. They cranked it again and waited. Still, no one came to the door, which was slightly open.

"It's like the old riddle, Harv."

"No time for your stupid jokes, Fly."

"So, when is a door not a door?"

"Not now."

"Can't help it, Harv. I get all riddley when I'm nervous, like my Aunt Louise. She always laughs when people trip or fall. A door is not a door when it's ajar. Get it."

Harvey didn't laugh. "And this one's ajar, so I think we should go in."

They gingerly opened the creaking door and stepped into the foyer.

"Anyone home?" Harvey yelled.

No reply. Fly shrugged his shoulders, and they walked to the grand staircase. The sun shone through the stained-glass window on the landing filtering the sunlight in deep hues of red and blue.

"Hello. Anyone here?" Harvey called out again.

Still no answer. They walked around the first floor, which was in total disarray.

"Just like the family," Fly observed. "Cattywampus."

They heard a groan coming from the kitchen and ran toward the noise. There on the floor lay Eunice, so weak she could hardly speak. Harvey got down on his knees and spoke to her.

"What happened?" he asked.

"Poi … poison."

"Fly, call 911."

Fly took out his phone and called.

"911, what's your emergency?"

Fly explained that the situation was dire and that poison was likely involved.

Harvey spoke to Eunice. "Help is on the way. Who? Who poisoned you?"

She raised her left hand and pointed to a paper cup that was lying on its side on the floor. The tumbler was the kind you might buy at a big box store. With labored, shallow breaths, she said, "Her." And then she passed out.

"Oh, man," Fly said. "This is bad, Harv."

"Look around for others, Fly."

"Is she gonna die, Harv?" Fly just stood there looking at the body, paralyzed by fear.

"Just go. Somebody might be alive."

Fly walked out to the foyer and gingerly walked up the old creaky stairway. No one was in the first bedroom, so he moved on to the next like a cat slowly stalking its prey. No one was there either. In the third bedroom, he found Carmela, Three's wife, in bed, fully clothed as if she crawled back there after once being up and getting dressed. She was breathing but seemed unconscious. Fly gently poked her arm. She groaned and babbled something incoherent. He poked a little harder. She sat up, looked at him, and let out a blood-curdling scream.

Fly jumped back. "You're alive. You're alive!"

She reached under her pillow and took out a pistol. "What are you doing here?"

Fly put his arms up. "Now, don't do anything rash. I'm a good guy. I'm here to help you. I'm Fly, the recycling guy. Remember me?"

She put the gun down just as Harvey ran up the stairs to see what the scream was all about.

"You okay, Fly?"

"Yeah. Guess I scared her."

"You okay?" Harvey asked the woman.

"I was in a deep sleep. You scared the b'jesus out of me. Why are you here?"

"Well," Harvey hesitated. "It seems that someone may have tried to kill Eunice."

"What? Where?"

"Here, downstairs."

"Is she okay?"

"EMS is on the way. She's alive, but barely."

Harvey looked at the woman. "And who are you?"

Carmela ignored the question. "Where's Felicia?" she asked.

"Good question. Where's her room?"

"In the tower. Up another flight."

They could hear a TV blaring at the top of the stairs, and they decided to walk up carefully. They found another door, opened it, and called her name. There was no answer.

"Felicia," Harvey called again.

The TV volume went down. "Who is it?"

"Felicia, it's important. We need to talk with you. We'll wait at the bottom of the stairs."

Carmela came out to the hallway straightening her hair as if she wanted to make a good impression on someone. "Hurry up, Felicia," she yelled up the stairs. "Eunice is half dead. Get down here."

Felicia came down looking unkempt and worried. They all went downstairs to the kitchen. They could hear the ambulance and police car sirens coming up Quarry Road as they looked at Eunice.

The police came in the front door, and Fly motioned for them to go to the kitchen. They checked Eunice's pulse. The EMS team arrived and took over, putting Eunice on a gurney and wheeling her to the ambulance.

"Know what happened?" Officer Cannon asked them.

Harvey told him that they came there on Chappy's advice and how they found Eunice barely breathing. "She said she was poisoned," Harvey said as he pointed to the cup. "I don't know if the poison was in that cup, but I suspect it was." Harvey took out his cell phone. "Chappy. Got a mess at the mansion. Get over here and bring Sanchez with you. Eunice is half dead. Looks like poison."

"Don't touch anything," he replied.

"Of course not."

Chappy arrived in short order with the phone in hand. He was talking with a police officer who was looking for speeding cars. He looked at Harvey and Fly. "I had the dispatcher put out an all-points bulletin to the county and forward the license number of the red car."

The police were already putting up yellow crime scene ribbons near the kitchen. The forensics team arrived, and they were taking pictures and packaging the poisonous container in an evidence bag. One of the forensic team members came up to Chappy.

"So, we have the one victim. I'm sure we're going to find poison in the cup. But there is another container on the kitchen table with liquid in it. It's like another person; maybe the perp was going to do himself in."

"Or herself," Fly chimed in. "We don't know who the other person is. Maybe Noah or Earlene, maybe the red car driver, or maybe somebody else."

"Fly's right. We need to keep our options open, especially this early in the investigation," Harvey added.

"Hate to admit it, guys, but I agree with Fly," Chappy said. "Only this one time, Fly, understand?"

Fly puts his arm around Chappy. "I knew you'd come around."

Harvey laughed. Chappy just shook his head, but there was a smile on his face.

Harvey knew that they would be in the way if they stayed around the mansion while forensics did their work, so he suggested that they leave and go see what was going on at Noah's.

"Be careful, men," Chappy said. "Noah is currently a suspect. He needs to explain why he was speeding out of here and chasing the other car."

"No problem," Fly explained. "I'm with one of the most seasoned investigators in all of Stillwell."

"I know," Chappy said. "That's why I said that!"

TRUTH AND CONSPIRACY THEORIES

Harvey and Fly drove back down Quarry Road to Noah's house and surveyed the property before they got out of the car. Noah's truck was not in the driveway, but Earlene's green Toyota Corolla was parked in front of the garage.

"So, you think she's home, Harv?"

"No, but there's only one way to find out."

"Get ready to be stonewalled again."

"When we get out, keep looking at the house. Don't walk up like you're admiring the buds on the trees, okay?"

"Of course, Harv. I'm all eyes, and my ears are peeling like I got sunburned."

They carefully got out of the car, intently walked up to the sun porch, and knocked on the door. Diesel started barking wildly until he saw Fly's face. Then he sat obediently, seeking attention.

No one responded to the knock, so Harvey walked around back. He felt the hood of the car and determined that it was cold. No one had been driving it for several hours. He knocked on the back door and again got no response.

When he came around front again, Fly was busily engaged in entertaining Diesel through the porch door window.

"I don't think anyone's home," Harvey said.

"That's what my algebra teacher said about me."

"Seriously, Fly. We're dealing with murder, and we don't know where Earlene and Noah are."

Harvey called Chappy again and let him know that no one answered the door at Noah's, but Earlene's car was there.

"Relax, Harv. We know where they are. Officers caught up with Noah speeding through town in his truck, and Earlene was with him."

"We didn't see two people in the truck when he was racing by. Did he pick her up someplace?"

"No, we stopped him as he chased that red Charger. She was with him the whole time."

"She must have ducked down when they saw us."

"Anyway, they're both here at the police station. Not saying anything. Mum."

"Interesting. Where's the Charger?"

"Got away. Outfoxed us. But we think we know where he went."

"Oh yeah? Where?"

"I can't say."

"Sure, you can, but you don't want to."

"It's for your benefit and Fly's, too."

Harvey ended the call. "Let's listen to some police radio, Fly. Might get a clue where the Charger went."

"Good idea, but I'm hungry. Didn't eat my Cocoa Puffs this morning."

"Ok. We can't do much more. Much as I'd like to, we can't go talk to Noah, so let's get something to eat at Tootie's. But be prepared. This will be like the bull going into the ring being attacked by a bunch of matadors."

"We're the bull?" Fly looked squeamish. "When I got up this morning, I didn't think I'd find an almost dead person and then go into a bullfight where I'm the bull."

"Ready?"

"Nope. How about we get takeout from the Quick Stop? We won't get jabbed there."

"C'mon, Fly. We might find out something at Tootie's that will help us."

Fly said nothing, a sure sign that he was flummoxed.

"Money. Think about the money you're going to get. We're close to figuring this out."

Fly thought for a couple of seconds, sighed, and smiled his toothy smile. "Ok. I'm good. Ready."

Tootie's was normally filled with noise and laughter. But this day was exceptional. People were abuzz with bits and pieces of news, and everyone was aware of the police sirens and the chase through town that morning.

As soon as Harvey and Fly came in through the rear entrance, they were pummeled with questions. "What happened at the mansion? Who died? Did they find Roscoe or Three?" The questions were endless.

Finally, Fly put two fingers in his mouth and made a loud whistling sound. Everyone quieted down, and Fly extended his arm toward Harvey.

"I know you all want to know what's going on," Harvey said. "Well, so do we."

"What about the murders at the mansion?" Rosie asked. "I heard they're all dead?"

"There are some things that are police matters, and we can't say."

"Police radio says there was one body and a couple of getaway cars," Rexie reported.

"Yeah, I heard that Noah Zark was racing away from the scene. Maybe he's a serial killer. Doesn't seem the type, though."

"Neither did Ted Bundy," Alice said. "Good looking. Charismatic."

"I wouldn't describe Noah that way," a man's voice chimed in from the back.

The group laughed.

"What about Earlene?" Rosie asked.

"She's all woven into this mess," Oscar said. "I remember her from years ago. Earlene Gody. Not a pleasant gal. Sour puss, actually."

"Kind of like the dead one on the mountain, Eunice," Jeb said.

"Who said it was her body they found or that any person is dead?" Alice said. Then a delayed thought popped into her head. "Hey, wait a minute. Gody. Wasn't that Eunice's maiden name?"

231

The group went silent.

"Holy cannoli," Fly blurted out.

Everyone turned toward him.

"Gody. She's a Gody like Eunice is a Gody. Sisters!"

That got everyone chattering away and making their own versions of the truth.

Harvey reached over and gave Fly a fist bump. "Aren't you glad we came in here?"

"You're not as dumb as you look, Harv!"

Harvey just smiled. "I think Chappy needs to know this. Order us a couple of sandwiches and drinks, and I'll give him a call."

Chappy answered on the first ring. "Whatcha got, Harv?"

"Another piece of the puzzle. We're over here at Tootie's, and the group's been chattering away about what's happening. Kind of like groupthink by the uninformed. But our trainee put something together."

"Not my trainee. Yours."

"Whatever. So, Earlene's maiden name is Gody."

"Yeah?"

"And Eunice's maiden name is Gody."

The phone went silent while Chappy absorbed this.

"You there?" Harvey asked.

"You think these two are sisters?"

"Sure looks that way."

"That means we've got one sister who was poisoned, and the other is racing away from the scene."

"Sounds right, Chappy. You still have Noah and Earlene with you?"

"Yup. And they're staying here until we find out what they've been up to."

"You know that there was a second cup there?"

"Heard about that. Not sure what it means."

"I think the poisoner was going to do the others in, at least one other one," Chappy said.

"Or herself or himself," Harvey said.

Harvey shifted gears. "Any more on the Charger guy?"

"You know I can't about that."

"Yes, you can, Chappy, because Fly has helped you tremendously in this case. You already owed him before; now you owe him again. Where did the Charger guy go?"

"I'll only say one word, and you use it however you'd like."

"Fire away."

"Philmont."

"Great. We have some connections to check there."

"And don't look for the car."

"Really?"

"We found it abandoned and wiped down. Not too far from the drug den in Philmont."

"Ok, thanks. I'll tell Fly to cross your debt off his list. Wait. No. Just cancel some of it. When we get the big bucks, he'll cancel the rest."

Harvey went back to the roaring crowd at the bullfight. Fly was surrounded by matadors and loved every minute of it. Harvey pulled him aside.

"You didn't say anything else, did you?"

"Me? Of course not."

"What else did you learn?"

"Been crowdsourcing, Harv. Your word, not my word of the day. All kinds of conspiracy theories. Like Earlene wanted to kill Eunice for her share of Junior's estate, and Earlene and Eunice wanted to kill Junior for the money. Get this. They said Noah killed Junior and then Three and Roscoe because they knew he did it."

"Any truth in these theories?"

Fly shrugged his shoulders. "Could be, but we need a lot more information. Can't jump to conclusions too soon."

"Brilliant, Fly. You must have had a good teacher!"

"Noah seems to be on people's minds. He has

233

access to the property and knows it inside and out. Rexie even said that he's thought all along that there was a body buried in the basement of the barn."

"There's a basement there?" Harv wrinkled his brow. "News to me."

"Yeah. Remember that day when I was raiding the dumpster near the barn? I got a little carried away and started harvesting metal."

"That's what you call it, harvesting?"

"Anyway, I went down the steps to the basement that they used to use as a root cellar. I'm standing down there looking around, and I hear your voice. You told me to get out 'cause the cops were coming."

"Yeah. I remember that. You were pretty slow getting out."

"As I was leaving, I saw another door in the basement that must have led to another room. Wooden door. Old, with rusted hinges and a padlock on it. Something was in there that somebody didn't want anyone else to know about."

"What do you think is there?"

"Treasure? Bodies? Your guess is as good as mine."

"We can't go breaking in there, and Chappy will need to get a warrant to go into that area. Capish?"

"Don't go laying foreign words on me. I only know a few Italian words like pizza and stromboli."

"Try this one. It's English—money. If we break in, we won't get any money."

"Understand?"

Fly nodded, but he wasn't smiling.

They got their lunch from Tootie, quickly ate it, and left. They had to figure out what was going on in Philmont.

THE LOST IS FOUND

"What do you think, Sherlock, Philmont?"

"You're Sherlock. I'm Watson."

"Okay. Watson, Philmont?"

"The devil's due a soul, I'd say."

"You read Sherlock Holmes, Fly?"

"Nah, I saw the movie. Good line, Robert Downey, Jr. Same idea."

"Maybe we will catch an evildoer today," Harvey replied.

They headed straight over to Philmont and planned to stop by Kiana's first. As they pulled up to her apartment, they saw the Charger being loaded onto a flatbed truck.

"Too much of a coincidence is finding the Charger here," Fly said. "We need to talk with Kiana."

They headed up the stairs to the fourth floor. Harvey was lagging behind and was huffing and puffing when they got to Kiana's door.

"Told you last time, you need a little cardio, Harv. Losin' a few pounds wouldn't hurt either."

Harvey ignored him, still catching his breath, while Fly knocked on the door.

Young Fly opened the door cautiously and smiled when he recognized Fly.

"Your mom in?" Fly asked.

"Hey, man, how ya doin', Big Fly?"

"Great. If I was much better, I'd be twins."

Young Fly laughed. "C'mon in. I'll get her."

They walked into the apartment as Kiana walked out of the bedroom.

"Hey, Kiana," Fly said. "You okay?"

"Just a little rattled, but okay."

"What happened, Miss," Harvey asked.

"Oh, Kiana," Fly said. "This is Harvey; remember him?"

"Sure, uh, well, this guy knocks on my door. Didn't

recognize him. He tells me who he is, and I remember us talking about those guys from 20 years ago."

"So, what was his name?" Fly asked.

"Oh, you know, not the one with the number name."

"Not Three," Harvey said. "Must have been Roscoe."

"Yeah. That's who he said he was."

"You didn't recognize him, huh? How do you know it was Roscoe?" Fly asked.

"Well, I only know his name because he told me. He didn't look much like either of the guys I knew back then."

"What did he want, K?"

"A ride. Said he needed a ride."

"I hope you didn't give him one."

"You kidding? I wouldn't get in a car with some guy I don't know. My Fly, not you, came out to the doorway and asked me if everything was okay. When the guy, Roscoe or whoever he was, saw him, he backed away. When I said Fly's name, it must have triggered something from the past 'cause the guy turned and went down the stairs like he was heading to a fire."

"I have that effect on people sometimes," Fly said.

"You must, too, Little Fly."

"He's bigger than you, Fly."

"Okay, how about Big Little Fly?"

Little Fly shook his head and smiled. "Why don't you call me what my friends call me?"

"What's that?"

"Maggot!"

"Gross. Got to do better than that."

"Ok. My mom calls me Midge."

"Midge? Why Midge?"

"Because that's a young fly. Get it?"

"Funny. Midge is easier than Big Little Fly."

Harvey got back to business. "Do you have any

idea where Roscoe was going, Kiana?"

"He said the train station. He wanted a ride to the train station."

"Better call Chappy," Harvey said. He took out his phone and called.

Chappy answered on the first ringtone. "Whatcha got, Harv?"

"Some guy calling himself Roscoe stopped at Kiana's place and wanted a ride to the train station. She lives right where they found the red Charger. It's the same place where we think Ebony died."

"How long ago did he leave her place?"

Harvey looked at Kiana. "When did he leave here?"

"Not too long ago. Maybe 20 minutes or a half hour ago."

"I heard that, Harv. He's probably looking for a train back to the Philly area. Those don't run but more than once an hour. There's a good chance he may still be at the station. I can send the Philmont PD over there to arrest the guy."

"Might be easier for us to identify him first and call them in, Harv," Fly said.

"Heard that, too. You're right, Fly. I'll stage them about a block away, and you can call 911 and say, 'Roscoe.' I'll tell them that means to go up on the platform and arrest the perp."

"Ok. We'll get a description from Kiana and drive right over there."

"Make it quick. We don't know when the train will come, and we don't want to lose him."

They ended the call with Chappy and asked both Kiana and Midge to describe him.

"Might be better if we went with you. We can identify him easier than you can," Midge said.

"Good thinking, son," Fly said. "Oh, wait. I don't mean son like I'm the father, just like an expression. You know, like an older guy calling a younger guy son. You know?"

They all laughed.

"No, we don't know, Big Fly," Harvey said, "but it doesn't matter now. Let's all get in my car and head to the station. I'm not sure where it is, so your first job is getting us there."

The trip to the station was quick since it was less than two miles away. They noticed three Philmont police cars at strategic locations. The parking lot on the ground level was almost full. They parked the car and agreed that they should not walk up the stairs to the platform together. They headed toward the southeast platform. Midge went first, and Harvey followed. There was a second set of stairs, and Fly and Kiana went up there. They all held cell phones in their hands.

A dozen or more people were waiting for trains on the platform, and another dozen were seated in the waiting room. As per their plan, Midge and Kiana were to comb the platform from different ends and text Harvey if they saw Roscoe. If they didn't see him, Fly was to walk through the waiting room and check the restroom. Harvey was to hang back and call 911 if they saw him.

Midge and Kiana swept the platform with no luck. They shook their heads as a signal to let Harvey know they didn't see him. Harvey signaled Fly to move into the waiting room. He casually walked around, trying to look like he was bored. He didn't see Roscoe, so he went back out to the platform to compare notes. Harvey went to the ticket master and found that the train to Philadelphia was due in about 10 minutes.

"Where could he be?" Kiana said. "He had plenty of time to get here."

"Did you check the restroom, Fly?" Midge asked.

"No. Not yet."

"OK. I want you to go in the men's room and look around," Harvey said. "If you don't see someone about your age in nice clothes, I want you to look under the opening in the stall at their legs and see if anyone has expensive-looking pants or shoes."

"What? How am I supposed to recognize the pants and shoes of a dude I've never seen? I suppose you want me to grab his ankle and take him down, too."

"No, Fly. Don't go near him. Come out and tell me, but be sure," Harvey said. "Midge, you go with him."

When Midge went into the restroom, he immediately noticed one man washing his hands and another in the stall. The hand washer was old and hunched over, but the man in the stall had on designer jeans and expensive-looking shoes. Midge recognized the clothing immediately, but he wanted to be sure, so he knocked on the door of the stall. It was locked as he expected, but the man inside said, "Occupied."

"Sorry," Midge said. He nodded to Fly, then he turned and walked out to the waiting room. He saw Harvey and made a gesture like he was making a phone call and walked over closer to him. "Call 'im Harvey. He's in the stall."

Just then, the ticket man made an announcement over the loudspeaker, "Train 504 to Philadelphia will arrive in three minutes. All passengers going on 504 to Philadelphia should proceed to the platform now."

Harvey had called in the police, but Roscoe could get on the train before they got there.

When the man came out of the stall, Fly turned so the suspect wouldn't recognize him. The team moved to their designated locations. Midge walked along the platform toward the first car on the train. Kiana moved toward the middle car, and Harvey headed to the last car. The man who called himself Roscoe came out of the restroom, walked through the waiting room, and went onto the platform.

"Roscoe," Kiana yelled as she waved her arm toward him. He looked up, recognized her, and walked toward her. As he did, the three men moved in and entrapped him in a human web. They didn't touch him, but he knew better than to move.

"Who are you guys? Let me get on the train."

"Not today, Roscoe," Fly said.

"Roscoe? I'm not Roscoe. You got the wrong guy."

"Then what's your name?" Harvey asked.

"Uh. Winslow. Bruce Winslow."

"Is this the guy that came to your apartment, Midge?" Harvey asked.

"Sure is. Wanted a ride here."

Winslow knew he was caught, and he tried to bolt. He punched Harvey in the stomach and broke away from the web. He ran down the platform, pushing people out of the way. He saw three police officers coming up the stairs, so he turned and ran toward the other stairway. People scattered, and Harvey yelled to the police. "Roscoe. Stop him."

Before he knew what hit him, Midge ran up behind him and pulled him back onto the platform. Immediately, the Philmont police officers swooped in and cuffed him.

"Who is this guy?" the officer from the PPD asked, looking at Harvey.

"We think he's a fugitive from the Marlowe case in Stillwell, but we're not sure what's up with him. He's the guy that was driving the red Charger you guys impounded," Harvey explained.

Officer Cannon from the Stillwell PD walked up to the platform. "I see you guys got one of our bad guys. Nice work."

"You want him?" the Philmont officer asked.

"Not really, but I think Chappy Chan would like to have him in Stillwell. Winslow, or whoever he is, has a lot of explaining to do." Harvey responded.

"We'll contact Detective Chan and figure out what to do," Officer Cannon said.

The Philmont officers thanked Harvey, Fly, Midge, and Kiana for their help in capturing Roscoe or Winslow or whoever the fugitive was. Harvey drove Kiana and Midge back to their apartment, and Fly rode with them.

"Thanks for your help, K," Fly said. "You, too, Midge." He laughed. "Not a fruit fly or a house fly, but a midge. Funny."

They all laughed.

"Stay in touch, Fly," Kiana said.

He smiled. "That's a good idea, K. I'll do that."

They parted ways, and Harvey and Fly headed back to Stillwell to see what was going on with their prey.

THE ZARKS

Harvey and Fly drove straight to the police station in Stillwell and called Chappy from outside to make sure it was okay for them to come in.

"Sure," Chappy said. "You're material witnesses. You found Eunice and led us to the capture of Noah and Earlene and Three or Roscoe or Bruce Winslow or whoever we have here."

Harvey and Fly went into the station and were led to the room where Chappy was sitting with Noah and Earlene.

"What are you doing here?" Noah glared at Harvey and Fly. "This has nothing to do with you or us."

"I invited them," Chappy said. "They observed you and the man in the red Charger speeding away from the mansion."

"So?"

"So, exactly. What were you doing?"

"Leaving the property. I work there from time to time."

"What were you doing there this morning?"

"Oh, just checking up on things."

"Did you go into the house?"

"I didn't."

"How about you, Mrs. Zark? Did you go in the house?"

"I started to. But why are you asking me questions? I didn't do anything."

"You were at the scene of the crime, Mrs. Zark. I suggest you answer our questions so you don't get charged with obstructing justice," Chappy said in a much stronger voice.

Fly's eyes widened. He was surprised to see this change in Chappy's tone.

"Legal gobbledygook."

"Call it what you will, but you have a choice, Mrs.

Zark. Either you cooperate, or we'll arrest you for obstruction. Do you understand?"

Noah reached over and gave Earlene's arm a squeeze. She looked at him, but no words were exchanged.

"Oh, alright," she said. "I went to check on the women, but this guy came running out of the mansion. Almost knocked me over."

"Out, not in. Then what did you do?"

"He kind of looked like one of the missing guys. You know, Roscoe or Three. Older, but he resembled them."

"Both of them?"

"Well, I didn't really recognize them after 20 years, and he was getting out of there fast. I wasn't sure who it was."

"Noah, can you tell me why you appeared to be chasing the car?"

"Well, you know, there's a big reward for information on the missing men. If that was one of them, I wanted to be in on the reward. Money's tight, you know."

"Was anyone with you in the truck?"

Noah paused.

"I was," Earlene said. "I ducked down when I saw Harvey's Mustang."

"And why did you do that?"

Earlene shrugged her shoulders.

"You know Fly and Harvey found Eunice semiconscious in the house," Chappy said.

Noah and Earlene looked surprised.

"Eunice? Who would want to hurt Eunice?" Earlene said.

"Maybe you could tell us, Earlene."

She shrugged again, and Chappy turned to Harvey.

"Can you tell us what you saw in the house when you went in, Harvey?"

"Well, we didn't see anything, but we heard groaning coming from the kitchen."

"You both went in the kitchen, right?"

"Yup. Both of us," Fly replied.

"Ok, Fly, what did you observe when you went into the house?"

"Observe. I love when you use those detective words."

"Fly!" Harvey said to get Fly more serious.

Fly wiped the smile off his face. "Oh, yes. I observed Eunice on the floor. There was a paper cup like you might get at a coffee shop next to her. She was hardly breathing."

"So, what did you do?"

"Harvey called 911, and he sent me upstairs to see if the other women were okay. They were except for the one with the gun."

"Which one?"

"I guess it was Carmela."

"Tell us about the gun."

"Well, it was a pistol, not sure what kind. Not a Glock like cops have."

"Did she point the gun at you?"

"Yeah. She thought I was there to hurt her."

"Did she shoot the gun?"

"No. I got her to calm down, and she helped us find Felicia to see if she was okay."

"Thank you, Fly. I think we need to talk with the other party, Mr. Winslow," Chappy said.

"You found the guy?" Earlene cleared her throat and coughed. "Don't know that name. Do you, Noah?"

"Never heard of him."

"We'll leave you two alone while we go see Mr. Winslow."

"Can we leave now?" Earlene asked.

"We'll let you know if and when you can leave," Chappy replied.

The men moved on to another conference room where Mr. Winslow was seated.

244

"I'd like to call my lawyer," he said.

"You'll have the opportunity to do that, but you aren't under arrest, Mr. Winslow."

Winslow looked at Harvey and Fly. "I don't want to talk to these two. They were part of that wolf pack that surrounded me at the train station." He paused. "My lawyer will be in touch with you two and the other guy, too. I suffered irreparable damage from your assault."

"Wait a minute, Wingnut," Fly said. "You're the criminal, not us."

Chappy ignored Winslow's and Fly's comments. "So, what brought you to the mansion today, Mr. Winslow?"

"I came to cheer up my aunt Eunice."

"Aunt, hmm. How is she related to you?"

"She was my father's sister, so she's my aunt."

"And why did you visit her today?"

"She has some issues and needs my support from time to time."

"What kind of support were you giving today, Mr. Winslow?"

"None. I no sooner got to the door when this lady came running out. Knocked me over, ran out to a truck, and got in. The truck took off."

"Did you go back into the house?"

"No. I chased the truck down the lane and down Quarry Road to town."

"Did you catch them?"

"I heard police sirens, so I decided to end the chase and head out of town."

"Where do you live, Mr. Winslow?"

"Near Philly."

"You drove here?"

"No. I came to Philmont by train and rented a car."

"Why did you abandon the car and try to leave by train?"

"I guess I panicked."

"Do you have something to hide, Mr. Winslow?"

"It's a long story."

"I'll bet it is. Do you know that Eunice was poisoned today?"

Winslow feigned shock. "Oh, no. Is she alright?"

"She's alive, but we don't know her condition yet. We talked with a witness today, who said that you needed a ride to the train station. This witness said you used a different name when referring to yourself."

Winslow said nothing.

Chappy continued to press him. "The witness said you called yourself Roscoe. Do you use that name?"

"She doesn't know what she's talking about."

"Who?"

"The witness."

"How do you know the witness is a she?"

"Uh, well, maybe it was a he."

"I think we just established that you were the person she talked with today and that you have a lot of explaining to do. Did you poison Eunice?"

"Of course not. I'd be stupid to do that."

"Really? Why?"

"Because Eunice is nice to me."

"Nice? Like money nice?"

"You could say that."

"So, you were going there today to get some money."

He silently nodded.

"And I'll bet this wasn't the first time."

"Nope."

"Why didn't you go into the mansion after you were knocked over by the lady?"

"I get a little impulsive, and I wanted to get even with that woman."

"Interesting. Did you recognize her?"

He nodded his head.

"Who was it?"

"Eunice's sister. Earlene."

Fly jumped out of his seat, "I knew it."

Harvey pushed him down and looked at the suspect. "Your name isn't Winslow, is it?"

The suspect didn't answer, but neither Harvey nor Chappy said anything. The silence was deafening.

Finally, the suspect spoke. "No."

"Are you Three or Roscoe?" Harvey asked.

Fly was on the edge of his seat. He elbowed Harvey and showed him three fingers. Harvey shook his head in disagreement.

"I guess this is part of the chess game where you say 'Check,'" the suspect said.

"So, who are you?" Harvey asked.

"Roscoe."

Fly jumped up again, and Harvey just smiled. *Liar,* Harvey thought.

Chappy intervened. "Ok, Roscoe. We've got a lot more to talk about. I think you know a lot, and you've known it for a long time."

Roscoe appeared to be relieved as if the weight of the world had been lifted from his shoulders. "I'm innocent of all charges, gentlemen, and I can prove it."

"Well, Mr. Savini," Chappy continued. "I think you will have an opportunity to do that, but we need to retain you as a witness in this case. We can't have you disappearing for another 20 years.

"But you need to know that the Zarks are giving a different story about the encounter at the mansion today. They say that you were the one running away and that you knocked Mrs. Zark over as you ran out the door."

"Well, who was chasing who?" Roscoe asked.

Chappy looked at Harvey.

"The truck was chasing the red Charger," Harvey replied. "Both were traveling fast like they wanted to get out of there."

Chappy, Harvey, and Fly went to a different

conference room to compare thoughts and plan their next move.

"What's your sniffer saying, Fly?" Chappy asked.

"Roscoe knows a lot, and I think he's telling the truth, well, maybe not all the truth."

"Harvey?"

"I agree with Fly, but I'd like to know why Earlene would poison her own sister."

"We're in agreement, but we need to get some evidence. Roscoe isn't going to be a credible witness in court after his escapades for the past 20 years."

"We need to positively ID him, too. Get prints and check them against the ones you got, Fly."

"What about the poison, coffee, and the cup?" Fly wondered.

"We've got forensics working on that."

"What about searching the Zark residence? Might be able to find some real connections there."

"Don't forget about the barn. Noah is real possessive of that place."

"The barn?" Chappy said. "That's a new one to me."

"Oh, yeah," Fly said. "There's a basement in the barn that was an old root cellar. But there's also another room in the basement with a padlock on the door. Something strange is going on there."

"We'll get a warrant and get that place checked out. Good work, Fly."

"Meanwhile, we're going to keep the Zarks and Roscoe here while we continue to investigate," Chappy said.

"We have a lot more to learn," Harvey said. "Like where are Junior and Three, who murdered Ebony, and who did Philip in."

"And don't forget your friends, the swamis, guys," Chappy said.

"Forget them," Fly said. "Too creepy for me."

"But when it comes to murder, you don't want to leave any stone unturned," Harvey said. "That's my tip of the day."

PRIME SUSPECTS

It took another day for the judge to issue a warrant to search the Zark residence. Itching to find out what they found, Harvey called Chappy at noon.

"Anything interesting?" Harvey began.

"Very."

"Like a similar cup?"

"Same brand cup and arsenic."

"Wow. Gold mine. This means that Noah and Earlene are the prime suspects."

"You've got that right. But why? Why would they want to do in Earlene's sister?"

Before Harvey had a chance to respond, Chappy ended the conversation in his signature way. "Busy day, Harv. Got to go."

Chappy had no sooner ended their brief conversation when Fly called.

"Anything interesting, Boss?"

"Very," Harvey replied. "I think they got the goods on Noah and Earlene."

"Goods? Not bad?"

"You're relentless. Goods. You know. Evidence. Stuff that can convict them of murder."

"Yikes. Your friend is a murderer?"

"We don't know if it's him or her. Remember?"

"I know. Shouldn't jump to conclusions 'til we know all the facts."

"Couldn't have said it better myself."

Fly wanted more information. "Why do you think they did it?"

"Might not have been them. Might have been him or her."

"They were both at the mansion."

"But only one went in the house."

"Earlene!"

"But Noah might have been involved. He drove the

250

truck that was getting away."

"But why would she do that to her own sister?"

"If we can figure that out, it might explain a lot about this crazy family."

"Wouldn't want to date those sisters."

Harvey laughed. "They're old enough to be your mother."

"Wouldn't want to date Momma either!"

"Don't forget. There were two sides to that story, Fly. Roscoe, if that's his real name, says Earlene was coming out of the house when he was going in."

"Yeah," Fly said. "And Earlene says Roscoe was coming out when she tried to go in. She says he went to his car and took off. Zarks followed."

"So, according to Earlene, Roscoe was in the house." Harvey speculated.

"I don't think it was Winslow or Roscoe," Fly said.

"Three? Hmm. Interesting, Fly. Is that your gut or your brain talking?"

"Both. They like to talk to each other."

Harvey smiled and shook his head.

"Will they take Roscoe's prints while they have him in custody?" Fly asked.

"They should."

"Then I bet they'll match the prints I found on the bottles and other stuff from the house. Betcha."

"Not taking that bet. I think you might be right."

They decided they needed more information to tie all these murders together, so they went back over to Philmont to interview Kiana with hopes of finding out how Ebony died and how Roscoe and Three may have played into it.

Fly took the lead as they walked up to Kiana's apartment. Midge answered the door. He immediately wanted to know what was going on, but Harvey told him that there was a lot they couldn't tell him because of the ongoing investigation.

Kiana came from the kitchen, smiled, and gave Fly a big hug.

"We're here to find out more about the death of Ebony," Fly began. "We're not sure where she died."

"So," she began, "did you find Three?"

"The guy we caught said he was Roscoe, not Three."

"Really? What's a surprise!"

"Why do you say that, Kiana?" Harvey wondered.

"Well, the guy that came here said he was Roscoe, but he looked more like an older version of the guy named Three."

"You've been thinking about it, huh?"

"Yup," she replied.

"Yeah," Midge said. "I was here, and that's what he said—Roscoe."

"He was going by Winslow, but we got a confession out of him," Fly said.

"Cool. Did you beat him up or smack him around with rubber hoses?" Midge laughed.

"Nope," Fly said. "Good interrogation by Snappy Chapman of the SPD."

"Back to Ebony," Harvey said.

"The night she disappeared, they were all here," Kiana said. "This is coming back to me now—Ebony, Three, and Roscoe. And the boys were arguing over Ebony right in front of her. I think she loved the attention."

"What happened?" Fly asked.

"I don't know. It was time for me to go to work, so I left."

"Did you see anything, Midge?"

"You kidding? Can't remember this at all. I wasn't born yet."

"Oh, that's right."

"When you came home, what did you find, Kiana?" Harvey continued his interrogation.

"Nothing. Ebony and the two boys were gone, and

the door was unlocked. Actually, it was slightly open."

"What time was that?"

"About 11:00 pm."

"Ever see any of them again?"

"Nope. None of them ever again."

"You ever tell the police about this?"

"You kidding? I didn't want nothin' to do with cops at that time of my life," Kiana said. "Say, did you find these guys?"

"We think so."

"Dead?"

"One, maybe, one is in jail."

"We think the guy that was here was Three," Harvey revealed. "He says he's Roscoe, but we have to prove he's Three. The other guy was found in a grave near Ebony."

Kiana put her hand to her mouth. "Oh, my God. And that all began right here."

Midge finally spoke up. "I've been doing my own research project on these guys. I've heard the story from Mom a few dozen times, and I was here when Winslow, or whoever he, is came by."

"You think you know who he is?"

"Well, I'm pretty sure who it is."

Fly looked at Harvey as if to say, "There goes the reward."

Harvey stepped on Fly's foot.

"I have age-progression software on my computer that shows what people might look like as they age."

"Cool," Harvey said.

"And I found pictures of Roscoe and Three when they went missing. Their pictures were in local papers, and they made their way to Google Images over the years. Google was still a young program when they went missing."

"You devil dog you," Fly said. "So, what did Sherlock Holmes Jr. do next?"

"I ran the aging app for both pictures. I actually had several pictures of both men, so I ran them all."

"And?"

"Excuse me for a minute," Midge said as he went to the bedroom. He returned with a pile of pictures that he had printed out. "Do you guys know what these two looked like when they were young?"

Fly and Harvey shook their heads. "Nope," Harvey said. "Neither one."

"Me neither," Fly added.

"I know which guy was here, and so does Mom. But only Mom knew them 20 years ago."

"This is killing me. Who is it, Midge? Who is it?" Kiana said.

He showed the youngest pictures of the men to his mother.

"Which one is Roscoe, and which one is Three?" Kiana pointed to the pictures of each man and said his name.

"Good job, Mom," Midge said. "Know how I know you're right?"

Kiana shrugged.

"Newspaper pictures had captions with both their names associated with their faces. Now let's look at them 20 years later."

Midge kept the two younger pictures out and pulled two older pictures from the pile. "Now, which is which."

"Oh, wow," she said. "That liar. Winslow isn't Roscoe; he's Three."

"Amazing," Fly said. "You know what this means?"

"Sure do," Harvey said. "But you say it, Fly."

"It means that Roscoe is the guy we found murdered on the mountain. Murdered with a hunting knife by Three."

"Good work Midge; you're headed for the right career."

Everybody gave Midge a high five.

"This also means that Ebony and Roscoe died about the same time. Maybe right here!"

"Don't start creeping me out, now, Fly," Kiana said. "Tell me they died someplace else."

"We don't know," he said, "but we know who knows the whole story."

Harvey was already on the phone with Chappy telling him to lock up Three.

MOTIVES

They all stood in silence for a minute, happy to establish that Three was the man they caught, but not sure what was next. "So, where are we with this mess?" Fly asked.

"Is that a rhetorical question?" Harvey asked.

"Why are you answering a question with a question?"

"Why did you just do the same thing?"

"Stop," Fly said. "I know the answer to my question."

"Then it's rhetorical." Harvey smiled. Fly shook his head and gave Harvey a knuckle bump.

"Ok. I think we were pretty close to what happened with our, get this word, Harv, speculation. Went down something like this. Three and Roscoe got into a fight over Ebony. Something happened to Ebony. Maybe she got pushed and fell or something like that. Probably an accident. I doubt either guy would hurt her on purpose. But whatever happened, Three and Roscoe were really going at it. Three pulled out a knife, and Roscoe was history. Then Three had two bodies to bury. Not sure if Roscoe was killed at Ebony's or in the field. He's dead either way."

"Not bad. Details are sketchy, but that fits with the four main causes of murder."

"Is this a detective lesson for me?"

Harvey just smiled. "The four Ls. Lust, Love, Loathing, and Loot. People are willing to kill for all these reasons."

"You're saying people love or hate each other, and they lust after other people and money. I think Ebony was killed because of love."

"Probably, Fly. Even if she died accidentally, love was probably the reason. Both guys loved Ebony. She died, and one of them ended up dying, too."

Fly continued to speculate. "Three and Roscoe didn't love each other. Jealousy and hatred. Loathing. Bad stuff. Ending up dead isn't cool, but having a theory about this stuff is cool."

"When you can figure out a motive, it makes it easier to find the killer."

"Like with Earlene and Eunice," Fly said. "Earlene wanted her sister dead. What's the motive? Not love."

"Not love, for sure," Harvey agreed.

"Loathing? Money?"

"Could be both. Could be neither. Definitely, speculation, Fly."

"Eunice was Mrs. Rich, and Earlene was Mrs. Poor, whose husband worked for the missing Mr. Rich."

"Jealousy can lead to hatred," Harvey said.

"This is cool. Keep going. What about Junior?"

"Well, we don't know where he is, but I know what I'd bet the motive is."

"Let me guess. Money. Three is saying 'give me the money,' and Junior's saying 'no way.'"

"Good theory, but no evidence yet."

"How about Philip?" Fly wondered. "The guy who knew too much. If we can figure out his secrets, we can probably figure out who killed him."

"I think we can do better than that."

"You know something I don't know, Boss?"

"Eunice was poisoned. The poison and the cup seem to have come from Earlene."

"Oh, gotcha. Philip was poisoned with arsenic, too. The cup could be the same brand as we found at Noah's house."

"Bingo."

"But what would be the motive with Philip? Would someone kill their stepson?"

"Which one of the motives?"

"Hmm. Definitely not lust or love. Maybe loathing or loot."

"Or both."

"I think we need to talk with Noah and Earlene."

"Eunice, too."

"And Felicia and Carmela. We got some talkin' to do."

Since the Zarks were still with Chappy, they decided to start with the sisters in the mansion. Eunice was sent home from the hospital thanks to the fast work of the EMTs when they got to the mansion. They began flushing her system with IV fluids before Eunice got to the hospital, and this saved her life. When she arrived at the ER, doctors immediately stepped up the treatment with further irrigation of her system. She was stabilized quickly and held in the hospital overnight.

When they went to the mansion, Harvey and Fly were greeted at the door by Felicia.

Fly whispered. "Well, at least we know she's here, alive."

"I heard you saved Eunice's life," she said. "Thank you. If you hadn't come to the house when you did, she probably would have died."

She invited them in, and Carmela joined them in the kitchen, which had been cleaned up.

"How's Eunice?" he asked. "I heard she was sent home from the hospital."

"Ha," Carmela said. "Cranky as usual. The poison didn't do anything for her mood."

"You know that the police know who poisoned her?"

Both women nodded.

"Earlene," Carmela said. "Doesn't surprise me."

"What do you mean?" Harvey asked.

"They don't see eye to eye on anything, especially money."

"Loot," Fly said.

The women looked at him as if he was weird.

"Uh, Flywheel, here is my mentee. He's learning to

258

be a detective."

"Well, Earlene wanted loot, alright. She figured that Eunice got all Junior's money, but she was wrong." Carmela said.

"What do you mean?" Harvey asked.

"Junior had all his money and investments tied up in the bank. He had trust funds for Eunice and Three."

"Not Roscoe," Felicia chimed in. "Only reason I can live here is because of Eunice, the cranky old battle axe that she is."

"Me, too," Carmela added. "She's a witch, alright, but she's okay most of the time. I wouldn't say she has a heart of gold, maybe rusted iron."

"That's the trouble with iron," Fly said. "Oxygen and iron are like oil and water, a bad mix."

"You should know," Harvey said, looking at the women. "Fly is known as the metal guy."

Fly smiled this toothy smile. "I lust for rust."

"So, do you think Eunice is up for talking about what happened?" Harvey asked.

"Sure," Felicia said. "She's ready to kill Three."

"Me too," Carmela said. "Some husband I had. No good egotistical bum. Thinks the world owes him a living."

"Loathing," Fly blurted out.

Harvey felt the need to explain that Fly was having another of his mentee moments.

The women led Harvey and Fly into the living room, where they had set up a cot for Eunice.

"Eunice, you've got company," Felicia said as she shook her awake. "These guys saved your life. They called the EMS for you. You were fading fast, Eunice."

Eunice looked at Harvey and Fly. "Thank you," she said in a barely audible voice.

"Do you know you were poisoned?" Harvey asked.

She shook her head up and down.

"Do you know how?"

"Coffee. Didn't taste it, but I guess it was there."

"Who gave you the coffee?"

"Not sure. Let me think." She closed her eyes and looked like she was going to fall asleep. "A woman."

"This is very hard for her," Carmela said. "Maybe you should come back another day."

"No," Eunice said. "My sister came to help me. I called her."

"I think this is too much for her, gentlemen," Carmela said as she tried to move them toward the door.

"No. I think it was...." She looked at Carmela. "You made some special coffee. In a paper cup, the ones left here by my sister," Eunice recalled.

Fly and Harvey looked intently at Carmela. "This is an interesting twist," Harvey said. "Did you give her the poisoned coffee, Carmela?"

"No, of course not. Why would I do that?"

"Well, let's see," Fly chimed in. "Lust, love, loathing, or loot or all of the above."

They all looked at Fly. "Motives. But which one?"

No one said anything for several seconds.

"I'll tell you which one," Felicia finally said.

Harvey and Fly turned toward the usually quiet Felicia.

"Loot. Carmela and her supposed ex-husband have been fleecing Eunice of her money for years."

"Shut up, Felicia." Carmela glared at Felicia with hatred in her eyes.

Eunice coughed. "True," Eunice said. "Carmela. No, you're no good. And that husband of yours is worse."

Carmela raised her arm as if she was going to hit Eunice. Fly quickly moved in and grabbed Carmela's arm, and pulled her away. "Better call Chappy," he said.

Harvey nodded and reached into his pocket for the phone.

When Fly let go of her arm, Carmela turned and headed for the stairs.

"My chase," Fly said as he ran up just behind her.

Carmela ran up the wide stairway, went into her room, and grabbed a rifle that was next to her bed. Fly was right behind her, and when he reached the doorway, Carmela was aiming her long rifle straight at his head.

"Here we go again," he said. "Don't go pointin' that thing at me."

"It's loaded this time. You're not going to arrest me, you two-bit cop."

"Yes, I am." Fly's chatter nerves kicked in. "It's going to be my first arrest, but technically I can't arrest anyone. Maybe just a citizen's arrest. You see I ..."

"Shut up."

She raised the gun and fired a warning shot above his head into the hallway behind him. The bullet hit the ornate chandelier spraying shards of glass all over the landing.

"Whoa," Fly exclaimed as he ducked and ran out of the line of fire."

As soon as he heard the shot, Harvey ran up the stairs, his arm extended with his pistol in his hand. Carmela came to the doorway and turned to face Harvey. She raised her rifle again, but Fly came up behind her, grabbed her around the neck, and pulled her backward. As she fell, she discharged another round into the ceiling. Harvey grabbed the gun, rolled her over, and put his knee on her back to hold her down.

"You okay, Fly?" Harvey asked.

"Sure. I'm fine. You know where the bathroom is?"

"Just get something to tie her hands with. I don't carry cuffs anymore."

Fly returned in a couple of minutes with a drape cord he found in the room near the bathroom. He tied her hands and walked her downstairs.

"You knew this would happen, Carmela," Felicia said. "You could only go on robbing Eunice for so long. Twenty years has been way too long."

They heard sirens coming up the lane, and before

261

long, Chappy was in the house. He spoke with Eunice, Felicia, Harvey, and Fly about what happened.

"Before you do anything, Chappy, I'd like to say something to the perpetrator," Fly said.

Harvey and Chappy looked at each other, hoping Fly wouldn't do something outrageous.

Fly spoke directly to Carmela. "Mrs. Carmela Marlowe III, I place you under citizen's arrest for the attempted murders of me and Eunice Marlowe and the murder of Junior Marlowe and Philip Rhinehart." He turned to Harvey and Chappy, broadcasting one of his signature toothy smiles.

WHODUNNIT

When the police arrived, they exchanged Carmela's drapery cords for handcuffs and ushered her to the police car for a trip to the Stillwell jail.

When she was out of earshot, Harvey yelled at Fly. "What? Under arrest? Junior? Philip? What's going on, Fly? You don't have any evidence for Junior or Philip's murders."

"That's what you think, Boss, but I've been talking with my protégée."

"Protégée? How can a mentee have a protégée?"

"Same way I can be a mentee to youtee. Hey, we can prove it all, Harv."

"Wonderful," Chappy said. "A retired detective turned celebrity with a detective wannabe who's putting people under arrest."

"You can't do this," Harvey said to Fly.

"I know I can't place anyone under arrest, BUT ..." He raised his arm with this finger pointing authoritatively. "But I CAN prove who killed Junior and Philip and who tried to kill Eunice." Fly nodded his head and smirked. "Oh, and I think we can explain Ebony's death, too."

"I hate to hear this, but who's your protégée, mentee?" Harvey asked.

"Midge. He's smart and can figure these things out."

"Do you have evidence?" Chappy wanted to know. "No evidence, no case."

"Working on that. But you have our main suspect. Need to tie some loose ends together."

"Let's hear what you have to say about Carmela. Why do you think she's involved?"

"You saw how she acted today. Faked being asleep with her clothes on. Hardly fooled anybody. Gun was a dead giveaway, too." Fly laughed and slapped his knee. "Dead giveaway. Get it?"

Chappy furrowed his brow. "I get it, but let me say what I think you're saying. Carmela put poison in a cup of coffee that she gave to Eunice."

"Arsenic. Midge says the victim can't taste it. He did the research."

"The cup was a paper cup like you might get at a big box store in large volume," Harvey noted.

"Lifetime supply for $15.99."

"Doubt that, but Carmela had some. Where'd she gets them?" Harvey asked.

"Probably, Earlene. Noah says Earlene's a shopper. Remember?"

"Not really, but I'll take your word for it."

Chappy wanted to pin things down. "So why would Earlene give her cups?"

Harvey laughed. "Ever been in their house?"

Chappy shook his head.

"Small bungalow. A couple of small bedrooms. One bedroom for Noah, Earlene, and Diesel. One bedroom for stuff. Looks like an annex for Frugal's Discount Center. She has a thing for paper. Toilet paper, paper towels, cups, you name it. She's ready for the next shortage of paper products. Bet she has a lifetime supply of the stuff."

"So, she gives the products away to family and others, right?" Chappy speculated.

"Guess so. I even saw some over at the swami's center. Cups, just like the ones that did the swami's son in." Fly said. "Didn't think much of it 'til now."

"Let's see if I understand this cup thing," Chappy said. "Eunice is poisoned with a cup that has arsenic in it. One of the same kind of cups you could buy at Frugal's. Right?"

"Yup," Fly said.

"Philip is poisoned with arsenic in coffee in the same kind of cup. Right?"

"Might say that," Fly said.

"Who else might have some of Earlene's paper cups?"

"I'd check the swami's place if I were you. Or maybe the protégée and I could do that for you."

"NO," Chappy said. "I don't want you messing up the investigation."

"Just joshing you again, Snappy. I'm not going back there again. Too creepy for me."

"So why should we check the swami … just for the cups that half the people in Stillwell also have?" Chappy grimaced. "We need a better reason than that to talk with them."

"Okay, how's this, Snappy? 'Cause swami's grandmommy knows a lot more than she lets on. Remember, she's Philip's mommy. Philip went by the name of Rhinehart, but that wasn't her maiden name. He got that name from the foster family who had him for a couple of years."

"What was her maiden name?" Chappy asked.

"Well, I had my protégée look into this. Amazing what you can find out about people on the internet."

"Cut the small talk, Fly. What was the swami's maiden name?" Chappy was growing impatient.

"You're not going to believe this."

"You're not going to be alive to tell us if you don't stop playing games. Spit it out."

"Same last name as two other people in this mess."

Chappy and Harvey looked at each other while Fly put on his toothy smile.

"Eunice and Earlene?" Harvey asked.

"Fly just smiled. You win an all-expense paid trip to the swami's house to get her to tell you."

"Are you saying she's a Gody?" Chappy asked.

"I'd bet my paycheck on it," Fly said. "She's a Gody, Earlene's a Gody, and Eunice is a Gody."

"I bet they were all taking food and coffee to Philip," Harvey observed. "In those paper cups and other paper products."

"Yup. They were all related to Philip. Swami's grandmommy, Aunt Earlene, and Aunt Eunice. Think any of them would kill Philip?"

"Doubt it unless Philip had something big on them," Harvey responded.

"This raises more questions," Chappy said.

"Carmela had access to the cups through Eunice. She kept Eunice pickled so she wouldn't really know what was going on. Sent her to the hospital often to show she wasn't well," Harvey said.

"Yup." Fly was still smiling.

"What about the arsenic?" Chappy wanted to know. "How would she get that?"

"Easy peasy," Fly said. "This is an old farm. They used arsenic as a pesticide, but they killed that idea years ago." He chuckled and slapped his knee. "But there was still some hanging around the barn. Betcha, we'd find some over there now."

"You don't need a lot," Harvey said. "Ollie said a teaspoon in a cup of coffee could kill you in no time."

"If we go with what Fly is saying, Carmela puts the arsenic in coffee and gives it to Eunice," Chappy said.

"Might have done the same to Felicia, too. She'd be a threat to Carmela when she learned for sure that Roscoe's dead." Harvey noted.

"Ok, men," Chappy said. "How did Carmela kill Philip, and more importantly, why would she do it? What did Philip know?"

"Ooh, you sound so detectivey, Snappy. I have to remember those questions when I have my own PI business."

"What did he know?" Chappy repeated.

Fly and Harvey didn't respond.

"This is where it gets tough," Chappy continued.

"We don't have a real motive for Carmela. We can prove she tried to kill Eunice, but we need more evidence for Philip's murder."

"Loot, Chappy," Fly said. "Heard the saying, 'Loot's the root'?"

"Never heard that one. I'm sure money was a big part of her motive, but not with Philip. I don't know that he had any money."

"She was there, though, at the gazebo, Chappy. Before the murder. Setting the stage." Harvey said. "Tell him, Fly."

Fly went on to tell Chappy how they went back in time reviewing Tootie's security cameras that captured the gazebo and sidewalk areas nearby. "Have Raven and her forensics team take another look at the gazebo video. You won't see anything until a couple of days before Philip is murdered. Go back in time from there, and you'll see somebody—Carmela—painting the camera lenses at the gazebo and other places, including Tootie's."

"I'll have them look at that, Fly, but I'm not sure they have the time. Video searching eats time. We also need to know why the mansion women went to see the swami each month," Chappy continued. "That must tie into this somehow. Let's do some more leg work and meet here tomorrow."

"Ok, Chappy," Harvey said. "I think Fly, and I might go visit swami Gody again. We need some straight talk from her."

On their way out, Eunice and Felicia thanked Harvey and Fly for saving their lives.

THE BARN

Harvey called Chappy to tell him they needed to check the barn to find arsenic and follow up on Fly's suspicion that Junior might be there. Chappy's initial response was to say that they didn't want to get a warrant to do the search, but Harvey pointed out that he could prove or disprove Fly's claim by checking. He changed his mind and said they would get a warrant.

The next day, they met at the Marlowe barn at 10:00 a.m. Fly, Harvey, and Midge joined Chappy and Ollie Kingston to tour the barn with flashlights in hand. Fly opened the pull-up door on the floor on the first level of the barn and led the group down the old wooden stairs to the basement level. The basement was filled with cobwebs and had a musty smell from its lack of fresh air.

"Over there," Fly pointed. "That's the old root cellar. There are old jars of pickled stuff in there. Don't eat anything. They didn't have refrigeration back then, so ..."

"Fly," Harvey said abruptly to get him back on track.

"Geez, just adding some color commentary." Fly pointed his flashlight at the door with the padlock on it. "This is where we think there might be something interesting."

Chappy rolled his eyes.

"My assistant, Midge, or Big Little Fly, brought along a hammer to break the lock. Okay, Snappy?"

Chappy nodded. Midge whacked the lock with all his might, and it popped open. He deferred to Chappy to take the lock off and open the door.

The dirt room was a mess, chock-full of old equipment piled helter-skelter. There was a very narrow pathway that led from the door to the back wall of the barn. The narrow room was only about 20 feet long and 10 feet wide. There were old car parts, old radio tubes, a very large TV with a tiny screen, some old paint cans, and whatever else the Marlowes wanted to discard over the years.

I wonder if Junior is discarded here, too, Harvey thought.

"I don't see anything, Wizard," Chappy said. "I think this is a lost cause."

"Excuse me," Midge said. "There's so much stuff in here that if something were buried underneath it, you wouldn't know it."

"I'm not taking all this stuff out of here," Chappy said. "I'd be wheezing from all this dust, and I don't see a single clue that would cause us to pull all this stuff out."

Fly looked at Midge, and they both looked at Harvey. They all nodded.

"Here's what we're willing to do, Chappy," Harvey said. "Since you don't want to look for the evidence, we can remove these treasures from the room one item at a time."

"I don't want you messing with the evidence."

"We know that, Chappy, so if we find something, we'll stop and tell you. If you aren't here, we'll call you at the donut shop."

"Don't get flip with me, Harvey. I don't like donuts, anyway." He tugged on the belt on his narrow waist, looked over at Harvey's potbelly, and smiled.

Chappy told them that he had plenty to do and should be called if they found something. "Officer Cannon will be here to observe. He won't be lifting any equipment."

"Of course not," Fly said.

They began by removing the stuff by the doorway. Item by item, they carried the debris out to the open area outside the room. They showed each piece to Officer Cannon, who looked thoroughly bored by the procedure. "Speed it up," he said.

"Want to help? It'll make it go a lot faster," Fly said. Officer Cannon didn't reply.

"Can I put this stuff in my truck?" Fly shook his

head, suggesting yes, and smiled.

"Wishful thinking," Harvey replied.

They continued to remove items piece by piece until the room was empty. Nothing but bone-dry dirt was left. They took an "air break" to clear their lungs. When they came back downstairs, they used their bright, LED Maglite that provided over 1000 lumens to check the dirt floor.

"Do you see that?" Midge asked. "Look up by the back corner."

"Looks like what the kids saw on the mountain grave," Fly said. "There's a slight depression in the dirt floor in the corner."

"Call Ollie," Harvey said to Officer Cannon. "He's been on standby."

Ollie arrived in about 20 minutes. He came downstairs and walked into the dirt room.

"Mr. Kingston, why is that area depressed when the rest of the floor is very dry and flat?" Midge asked.

Ollie looked at the area and then the rest of the room. "It's different, that's for sure. Excuse me. I want to call Chappy." He climbed the stairs, made his call, and quickly returned.

"We think we should dig that area up," Ollie said. "Chappy is sending the forensic team out, and we'll take it from here. You all can leave now."

The men started to walk up the stairs.

"Wait," Fly interrupted. "Before we leave, we should look at what's in the containers in the other section of the barn. We'll need Ollie's help on that one, too."

The troop reversed themselves and walked to the other end of the basement.

"Mr. Kingston," Fly began. "See all these containers?"

Ollie nodded.

"Do we know what's in them?"

"Probably some old fertilizer or chemicals used on

the farm."

"Recent stuff?"

He shook his head. "Old, very old."

"Like back when they used arsenic to get rid of pests on plants?"

"Could be."

"If any of these powders is arsenic, could it still be deadly?"

"Possibly," Ollie said, "but we'd need to test it in the lab."

"This could be the murder weapon, right?"

"Possibly, Fly," Ollie said.

Midge spoke up. "If you look at them, all but one of the containers hasn't been touched in years. One of them looks like it's been opened more recently than the others."

Ollie went over to the container in question. He took a picture of it as well as one that had not been disturbed. He took a plastic bag from his pocket and put a small scoop of the powder in it.

"If it's arsenic, we'll know soon," Ollie said. "Good work, young man."

"That's my boy," Fly said. "Oh, no, I mean, way to go, son. No, no, good work, Midge."

Harvey and Midge laughed. Ollie looked confused. He didn't get it.

Ollie waited for the forensic team to come and dig up the suspicious area in the dirt room. Harvey, Fly, and Midge headed back to Harvey's house to await the news in the Situation Room.

Within hours, the team found remains of a body in the basement grave. They photographed the site and body, looked for other clues, and then took the body back to the morgue. The forensic examiner who came to the site looked at the powder they had bagged and gave a preliminary finding of arsenic.

Finally, around 4:00 pm, Chappy called Harvey,

who immediately put the phone on speaker. "Guys, are you ready for this?"

"You kidding? Tell us, c'mon," Fly said.

"Well, you nailed it, Fly. You and Harvey nailed it."

"Midge, too." Fly reminded him.

"There was a body under the dirt like you predicted. I don't know how you predicted it when the room was locked."

"His nose and his gut, Chappy," Harvey said. "I don't get that, but he's got a nose like a bloodhound and a gut that's wired to his brain."

"Aw shucks. You're embarrassing me," Fly replied.

"But we still have one more thing to figure out," Chappy said. "Philip. Fly, you said Carmela killed Philip, too."

"She did," he replied

"But we found the same cups used to poison Eunice in Earlene's house."

"Find any arsenic?" Harvey asked.

"Yeah. Noah said that was old stuff. Hadn't used it in 30 years."

"But we also found arsenic in the barn at the mansion," Fly added.

"Hmm. You have a point."

"And if you look further in the mansion, I bet you'll find a whole mess of those cups. I don't think the sisters like to do dishes," Fly said.

"Could be Three or Carmela," Midge observed

"I think they were both in on all these murders," Fly said. "Three was either murdering or helping. He probably did a lot of digging, too."

"We've got the clincher on Carmela, Chappy," Harvey said. "Did your team look at that video of the gazebo we told you about?"

"Not yet. We're really ..."

"Busy, we know," Fly interjected.

"Better have them get on that, Chappy," Harvey

said. "It proves that Carmela was at the gazebo and painted the cameras so she could poison Philip."

"And while you're at it, Snappy," Fly said. "Check out the sneakers Carmela was wearing when you put her in jail. They look mighty familiar, especially when you compare them to the videos of the person painting the camera lenses near the gazebo."

"Ok. I'll get on it right away. We also need to interview Noah and Earlene again to see if they will implicate these two."

"We still have one more bit of detective work to do," Harvey said.

"We do?" Fly looked curiously at Harvey.

"Yes. We have to figure out why the sisters visited Madam Dubois once a month."

"We know that she's Philip's mommy," Fly said.

"But that doesn't tell us much. We need to pay another visit," Harvey said.

"No. That's where I draw the line. No way. I'm not getting freaked out again."

"I'll pick you up at the park in an hour, Fly."

"If I'm not there, you go on without me."

"You'll be there. This might have something to do with one of the 4Ls, Fly. Loot. Our loot!"

"See you in an hour, Harv. Green's my favorite color."

ANOTHER SWAMI VISIT

Fly was quiet on the ride over to the Clairvoyant Center. As they approached Groveland Street, his Jimmy's knees started jiggling.

"What are you worried about, Fly?" Harvey asked.

"Can't help it."

"Swami grand mommy thinks you're her hero. We were fine last visit. If fact, you calmed her down, remember?"

Fly wasn't smiling. "Let's just get this over with. Just need to know why the sisters visited."

"And we need to listen for more information. We need to know what Philip knew. I'll take the lead in this interview but chime in, Fly, if you see or hear something that needs follow-up. But no wise guy stuff or I'll ask her to do a creepy reading just for you."

Fly shivered as a cold wind blew past him. They walked up to the door, rang the doorbell, and the organ music began to play. Fly pivoted and started to walk back toward the car. Harvey grabbed his shirt and yanked him back just as Madam Marlena opened the door.

"Oh," she said. "I didn't expect to see you men back here, but come in. Mother has been upset. I think she's still mourning Philip's death. To tell you the truth, I'm still trying to get a grip on the fact that he was my brother."

"We'd like to talk with your mother if that's okay. We think we may have a suspect in Philip's death. She might clarify things."

"Certainly." Madam Marlene gestured for them to come in.

"Just one thing, Madam," Fly said. "Could we talk here in the living room? No readings or talking to Philip. Okay?"

She smiled and nodded. "I'll bring mother out here. Please have a seat."

"Oh, and one more thing," Fly said. "Could you

please turn off that organ music? It gives me the willies."

Marlena smiled and left the room. Harvey looked at Fly. "The willies? That's a new one, Fly."

"Haven't said that in a long time. Used to say it whenever we were going to watch The Wizard of Oz as a kid."

"Not that again. Have you seen a therapist about that movie?"

"Wasn't just the movie. My brother used to laugh like that creepy witch when he wanted me to freak out. Creepy things like organ music and talking to dead people give me the willies."

"Well, my little pretty," Harvey whined and then laughed.

Fly shivered. "Stop it. That's what he used to say."

The curtain to the parlor was pulled back, and swami's grandmommy appeared in her flowing turquoise gown. "Good morning, gentlemen. I'm glad to see you back here. How may I help you?"

"We'd like your help, Madam DuBois," Harvey began.

She nodded.

"And we'll be as open and honest with you as we can be. We'd appreciate you reciprocating."

"I'll try," she said.

"We are trying to solve Philip's murder, and we think we have a suspect."

"That's good. I want to get to the bottom of this. I may have been a horrible mother, but I want to see justice done."

Harvey let the comment pass. "For starters, we believe that you would bring food and drink to Philip. Right?"

"Yes."

"And you used to bring drinks in paper cups. The tall kind that you can get at big box stores like Frugal's."

"That's right. Usually coffee. He always liked his

coffee, especially at night in the winter."

"How often did you visit with him?"

"At least once a week, sometimes twice."

"Did he ever say anything to you about the women in the mansion... the ones who would visit you each month?"

She was silent for what seemed like an eternity. "Well, yes. He didn't like them. Said they were dangerous, and he didn't trust them."

"All of them?"

"Not Felicia. She's like a pussy cat. Quiet."

"Eunice?"

"She was okay for a long time. They used to just come over to visit. You know, sisterly, even though Felicia wasn't my sister."

"Did anyone else come with them?"

Madam DuBois paused, then said, "Most of the time, it was just Eunice and Felicia."

"What about Carmela?"

"Oh, that's when things got nasty. She wasn't here for a long time. I didn't see her for almost 20 years. Then a couple of years ago, she just showed up."

"So that's why I only met two women when I used to visit them," Harvey thought aloud. "So, let's see if I have this right. When Junior and Three went missing, it was just Eunice and Felicia in the house."

"That's right," Madam Dubois said.

"And then Carmela arrived."

"Out of the blue, she just showed up." She paused to digest a bad memory. "That's when she came here to visit me and pressure me for money."

"Right in front of Eunice and Felicia?"

She nodded. "She made me sign an insurance policy with her as the beneficiary. A million dollars. I didn't have a choice."

"Why did you feel so pressured to sign it?"

"Philip. She threatened to expose me as his mother.

Even hinted that she might kill him and leave evidence that I killed him."

"Whoa," Fly chimed in. "That's horrible."

Harvey returned to the questioning.

"What else might Philip have known that might cause her to want to get rid of him?"

"You know he worked for the Marlowe family when Junior disappeared. Right around the time when Three and Roscoe disappeared."

"Yes. What did he do?"

"He was still young, around 20. Did odd jobs, anything they needed help with."

Fly entered the conversation. "Excuse me. Did he know Three and Roscoe?"

"Sure. Unfortunately, they introduced him to the joys of drugs. That was his downfall. Got into all kinds of drugs. He found it safer as a homeless man than being around Three and Roscoe."

"Smart. But being around those guys was dumb."

"Yes," she replied. "And being addicted means you make poor decisions. You can't tell smart from dumb sometimes."

Harvey wanted to get to the core of what they needed to know. "So, Madam, we're trying to figure out what Philip knew that made him a threat to someone else."

"Ha. What didn't he know, especially about those women in the mansion?"

"Like what?"

"For starters, Felicia and Eunice were held like prisoners in that place."

"By?"

"Carmela. Sweet Carmela. Talk nice to your face, but don't turn your back on her. Devil in sheep's clothing."

"What were they like when they came here?"

"Pathetic. Eunice and Felicia were like sheep, and Carmela did all the talking. It was a shakedown. She knew I knew she had something to do with the disappearances. I learned that from Philip."

"Wow," Fly said. His knees had stopped shaking.

Harvey continued. "Was Three still involved with Carmela?"

"Sure. He came to see her, and she went someplace outside Philly to see him. He was on the run from the law, and she was holding his secret together."

"And what's that secret?"

"That they killed Junior to get at his money sooner. In their view, Eunice was a second wife, and as the first son, Three thought he should receive most of the estate. I never heard what the will said, but Three didn't care. He was hell-bent on getting the money."

"Loot," Fly blurted out.

"Excuse him, Madam," Harvey said. "Fly is referring to the fact that money was the motive here."

The madam continued. "The women used to visit Philip. They brought him coffee in Earlene's cups. That's what they called them. She hoards paper goods like there's going to be another pandemic. She gave us all paper products—cups, plates, bowls. Napkins and paper towels too. And, oh yes, lots of toilet paper."

Harvey looked intently at Madam Dubois. "Philip knew that Carmela was controlling the mess in the mansion."

"We all did. The sisters."

"Sisters?"

"You know that Eunice, Earlene, and I are sisters, right?"

"Well, flip my pancake," Fly interjected, pretending this was news to him. "You three are sisters? Wow."

Harvey winked at Fly.

"We're pretty sure that Carmela poisoned Philip. We just need some evidence."

"I'd look for some poison, for starters," she said. "Then take a look into Carmela's insurance. I'm pretty sure she used some of the money she got from me to pay for a

278

big insurance policy on Philip. Probably got him high on crack and had him sign a substantial insurance agreement. Probably cashed it in already."

"Did she ever try that with your sisters?"

"I know Eunice made her the sole beneficiary, and I did, too."

"If we can find some arsenic, get Earlene to tell us that she delivered cups to Eunice, and get hold of insurance policies for Philip and Eunice, we've got her," Fly said.

"But what about Junior? Looks like Three did him in, but we need to prove that."

"There's still work to do, Boss," Fly said.

They looked at Madam Marlena, who appeared to be in shock.

"Mother. Why didn't you tell me all this was going on?"

"I didn't want you or the grandkids involved. I made them come here when the kids were in school and you were out of the house."

Madam Marlena looked at Fly and Harvey. "Gentlemen. You have our full cooperation. We want these criminals arrested and sent where they belong. Thank you for bringing this to our attention."

They thanked the two madams for their information and left. When they got outside, Fly said, "You were good in there, Boss. I took a lot of notes."

Harvey looked puzzled.

Fly pointed to his head. "Mental."

They called Chappy and made arrangements to tell him what they had learned.

BACK TO THE ZARKS

The Zarks had been released from custody and were at home. Harvey felt that it would be best to just show up to the house unannounced and try to let them know that they know a lot more about the dynamics of the Marlowe family.

Both men drove separately and, for once, arrived at the Zark's house at the same time. They got out of their vehicles, and Harvey pointed to Fly to make him go first to avoid having Diesel jump on him. As if on cue, Diesel ran right to Fly, sat down, looked longingly at him, and wagged his tail. Fly patted his head, scratched his ears, and signaled for him to lead them to the front door.

Noah was standing outside the door by the time they came up the walk. "I'm not talking to you. I had nothing to do with murder, understand? And Earlene had nothing to do with this mess. So as far as we're concerned, this case is closed for us."

"We know how you must feel, Noah," Harvey said in his most sincere voice. "We just need to talk with Earlene to clarify some facts. We think we know who killed Philip, Junior, Roscoe, and Ebony and who almost killed Eunice."

Noah thought for a minute, and Harvey and Fly knew better than to say anything.

"Just a minute." He opened the door and yelled in. "Earlene. Think you need to be part of this conversation. Come out here."

Earlene came right out, and they all stood scowling in silence on the lawn. Finally, Noah broke the silence. "Ok. Men. You came here, so tell us what you want."

"Yes," Harvey began. "We can't tell you everything you'd like to know, but we are seeking information about your paper collection, Earlene."

"What? People are murdered and almost murdered, and you want to know about paper?"

Fly jumped in. "Could we see a sample of the cups you have? The ones you bought at Frugal's."

Still confused but willing to find out what was going on, Earlene went into the house and brought out a paper cup.

"Is this the only kind of cup you have?" Fly continued.

"Yup. The only kind that Frugal sells. I'm a power shopper there, you know."

"Yes, we know. Mind if we take this with us to compare to other cups?"

"I can tell you you'll find some at Eunice's. And at my other sister's too."

Feigning ignorance, Fly said, "And that other sister would be?"

"Come on, Mr. Fly. You know as well as I do who she is."

Fly broadcasted a big smile. "Sure. Swami grandmommy."

"What?"

"That's what we call her. Grandkids call her that, too."

"She goes by Madam DuBois, but to me, she's just Mia Gody, my big sister. She has nothing to do with the murders."

Harvey stepped in to reassure her. "Of course, we know that, but all three of you had interactions with the other person living at the mansion. Carmela."

Earlene scowled again. "You have no idea. She's evil. The wicked witch is what we call her."

Fly shivered, and Harvey put his hand on his shoulder. Fly imagined the Wicked Witch of the West, stooped and green-skinned, dressed in black.

"Yes," Harvey said. "We've heard she's somewhat controlling."

"Somewhat controlling? Try downright threatening. Murderous. Evil."

"How did she try to control you, Earlene?" Harvey asked.

"Every way she could. Blackmail. Lies. Threats. If it wasn't for Noah, I'd probably be in prison for trying to kill her."

"Well, we're glad you're here. But you use some strong language to describe her. How do you think she's tied into these missing men and the murders?"

"Let it out, Earlene," Noah said. "This mess has been buried for way too long."

"Ok. I'll tell you the truth. First, you may know that my sister and Noah were an item back when they were in high school. And, well, you sure you want me to say this, Noah?"

"I'll say it," Noah said. "I fathered a child with Mia, and that child was Philip."

"Momma Mia," Fly blurted out.

Harvey glared at him, but Earlene broke into laughter. She laughed and laughed. "Here we go again," she said and laughed some more.

"I'm sorry, Earlene," Harvey said, but Earlene was still laughing.

"Oh, don't be. I haven't laughed in a long time. Thank you, Mr. Fly."

Fly was showing his toothy smile.

"So," Harvey said. "It would be very helpful if we could know what you know about Carmela and possibly Three."

Earlene repeated the same allegations that Madam DuBois said, including making Carmela the beneficiary of a million-dollar insurance policy. She knew that Philip had signed a similar policy. As soon as he did, he was in trouble. A candidate for murder.

When they felt that they had their questions answered, Harvey thanked the Zarks, and Fly looked at Earlene. "When you see your sister next time, you know what to call her."

Earlene just laughed and gave Fly a hug. "You might be terrible at paying your debts, but you know how to cheer me up."

They were all smiling as Harvey and Fly headed back up the sidewalk. Diesel started barking. Harvey turned around to see him galloping at full speed toward him. "Oh no," were the last words Harvey said before Diesel leaped up and pushed him with his two strong front paws.

"Diesel," Fly yelled. "Go." The big dog dutifully went back to Noah, and Fly grabbed Harvey's arm to help him up.

They continued to the vehicles, with Earlene's laughter providing background music for their exit.

CONFESSIONS AND REWARDS

When they left the Zark's house, Harvey and Fly headed straight to Chappy's office.

"The super sleuths," Chappy greeted them.

"Aw shucks, Snappy, you're making me blush," Fly said.

"Right," Chappy said. "Let's make this a wrap."

"Did you see the security video from before Philip's murder yet?" Fly reminded Chappy.

"Oh yeah. Let me call Raven over at forensics right now. She was the one that looked at the security video." Chappy placed the call, and Harvey and Fly listened to his "uh huh" and looked at his head nods while Raven updated him. Finally, he ended the call.

"Well, Fly," Chappy said. "That was good evidence. According to Raven, those shoes belonged to Carmela, and the body type and gait were like hers. They're going over to the mansion to look for the hoodie. Nice job, guys."

"You can thank Fly for that one," Harvey said.

Fly and Harvey brought Chappy up to date with minimal details about their trip to see Madam Dubois. They made him swear to secrecy about anything they would say about Madam Dubois, Noah, or Earlene. Chappy knew Philip's parentage, so they only told him that both Noah and Madam Dubois were being blackmailed by Carmela. They also told him that Carmela was basically holding the two other women hostages in the mansion.

"That's the part I don't get," Fly said. "Why would those ladies put up with her?"

"Why does anyone put up with being bullied?" Harvey said. "Fear is a powerful weapon. These ladies were afraid for their lives. Look what happened to Eunice."

"You're right, Harvey," Chappy said. "We see this all the time. Bullies lie, cheat, threaten, and do anything to reach their goals."

"Loot," Fly blurted out. "They wanted Junior's

284

money."

"And they got some of it, twenty years' worth," Harvey said. "But they wanted it all and then some. Millions that rightfully belonged to Eunice."

"Speaking of money," Fly said.

"Don't," Harvey said.

Fly ignored him. "There's a reward for whoever solves this case. $150K, I think."

"Nope," Chappy said.

"What?" Fly's eyes widened. "We worked hard for that money, and now you're saying we aren't getting it?"

"Focus, Fly," Harvey said. "He didn't say we aren't getting it."

"Well, men," Chappy was being deliberately slow with his explanation. "It seems that the surviving victim, in this case, is very grateful. Eunice is so grateful that she's doubled the reward. You guys now have $300K to split."

"You kidding?" Fly said. "$300K. You hear that, Harvey?" Fly stood up and started to dance around the conference room. He gave Harvey and Chappy high fives.

"We're going to have a special ceremony next week to celebrate the end of this case and to honor the fallen victims. You'll get your checks then. Be thinking because you'll be expected to say something," Chappy said.

———

A week later, at 2:00 p.m. on a warm and cloudless spring day, crowds gathered at the gazebo in the square for the award ceremony. Tootie's closed down for an hour so she could attend. Most of her regulars, as she called them, were also there—Rex, Oscar, Alice, Jeb, and Rosie. Noah and Earlene were there, as were Madam Marlena and Madam Dubois. Even Donut was there, standing by an ambulance in case there was an emergency among the attendees. Eunice and Felicia came to the event dressed in their finest attire.

The dignitaries sat in chairs on the gazebo, and

Harvey and Fly chose to sit on the bench where Philip spent most of his time. Chief Jenkins, Chappy, Ollie Kingston, and Mayor Feedler were also seated in the gazebo.

There was a large crowd of local residents who had been following the case for many years and wanted to see the local heroes get their reward. Channel 8 news reporter Heather Compton and a camera crew were broadcasting the event live, and Gazette reporter, Bob Gilpain, had a voice recorder hanging around his neck and was taking copious notes as he asked the crowd to comment on their feelings about the murders and the solution of the crimes.

A Scout from Troop 46 led the group in the Pledge of Allegiance, and the Stillwell High School band played the Star Spangled Banner. Greta Gringwald, Tootie's cousin and head of the town council, welcomed everyone. She told the crowd that today everyone was safer because of the selfless acts of heroism performed by Harvey and Flywheel. The crowd cheered.

Next, Chief Jenkins praised the work of his department, especially that of Chappy and Ollie. The crowd cheered again.

Mayor Feedler spoke next and told the crowd how proud he was of the Stillwell Police Department as well as the guests of honor. He went on to cite the many accomplishments of his administration and how open he was listening to the citizens. He never mentioned that he would be running for re-election later in the year.

The mayor concluded by bringing Harvey and Fly to the podium and presenting each one with a check for $150K. He thanked Eunice for her generosity and expressed his remorse at the loss of her husband.

Finally, it was time for Fly and Harvey to speak. Harvey spoke first, expressing thanks to Eunice, Chappy, Ollie, and especially Fly.

"My partner in this cold case has been a man that most of you know. The man with a nose for metal, a gut for detective work, and a heart of gold. The man we call Flywheel."

The crowd rose to their feet and gave Harvey and Flywheel a standing ovation punctuated by cheers, hoots, and whistles.

When Fly got up to speak, he noticed Kiana and Midge standing toward the back of the crowd. He thanked everyone, especially Harvey, who he said "taught me how to be a gumshoe. So, I guess I'm a metalhead with gum on my shoes." The crowd laughed. Then Flywheel got serious. "You know, these murders were all because of loot. Money." He held up the check. "I got into all this because of loot. I wanted this reward as much as I wanted to catch the bad dudes and dudettes. But along the way, I discovered someone who helped solve this case. He's smart and will one day make a great detective. His name will sound familiar. He's the only other person who has my name, Flywheel." The crowd applauded, and Midge raised his hand and smiled as a gesture of thanks.

"Midge, that's his nickname, folks," Fly said. "Midge, you know that's a young fly. Come up here, Midge." The crowd laughed.

Midge hesitated, but Kiana gave him a nudge, and he walked up the steps to the gazebo. Fly continued. "You know, when I started with this case, I had no idea what I was doin'. I mean, I knew nothin'. Cops were people I stayed away from. The only reason I joined up with Harvey was for the money." Fly raised his right arm like he was taking an oath. "Truth. That's the truth. But the more I got into it, the more I realized how complicated figuring out crime is. But then, I met Midge here. Smart buzzard. Really helped us solve this case."

The crowd applauded and cheered.

"So, here's what I'm going to do." The crowd hushed, and Fly looked at Midge. "I'm going to help you with your education, Midge. Next year you're going to State as a Junior. I'm going to pay for all your expenses—tuition, room, board, or whatever until you graduate."

Midge was speechless. He hugged Fly and whispered to Fly. "You're like the Dad I never had. Thanks."

Kiana looked like a proud mother as she wiped away her tears of joy.

Chappy got up and shook Midge's hand. "Midge, when you finish your degree, call me right away. And keep up the good work."

Harvey was feeling moved by the moment, so he stood up again. "Ladies and Gentlemen, what Fly has done will make all the difference in Midge's life. Nice, Fly. I'd like to make a difference in someone's life, too. Therefore, I'm giving my reward, all of it, $150,000, to the scholarship fund at Stillwell High School. I want this money invested and the interest to go for a scholarship for a student with lots of potential but little money. I'd like this to be called the Philip Rhinehart Memorial Scholarship. Like Fly, I realized along the way in this journey that I was chasing the wrong reward. It wasn't all about the money. Justice is far more important than money." The crowd went wild.

As the program ended, the reporters rushed to the gazebo to get quotes from Harvey, Fly, and Midge.

DEBRIEFING AT TOOTIE'S

The next day, the Gazette headlines and Eyewitness News reports were more upbeat and cheerful than they had been for over 20 years. Both Heather Compton and Bob Gilpain captured the award ceremony in detail and ran it as the lead story.

Harvey and Fly showed up for the meeting of the regulars at Tootie's. The café filled with whistles and cheers when they arrived. There seemed to be more people than usual at Tootie's. The famous duo was flooded with questions. Patrons wanted to know every gory detail of the cold case.

"Saw both your pictures in the Gazette this morning," Tootie said as she held up the paper. "This is much better than that other shot of you a few weeks ago, Harvey."

"I don't know about that," Rexie said. "This looks like the kind of shot that you get when you are awarded for saving a dog stuck on the ice at Milford Lake. But a butt shot, that's special."

Rosie wanted to get to the nitty-gritty. "Ok, guys. So, what was Carmela doing while her husband or ex-husband or whatever he is was out doing who knows what?"

Fly laughed. "I'll tell you what, Rosie. When he was out doing who knows what, she was here scooping up hush money from Eunice, Madam Dubois, Noah, and Earlene. She was busy spending what she wanted and keeping Three in cash wherever he was."

"I don't get it," Oscar chimed in. "How did this mess go undetected for so long? He must have visited here, and she must have visited him."

"She left with Three after Junior was killed and didn't return for about 18 years," Harvey said. "A relationship built more on money than love. In fact, I don't think love was part of their lives at all."

"He must have killed Ebony and Roscoe at about the same time. Maybe Junior, too," Jeb speculated.

"The way we think it happened, with a big emphasis on think, is that Three and Roscoe were arguing about Ebony in Kiana's apartment," Harvey said. "A love triangle. The three of them were the only ones there. The argument became physical, and Ebony tried to break it up. She got pushed really hard in the scuffle, and she hit her neck on the edge of the table and then the floor very hard. She probably broke her neck and died right there on the floor. That's pretty much what Three's version of the story is."

"So then, Three kills Roscoe?" Alice wondered.

"That's not how Three tells it," Harvey said. "He says Roscoe ran away and must have been killed by someone else."

"Bogus," Fly said. "Only Three would think to bury both bodies in the upper field near the limb maker's house."

"Heard you guys found the knife used to kill Roscoe," Oscar said.

"Fly did," Harvey said. "Tell them about it, Fly."

"Stainless steel with a great bone and wood handle. Had a symbol on it with three triangles. Intertwined."

"What's it mean?" Oscar continued.

"A Valknut. An old Viking symbol that means 'knot of the slain warrior.'"

"How did you link it to Three?"

"He wasn't really careful with stuff, Oscar," Fly said. "When they arrested him, they found a card with the same symbol on it in his wallet. One of those secret societies you can join online. Dummy should have gotten rid of the knife better, to begin with."

Tootie tried to summarize the events. "So, Fly, you're saying that Ebony may have been killed by accident, and Three deliberately killed Roscoe out of hatred for him."

290

"Loathing," Fly said. "One of the four Ls that are motives for murder."

"Look at you," Jeb said. "A regular Sherlock Holmes."

"The real culprit in this is Carmela," Harvey added. "She likely planned to murder Junior with the same poison she tried to use on Eunice, but he and Three got in a fight, and he left. Three probably caught up with him, murdered him, and found a good place for him in the barn. Carmela probably helped him dig the hole and padlock the room."

"Felicia and Eunice must have known about this. How could they not know?" Tootie said.

"Well, if Felicia was a recluse and stayed in the tower all the time, and Carmela kept Eunice plied with liquor, the women would not know half of what was really going on. Three had already done Roscoe in, so they took out as much money as they could get from Junior's account," Harvey said to his attentive audience.

"The women in the mansion didn't report Roscoe, Three, or Junior missing for weeks," Fly added.

"But poor Philip," Rosie said. "I used to love talking to him."

"I bet you did, Rosie," Rexie said. "You're always on the lookout for a juicy story."

This broke the tension of the discussion, and everyone laughed.

Harvey continued. "Philip just knew too much. He used to work for Junior and was let go after Junior was missing. But he must have known where Junior was. I remember asking him one day if he knew where Junior was, and he said, 'not far away.' And when I asked him if he was dead or alive, he repeated, 'not far away.' Then I told him that Junior was found up on the hill, and he said it wasn't him."

"Wow. So, he probably knew exactly where Junior was," Jeb said. "I wonder why he didn't say anything."

"Loot," Fly said. "Gettin' money from Carmela,

291

maybe Noah and the swami, too."

Harvey kicked him.

"Uh, disregard what I just said. That's what we call speculation."

But Alice picked up on his comment. "Why would the swami and Noah pay Philip?"

Harvey kicked Fly again so he wouldn't say anymore. Harvey picked up the answer. "All I'll say is Philip knew a lot about all of Stillwell's secrets, and most of them died with him. So, folks, that's all the news from Stillwell this morning. Sorry to leave you, but Fly and I have some money we need to deposit."

Tootie waved her arm when Harvey reached for his wallet. She winked and nodded at him as he and Fly headed out the back to the parking lot.

They looked at each other. Few words were needed at this point. "Thanks for your help, Fly," Harvey said.

"You're the man, Harv. Taught me everything I know."

They shook hands. "Let me know if you need more help. You know, next case," Fly said.

"Next case. Sure. You'll be the first to know."

"Now that I'm a metal-headed gumshoe, maybe I'll be letting you know about the next case."

Harvey got in his Mustang and Fly in his beat-up truck. They drove off in opposite directions, both feeling proud of their accomplishment but somewhat sad that the case was closed.

DINNER AT HOME

Solving the missing Marlowe case took its toll on Harvey, but winning the big prize made it worthwhile. He took a nap and woke up around dinnertime. No TV dinner tonight, he thought. He made a phone call to his favorite steakhouse, Beef Galore, and ordered a filet mignon dinner with fries and salad. He topped the order off with a large piece of cherry cheesecake and arranged to have a food delivery service, Food4U, bring it to his house. He opened the fridge, popped a beer, and sat down to catch up on the evening news until his food arrived.

Within ten minutes, the doorbell played Take Me out to the Ball Game.

Wow, he thought. *That didn't take long.*

All smiles, he went right to the door and opened it.

"Surprise," the two women on the porch yelled.

"We thought you'd want some company," Thelma said. "So, I brought grandma with me to cheer you up."

"Hi, big boy," Grandma said. "Let's party!"

Harvey was speechless.

SHARE THIS BOOK

I hope you have enjoyed *Where Are They?* If you liked it, please let others know about the book by writing a review, posting on social media, emailing friends, posting on the publisher's site, or telling others by word of mouth. You can learn more about my writing projects at my author website: http://www.dcochran.net.